The Garden of Perfect Brightness

MELISSA ADDEY

For Paul and Rachel.
Thank you for such a wonderful experience.

Your Free Book

MELISSA ADDEY

the
Cup

The city of Kairouan in Tunisia, 1020. Hela has powers too strong for a child – both to feel the pain of those around her and to heal them. But when she is given a mysterious cup by a slave woman, its powers overtake her life, forcing her into a vow she cannot hope to keep. So begins a quartet of historical novels set in Morocco as the Almoravid Dynasty sweeps across Northern Africa and Spain, creating a Muslim Empire that endured for generations.

Download your free copy at
www.melissaaddey.com

Spelling and Pronunciation

I have used the international Pinyin system for the Chinese names of people and places. The following list indicates the elements of this spelling system that may cause English speakers problems of pronunciation. To the left, the letter used in the text, to the right, its equivalent English sound.

c	=	ts
q	=	ch
x	=	sh
z	=	dz
zh	=	j

1 Engraved Moon and Unfolding Clouds:
The Peony Terrace

2 Hall of Fulfilled Wishes:
Castiglione's Painting Studio

3 Grand Palace Gate
to the Garden of Perfect Brightness

4 The Rear Lake
And the 9 Continents Clear and Calm

5 Sea of Blessings

6 The Maze

7 The Western Palaces

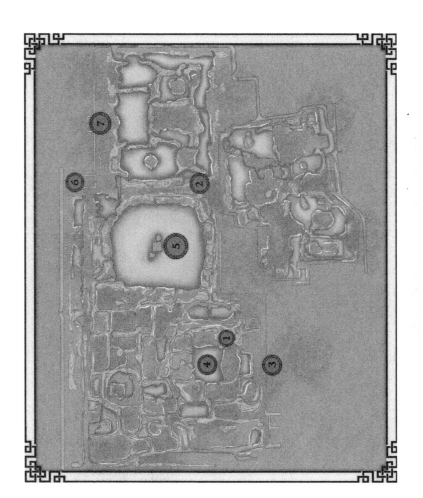

Main Characters

Emperors, their concubines and children

The Kangxi Emperor
- Multiple concubines including Lady Que Hui
- Over 30 sons, including the Crown Prince, Prince Yong and Prince Zhi

Prince Yong, later the Yongzheng Emperor
- Lady Nara, Primary Consort, later Empress
- Lady Niuhuru, concubine to Prince Yong, mother to Hongli, later Empress Dowager
- Lady Qi, mother to Hongshi

Hongli, later Prince Bao, later the Qianlong Emperor
- Lady Fuca (Foo-cha), Primary Consort, later Empress
- Lady Ula Nara, later Step Empress

The Jesuits

- Giuseppe Castiglione, painter, also named Lang Shining (Shur-ning) (Italian)
- Laura Biondecci, painter (Italian)
- Brother Costa, surgeon (Italian)

- Brother Michel Benoist, engineer (French)
- Brother Jean-Denis Attiret, painter (French)
- Father Friedel, Superior of St Joseph's (Austrian)
- Brother Michele Arailza, painter (Italian)
- Brother Ferdinando Moggi, architect (Italian)
- Brother Matteo Ripa, copper-engraver (Italian)
- Giovanni Gherardini, painter and Castiglione's predecessor in China (Italian)

Servants

- The Chief Eunuch
- Yan, maid to Niuhuru
- Kun, eunuch gardener, later husband to Yan
- Chu, adopted daughter of Yan and Kun

Others

- Nian Xiyao, court official tasked with introducing Castiglione to court life
- Madam Guo, a Chinese Christian
- The Lei family of imperial architects, including Jinyu Lei, head architect

This whole inclosure is called, Yuen-Ming-Yuen
(the Garden of Perfect Brightness).

There is but one Man here; and that is the Emperor. All pleasures are made for him alone. This charming place is scarce ever seen by any body but himself, his Women, and his Eunuchs. The Princes, and other chief Men of the Country, are rarely admitted any farther than the Audience-Chambers. Of all the Europeans that are here, none ever enter'd this Inclosure, except the Clock-makers and Painters; whose Employments make it necessary that they should be admitted every where.

Letter from Jesuit painter Jean-Denis Attiret. Beijing, Nov 1ˢᵗ, 1743

Memory Palace, definition:

1: Originally and chiefly historical, an imaginary building thought of as comprising various rooms and areas, each containing mnemonic objects and features that symbolize particular ideas, which can be visualized mentally as a systematic method of remembering those ideas.

2: A building, place, or structure that holds or evokes memories.

The Oxford English Dictionary

Early 1700s

The Crow's Summons

THE EYES OF EVE, AT the very moment of her greatest sin, offering Adam the apple in her hand, gave me pause. I looked down at the designs and shook my head. There was something too knowing about her expression. The moment of mankind's downfall should not contain malevolence, except from the snake, already painted yesterday, which watched with glittering wickedness for its plan to come to fruition. My pencil moved and now Eve gazed at her mate with a loving innocence. Her hair, long and dark, fell to cover part of her naked breast. The Garden of Eden might have been a place without shame, but the priests would throw up their hands in horror if I were to deliver them a fresco of a naked Adam and Eve.

Around me the church echoed to curses and the loud noises of the fresh plaster being prepared – scraping, mixing, water pouring.

"God's bones! Do you have to make such a din?" I finally bellowed. "I can barely think!"

"Sorry master," said the foreman. "Won't happen again." He cuffed his young assistant round the head and there was something approaching a blessed silence for a few minutes until one of the other labourers muttered something about the master having a sore head from too much drinking and the whole group burst into laughter.

I considered threatening to dock their pay but my head ached enough to persuade me to wait a few more minutes until they were done and gone, when silence would be restored and I could work without interruption. I nodded to my own assistant, who had prepared my paints for the day and dismissed him with a wave. He would return at midday with my lunch, for once the fresh plaster was up I was working against Old Father Time himself to paint what I could of the fresco, which was very large. The quicker the work was done the better, for each day's work left telltale marks between one section and another, which offended my eye even after blending the paints between the two areas as much as possible.

"All done, master," said the foreman. "Smooth as you like."

I did not inspect his work. Vannozzo's plastering was without equal, he was in demand all over Milan by artists painting frescos. I was lucky to have secured his services early in the morning, allowing me a longer working day before the plaster set and I could no longer paint on it.

"I'll see you tomorrow," I said.

"As God is my witness, master." He waved goodbye and took his labourers and noise with him.

Time passed and my headache began to subside. The quiet around me, the focus on my work, these things calmed me. Fresco work made some painters anxious, for there was no room for error: when the paint touched the wet plaster the brushstrokes must be accurate. Oil on canvas could be layered and then layered again to cover any mistakes or create desired changes. The only way to undo fresco work was with a chisel. But I loved its delicacy, its speed as well as the need for certainty and found a sense of calm in the work.

The quiet of the church was broken by quick steps, followed by a lingering pause, which irritated me, for it meant that someone was hovering behind my back without having the courtesy to introduce themselves. I have never cared to be overlooked whilst painting, much less by a stranger. I spoke without turning.

"Who's there?"

Further quick steps brought a man before me. His tall black hat and long dark robes, combined with an inquisitive air, made me think of the loitering crows near my family's home. I half expected the Jesuit's voice to emerge as a caw.

He made an inelegant bow and having introduced himself in a thick Milanese accent he paused, as though waiting for my own name, although surely he knew who I was, having sought me out in my place of work.

"Giuseppe Castiglione," I said at last. "Son of Pietro Castiglione."

He nodded but seemed uncertain of his mission, gesturing awkwardly at the fresco as though to buy time. "May I?" he asked.

I waved him towards it without pointing out that as he had hovered behind me for a lengthy period he must surely have seen the image already.

He fluttered closer to it and stood regarding the image. On the wall, as though seeing through an open door, was a glimpse of the Garden of Eden, with Adam and Eve standing beneath the Tree of Knowledge, their hands touching as the fateful apple passed from one to the other. The use of a forced perspective meant that the image would appear real, as though one might step through the door and into the Garden, to warn against evil or perhaps to partake in it.

The crow held out his hand and let his fingertips brush against the cold surface of the wall. "A remarkable illusion," he said.

"It is called *trompe l'oeil*," I said.

"To deceive the eye," he said, nodding. "I have seen it done before but not, sir, as well as it has been done here."

I waited. If the crow was intent on flattering me then it was likely he wanted something from me. Whatever he wanted, he needed to hurry up and make his request. The plaster was drying even as we spoke.

"Do you enjoy your work?" he asked at last.

I nodded but this did not satisfy him.

"The subject matter?" he pressed. "Images of a religious nature?"

I nodded again. Much of my work was of a religious nature, for the Church paid handsomely and there was scope for the imagination.

"Are you inclined towards the Church yourself?" he asked.

I shook my head. He seemed disappointed. "My brother Giovanni is a priest," I offered, as though this might console him.

He brightened at once. "Indeed?" he asked. "And would you consider a similar path yourself – but one where your talents as a painter might be put to service for a higher purpose?"

I frowned. "A painter-priest?"

Now he was all smiles. "Exactly!"

"I am already a painter. Why would I have need to become a priest?"

The crow smiled at my confusion. "May we talk?" he asked.

I had thought we already were, but I allowed him to draw me to one side, to a pew at the back of the church where we both sat, turned awkwardly towards one another. I looked at him, waiting for him to speak, while thinking of my fast-drying plasterwork.

"The Jesuit Brotherhood has a Mission in China," he began. "We wish to convert as many souls as we may there, that they may know the love of God. But in order to do so, we hope first and foremost to engage with the Emperor of China, that he may allow our work to continue there, but also perhaps hear the word of our Lord for himself."

I had heard of their missionary work and in particular of one of their missionaries, now long dead, a certain Matteo Ricci. He had a notion that I myself have used to great effect throughout my life, the creation of a 'memory palace', a building created and held within one's own imagination, in whose rooms one can store memories such that they can be easily retrieved. I began to speak of this with enthusiasm, noting that for a painter, such a technique was of particular interest, allowing one to store details which might seem trivial to others but which gave paintings true verisimilitude – the broken twig, a particular pose or colour, the ways in which water moves when touched by the breeze and more. I would have gone on but the crow only nodded and smiled.

"Indeed, indeed," he said. "It is through such talents that we hope to make our mark with the Emperor. We have taken him gifts of telescopes and other marvels of our own world and he has been much pleased with them. But his greatest interest is reserved for the men of skill that we have brought to China to serve him. Botanists, clockmakers, astronomers, mathematicians and architects. They have been chosen to serve him personally and through seeing their talents serve his needs he has in turn shown much graciousness towards our mission."

"Has he converted?" I asked.

The crow shook his head sadly. "Not yet," he said. "But we hope that he may still do so, despite his advancing age – indeed, many men convert as they grow older and come to think of their own demise."

"Who is this emperor?" I asked.

"The Kangxi Emperor has ruled for over forty years, since he was a young child. He is now approaching fifty years old. He has brought about stability and wealth for his country, but he is also a great lover of new ideas." He paused, as though thinking how best to frame his next words. "He has requested a new painter," he said at last. "Our Mission had previously supplied him with such a man, by the name of Gherardini, from Bologna. He arrived in China in 1699 and served the Kangxi Emperor well enough, but he could not accept the missionary lifestyle and left the Mission of Beijing after less than ten years, against the will of the Brothers there. Before him, there was a painter by the name of Fiori, who also tired of the life there and returned home to his native city. At present, therefore, we are without a painter." He looked at me expectantly.

"You wish me to go to China as court painter to the Emperor?" I asked, my voice betraying my excitement. Already I was imagining the long sea voyage, the arrival in a foreign land, the many new sights I would see, the service (highly praised and rewarded, of course) to an Emperor, no less. I laughed out loud, all irritation with the crow suddenly gone. "Well, I believe I am your man – it will be a great adventure and a fine story to tell my friends and family on my return!"

The crow gave a half smile at my newly found enthusiasm but was already shaking his head. "I have not made myself clear," he said. "Fiori and Gherardini were not Jesuits and therefore they were free to leave our Mission, but their leaving was not looked upon kindly by the Emperor. It has therefore been decided that the next painter we send to China must be a Jesuit, so that he will be obliged to follow the directives of our Order. The painter whom we choose must undertake to remain in China and to serve the Emperor and his descendants for the term of his natural life. The man we choose must take the vows of our Brotherhood: Poverty, Chastity and Obedience, within two years of reaching Beijing. He will go to China and never return."

We talked a while longer, that I might know what would be required. Behind us, the plaster dried. I did not care. A voyage by sea, not without danger, of over a year, followed by a further shorter journey across China to reach the Emperor's capital, Beijing. Unquestioning service to be rendered to the Emperor and any future successors. Painting commissions to be carried out according to his orders and taste. Above all, that once committed to this mission I would never again see Milan, nor my friends and family. When he left I sat before the fresco on which I should have been working, my eyes unseeing, my hands still and tools untouched, my heart beating fast. At last, an outlet for my ambition! Adventure, new sights to capture, a whole new world opening up before me. In my naivety the price to pay seemed low enough. The company of women? Well, I had met a few who had charmed me, in their own way, but they could not, must not, stand in the way of my career as a great painter – for such I wished to become – and so I might as well forswear their companionship. Some of my friends told great tales of love, but I had yet to experience such devotion as they described and indeed, rather suspected them of exaggerating for effect. I would be clothed and fed and housed, whatever vows of poverty might be made. Above all, shining above all, was the promise of an imperial patron. For me, there was no decision to be made. My assistant brought me food, which I did not eat. I dismissed him for the rest of the day, much to his amazement, then left the church without finishing my work. Vannozzo would curse all the saints tomorrow when he had to chip away the plaster I had left to dry unpainted. I could not wait to tell my family and friends about the adventure before me.

My mother Anna Maria was aghast when I told her my plan. She wept. "I will never see you again! I have already given a son to the Church. Why is this sacrifice demanded of me? I will never see my son again, never have grandchildren."

My father patted her awkwardly on the back. He did not like crying women, they made him ill at ease. "I am sure Giuseppe will make our family proud," he said, with excessive cheerfulness. "There is no higher position for a painter than to have a monarch as his patron. Our son's talent is already reaping rewards."

I nodded, smiling. This was a position I had dreamt of. Most painters would have to become better known, older, with a studio of their own, before being summoned to receive royal or imperial patronage. I was about to make the leap while barely out of my

23

apprenticeship. I made my excuses and left my mother to weep while I made my way to the local tavern. My friends, at least, would be impressed.

"No women?" Antonio cried. "None at all? Your dick will fall off through lack of use!" He leaned against me, simpering like a girl, tugging at the corner of his eyes to make them seem Oriental. "And what if you were to meet a Chinese beauty such as myself, young sir? Would your heart not melt? Would your rod not stiffen, eh? Eh?"

The others roared with laughter.

I shoved him away. "You have no ambition, Antonio," I told him. "You only think with your dick. Imagine being painter to an Emperor! You'll be lucky if you ever attend a court, let alone be attached to one."

"The Emperor of China can go hang," said Antonio. "Give me a pretty girl any day."

"Then that's all you'll get," I told him. "Whereas I shall be a renowned painter. My work will be admired across the world while you spend the rest of your life painting portraits for merchants."

Antonio shook his head and waved for another jug of wine. "So *proud*," he said. "So full of yourself. Always certain you are destined for great things."

"I am," I told him. And I believed it.

My master Filippo bid me a kind farewell. "I am sure I will hear your name again," he said. "You have been an apt pupil and your talent is real. In particular your skill in depicting textures and illusions. I shall miss watching you develop further."

I raised my chin. "I will honour your name," I assured him.

He nodded. "A word of advice."

I sighed a little to myself. I was growing somewhat weary of advice and warnings, from opinions on the vow of chastity to my mother's endless weeping. I knew my own mind and considered it made up. "Master?"

"You may find their painting methods very different. And perhaps worth learning from?"

I nodded politely, although I doubted his point. If they were happy enough with their own painting skills, why call on mine? Surely because they wished to learn from a more advanced style? I was certain that I had much to teach them. Now I can only smile at the thought of my master's advice and Antonio's warnings. I should have heeded them both. And bid my mother a gentler farewell, poor woman. It is hard to see a son come into his own and then leave your side for greater things, as I now know for myself.

Perhaps it was only on bidding my grandmother Maddalena farewell that I faltered. She did not weep, even though she was very old and knew full well she would never see me again. She only laid her hand on my head and blessed me, her kindly smile never wavering. I held her warm soft hand in mine and had to briefly bow my head to her, less out of the respect I owed her than from a young man's pride in hiding the sudden shining in his eyes that might suggest a weakness of resolve. Then I left her, walking through her sweet-smelling garden, the place where my brother and I had played together as children, my head held a little too high, hoping that pride would conquer sadness.

If I had thought that I would leave for China at once, I was sorely mistaken. First, I had to spend a great deal of time with the Brothers in the city of Genoa, to be educated in their ways. I, who had never been called to the church as my brother had, was now obliged to hear Mass a great many more times in a month than I had thought possible, to listen with a solemn face to holy readings and be lectured on my future obligations as a Brother. I was given the task of completing a series of religious paintings on the walls of the Jesuit refectory there, perhaps in part to further demonstrate my talents. I painted *Tobias and the Angel, Abraham and Sarah* as well as other works, each meant to provide instruction and a point of contemplation and reflection for the Brothers as they dined. These works done to their satisfaction, I took my initial vows, admitting me as a lay brother to the Order, although my binding vows of poverty, obedience and chastity would not be made until I had been with the Brothers a couple of years, to prove my worth.

"Better make the most of not having taken them yet, then," suggested Antonio, visiting me in Genoa. He remained staunchly appalled at my choice and made it his business to point out every good-looking woman who came within sight, reminding me that I would be forswearing their company forever.

"I had better do no such thing," I retorted. "I am to travel to Portugal to await a ship and while I am there I have not one but two commissions. I am to paint frescos for a chapel there but I will also paint portraits of the Queen of Portugal's children. So you see I am already painting royalty, while you are painting nothing but the fat wives of merchants."

"I like something to hold on to, myself," laughed Antonio. "The wives of merchants show a great deal of interest in the man painting their portrait."

"And you show too much interest in them," I said. "You'll get yourself punched in the face one of these days, or worse." But I was sorry to bid him farewell, he was a rogue but I had known him since childhood and the thought of never again hearing his raucous laugh saddened me.

And so I left for Coimbra in Portugal, excited and ambitious, only to find that the tides and the Queen of Portugal alike were capricious. One ship and then another was promised and then postponed, while I painted her noble wailing babes and unruly brats, and when at last ships were ready the Queen pronounced herself so happy with my work that she commanded I must miss more than one sailing in order to wait for her new pregnancy to be complete, so that I might paint the portrait of yet another royal offspring. Meanwhile I struggled to learn Mandarin with nothing but Portuguese echoing in my ears, puzzling over meaningless symbols, not the simple two dozen of our own but the many thousands I had been told I must acquire to read even the simplest of texts. Speaking it was worse, for every sound was to be pronounced up or down, flat or high, in a way that drove me to distraction. More than once I doubted the choice I had made and yet when I saw one ship and then another leave the shores, bound for adventure and glory, I chafed at being left behind. I wrote repeatedly to the Father General of the Jesuits in Rome, reminding him of my great desire to begin my service in China as soon as possible.

My hopes rose of an imminent departure when I was joined by two new recruits to the Order. A Brother Costa, by profession a surgeon, arrived from Naples, his medical skills needed in Beijing. He was a taciturn man, not much given to idle chatter but apparently highly skilled in his profession. Another painter, Biondecci, this time from Rome, younger by ten years than myself, was to join me as an assistant. I went to meet Biondecci and was startled to find a young woman, scarcely more than a girl, whose thrown-back hood revealed an unusual mass of thick blonde hair, suited to her name.

"Biondecci?" I asked, disbelieving.

"The same," she said. "Laura."

"Giuseppe," I said.

Her expression lightened. "Ah, you are my new painting master. I am pleased to meet you."

I gestured to her to follow me and gave a small coin to a man to carry her trunk. "I did not expect a woman," I told her. "The journey will be arduous and once we enter the Emperor's employ we cannot leave again unless he or the Mission dismiss us."

"I know," she said. "I have dreamed of China since I was a child. My father had maps in his study and I would pore over them. After he and my mother died, I joined the Order as an apprentice painter. I have begged to serve in China for years and when I heard that there was a painter leaving I asked to be made your apprentice."

I could not but have doubts about the prudence of sending a woman, especially one so young, on such a long voyage to a distant land, surrounded by men. One might suppose the Brothers would protect her, of course, but there would be sailors about, possibly pirates, during the voyage and once we reached our destination, who knew how the local men might treat a foreign woman?

Still, Laura had talent, this I quickly ascertained from examples of her work and she had applied herself diligently to learning Mandarin. It having been decided that being a woman she would not have need to read or write the language, she had worked the harder on her speech and put my own efforts to shame, the odd tones seeming to come to her more easily. Thus our last days before boarding the ship were spent together attempting to speak only in Mandarin, something that reduced our conversation to the level of small children and gave us occasion to laugh at our efforts. Brother Costa only shook his head at us and practiced his writing of the symbols, his surgeon's exactness perhaps standing him in good stead.

Enough. My time in Portugal seemed endless to a young man and yet seems so very long ago now. The heaving boards of the ship, Our Lady of Hope, thrilled me to my very core.

My memories of that voyage, long as it was, are not unpleasant. For all the wild tales the sailors told us, boasting of encounters with savages and pirates, we travelled peacefully to Madeira and on to Cape Verde before making brief stops in Senegal and the Gambia.

"Stay close to me," I warned Laura, after our first disembarking on the tiny island of Gorée near Senegal. Her golden hair drew more attention than was desirable, the local people even approaching her quite boldly to touch it, rubbing it between their dark fingers as though to ascertain its quality, like goods in a marketplace. "Be off with you," I added, to one woman. "Do not touch her."

The woman smiled without letting go.

"They are friendly enough," said Laura peaceably. "I am sure they mean well. They cannot have seen many women with hair this colour."

"They should show a little respect," I said, gesturing to the woman to move away, which she did, reluctantly, only for a man to take her place. "I shall have to carry a stick with me next time we come ashore," I said, exasperated, "or leave you on board until we reach China."

"Why, are the women of China blonde too?" Laura asked, laughing. "We must grow used to being objects of curiosity on our travels, Giuseppe."

We saw much that still remains in my mind. The dark shape of whales, rising up through the depths, the fish that leapt from the water as though they might sprout wings and fly. By night the stars seemed brighter than we had ever seen them before and although the heat made us long to swim, we were advised not to by the older sailors, who swore that more than one of their comrades had been dragged down by the sharks whose fins we glimpsed from time to time. The sailors claimed that the creatures were ever hungry for human flesh. We were lucky to brave only one bad storm, in which Brother Costa's skills were called on to save the life of a man struck by a falling broken mast and many Brothers of the Mission were kept busy hearing the confessions of those with troubled minds who believed they might be about to meet their Maker. By the time we reached the Portuguese colony of Goa many of us on board were suffering the swollen legs and peeling gums of scurvy, having run out of the oranges we had previously taken on board. We were glad to eat fresh fruits and vegetables again, albeit they were strange in taste and form to us and the whole company soon recovered. Altogether, we were at sea for almost a year by the time we knelt in gratitude to sing Te Deum when the shores of Macau were sighted and we knew that our journey was almost over.

Once disembarked we heard Mass in a tiny plaster chapel decorated with a red and blue glaze which we were told was common of the local style. My legs still felt strange on land and I felt as though I staggered. About us was all the usual noise of the docks. I had thought of course to hear Mandarin spoken, but the locals mainly spoke either a mangled sort of Portuguese or Cantonese, neither of which we understood and so we were entirely reliant on the Brothers to translate for us. It seemed strange to see Portuguese custard tarts for sale at street stands and we were served a dish named Portuguese Chicken which bore no resemblance whatsoever to food from Portugal, being served with a yellow curried sauce. But it was a great relief to stand once more on the firm earth and know that from now on we were done with our sea journey and all its privations.

As we made our way round the local streets in an attempt to get our bearings we were surprised to see small piles of food left by the sides of the road, often with sticks of incense burning before them.

"It is the Hungry Ghost festival," a Brother informed us. "The local people believe their ancestors return to visit the land of the living and must be fed. Ancestral veneration is of great importance here."

We were soon settled in the local Mission, there to be instructed by senior Brothers on the behaviours we must learn in order to be accepted into this new land and in particular its court. Our spoken Mandarin was pronounced atrocious and a local convert to the faith was appointed to give us daily instruction. Certainly hearing the language spoken by a native made it easier to improve our own efforts.

I was given long black robes to wear, with oddly baggy silken trousers underneath. I was told this was what the Chinese scholars wore and that the Jesuits had thought it prudent to wear the same, to indicate our standing as men of intellect and skill. The robes felt odd, my legs unprotected beneath rippling folds of silk more befitting to a woman. Besides, there seemed little difference, to my untrained eye, between the men and the women's clothes here: all of us wore these long robes, from simple cotton for the maids to highly decorated silk. All were shapeless. Gone were the half-glimpsed cleavages of women, their tight waists pulled tighter still by unseen corsets and their billowing skirts. Gone were the well-turned calves of men in their stockings below form-fitting britches and waistcoats, jackets cut tight to show off the width of manly chests. I found myself tugging at the robes or irritably rolling my shoulders in them, trying to become accustomed to the feel of them. The black hat I was given was also odd, round but rising to a square, with two long strips of cloth which hung past my ears and which I found myself pushing back when they dangled at the edges of my sight. Laura laughed at me when she saw me and I in turn told her that her blonde hair looked most odd pinned up on a thin black lacquered wooden board.

"You should have them lacquer you a board in yellow, it would suit your hair better," I told her. "I am certain the black is supposed to be hidden by your hair being the same colour."

She shrugged. "I am not bothered about my hair," she said. "Look at my shoes."

They were odd, certainly, for while the tops were made of a pretty enough embroidered silk, below the sole was a high wooden block, lifting Laura's short frame to a loftier height, something like the wooden pattens a woman might have worn at home to keep her good shoes out of the mud, though these were higher and Laura stumbled more than once while she grew accustomed to them.

We were shown how to behave in the presence of the Emperor. We were to stand with feet together and hands at our side, this being a modest and respectful pose, before, at a given signal, kneeling and prostrating ourselves, our heads to touch the floor three times. We were then to rise and repeat the whole salutation a further two times, our foreheads to touch the floor nine times in all. This, we were informed, was correct on our first meeting and at any further great occasions such as New Year or the Emperor's birthday. Once would be sufficient on less formal occasions. It proved a difficult act to perform with any grace, although Laura seemed to manage it better than Brother Costa and myself.

Brother Costa was warned against practicing medicine on the Emperor himself, for there had been tales of local physicians who had attempted to cure the Emperor of some minor malady and having failed had been lashed and then jailed in heavy chains. They had been released only on condition of treating another member of the imperial family and on doing so successfully had still borne the shame of being obliged to wear a small chain and clasp about their necks for the rest of their lives, as a warning and reminder of what might befall them.

We were also given some guidance as to the Mission's reputation at court.

"There have been difficulties," admitted our instructor, an elderly Father. "There has been controversy over the permitted religious rites."

Laura and I raised our eyebrows, while Brother Costa nodded. Clearly he had already heard word of this.

"To better encourage our Chinese converts to adopt our religion we have allowed them to include ancestor worship as part of the Christian rites. Ancestral worship is of great importance to the Chinese, it would be very difficult to persuade them to convert were this forbidden. And of course it is entirely appropriate to show respect towards one's ancestors. And our leniency in this matter encouraged the Kangxi Emperor to allow us great freedom in preaching the Word. He issued an edict many years ago protecting both our Mission and our churches throughout the empire." The Father sighed. "However His Holiness Pope Clement the Eleventh has, in his infinite wisdom, just issued a Papal Bull disallowing ancestral worship, which he views as irreligious since it might be seen as making icons or indeed venerating ancestors as divinities, which of course cannot be allowed."

"And does the Emperor accept this ruling?" I asked, already feeling that I knew the answer.

"He does not. It has irritated him beyond all measure. We have just received word here of his response." He took out a folded paper written in a rich red ink, which I was later to find out was a colour reserved exclusively for writings by the Emperor himself. Peering closely at it, he read out: "'Reading this proclamation, I have concluded that the Westerners are petty indeed. It is impossible to reason with them because they do not understand larger issues as we understand them in China. There is not a single Westerner versed in Chinese works, and their remarks are often incredible and ridiculous. To judge from this proclamation, their religion is no different from other small, bigoted sects of Buddhism or Taoism. I have never seen a document which contains so much nonsense. From now on, Westerners should not be allowed to preach in China, to avoid further trouble.'"

"Does His Holiness not understand that the Mission would be damaged by this ruling?" asked Laura.

"We cannot question His Holiness's ruling," said the Father, although his tone lacked much reproof. "It is, however, all the more important that your work and service to the Emperor be most excellent, to perhaps soften his feelings in this matter."

"We are still waiting to be summoned to court," pointed out Laura.

But word of our arrival had travelled swiftly, even at such a great distance. A summons soon reached us that the Emperor Kangxi was impatiently awaiting us at court. Our education would have to be continued in Beijing. Laura's eyes shone when she spoke of the Grand Canal on which part of our journey would be made, though I knew little of it and had grown weary of travel.

"I will be glad when we arrive," I told her. "For then my work can truly begin."

"Our work," she reminded me.

"You are my apprentice," I said, perhaps a little arrogantly. "The Emperor has requested my service and I am anxious to begin."

"You are only anxious to be praised," said Laura, a little mischievously. She should have been more respectful to her master, of course, but she was very young and we had struck up something of a friendship, given the long voyage.

"And I will be," I said with certainty. "I will be."

I had thought to see something of the country as we passed through it, to have the leisure to accustom ourselves to the look of it, the buildings, the inhabitants and their way of life. Instead we found ourselves seated within a carrying litter, cramped and in half-darkness, day after day. I said that I was well able to ride a horse and indeed would prefer to do so, but was told in no uncertain terms that this would not be fitting and that we would travel as had been arranged. Brother Costa suffered from nausea at the constant motion of our litter and Laura and I grew ill-tempered with one another, confined as we were to close company with little to vary the monotony of our daily travels. By night we would stop at inns. They were poor places often riddled with various small creatures in our beds, which disturbed our sleep. I was also concerned for Laura's safety. I bid her to keep her door closed and to push some item of furniture against it, if possible.

When we finally reached the Grand Canal we caught but a glimpse of the quayside before we were ushered into the boats in which we would continue our journey. Laura's disappointment in finding that there was no way of looking out of the boats brought on a fit of weeping, which I could not condemn, for I was as frustrated as she at our shuttered journey. Brother Costa seemed more phlegmatic about our confinement, being more concerned with the movement of the boat and its effect on his digestion, but then he was not a painter like Laura and me, yearning for some form of visual simulation.

"The Emperor himself is never seen by the common people," said one of the accompanying guards, when we complained.

"How can he not be seen? Does he never leave the Forbidden City?"

"Oh certainly. But screens of bamboo and cloth are erected on either side of the road, so that he may not be seen."

"How absurd," I muttered to Laura and Brother Costa.

Laura passed the time by making small sketches and I passed comments on her work, correcting her shading or encouraging her to improve her technique in certain respects regarding movement and texture.

"Think of a bird," I suggested. "How it flaps to the ground, not the slow swoop of its wings when it soars high up in the sky but the last moments before it lands, the tremble of its wings, the delicacy of each feather."

She obliged and I nodded when she drew for me a tiny sparrow, its wingtips aflutter as it sought out a fallen crumb.

The black crow-robed figure of the Jesuit still perches on the high outer wall of my memory palace, cawing to me daily when I pass his post, his call always the same. "China! China!"

Hundreds of Butterflies

IT'S HOT AND STICKY. MY robe feels heavy. I try to loosen the collar a little to let some air reach my skin, but there is no air. Just more heat. I've never worn this robe before. It is my mother's best, the finest in our house and the only thing appropriate for today. It's too short on me, although it lies baggily on my still-flat chest. My mother tutted over the fit and scolded me for being a beanpole. I shift my weight from one foot to the other. The girl on my left has stood perfectly still for over two hours. In fairness, she's balancing on the tiny curved blocks that support cloud-climbing shoes, so perhaps shifting her weight back and forth is not a good idea or she might overbalance and end up falling on her backside. I'm grateful I have nothing so elegant to wear, for at least in my simpler cloth shoes I can rest one foot at a time. The only sign that the girl is even alive is the damp cobblestone at her feet, wetted one tear at a time from her expressionless face. I don't know why she's crying. Half the girls here are crying. There could be any number of reasons.

Before the eunuch guards and officials arrived to bring us to the Inner Court of the Forbidden City we were allowed to mill about while we waited. At least two of the girls were already weeping and wringing their hands because they were in love and wished to marry their sweethearts. They were afraid of being chosen to marry the Emperor or one of his sons and never seeing their beloveds again.

One older girl was unhelpfully passing on gossip she'd heard. She claimed one of her aunts was a lady-in-waiting in the Palace and that a distant cousin served one of the princes in his palace in Beijing. More and more girls gathered about her, their heads bent close to hers. I joined them.

"... there's the Crown Prince, my aunt said he chooses very young concubines, even ones who aren't yet of marriageable age... she's heard crying from his palace and seen bruises..."

Some of the girls whimpered and I turned away. I didn't want to be frightened by some busybody's gossip. I turned to the nearest girl, whose eyelids were puffy from crying.

"I'm Niuhuru."

The girl nodded and tried to wipe her eyes. "My father says he'll beat me if I'm not chosen," she confided. "He says girls have been chosen for imperial marriage from our family for generations and I'll bring dishonour to our family name if I'm not. Will you get in trouble if you're not chosen?"

I shook my head. "No-one's expecting me to be chosen," I said. "We're not very important. And anyway," I added, "my mother said I'm too tall and clumsy and I've got funny-coloured eyes."

"Lucky you," sniffed the girl. I wanted to tell her that if she made herself ugly by sobbing she was even less likely to be chosen, but thought that the idea would probably only make her cry more, so I stayed quiet.

Now I try not to let my lips move and keep my eyes straight ahead. "How much longer do you think we'll be here?" I whisper to the girl.

"Silence!" yells the eunuch who's watching over us. Curse him, he has ears like an elephant. I could barely hear my own voice when I spoke. I roll my eyes and he glares at me. I don't care. I'm not that keen to be chosen, so if he dislikes me, so much the better. Perhaps he'll tell the more senior eunuch I'm not suitable and then I'll be free to go home. I yawn and don't bother to hide it. They have over two hundred of us standing here, they're not short of girls to choose from.

There's a small commotion somewhere in the courtyard as a girl faints. When the first one went down everyone stared, now we only glance at the girl as she's carried out, to be revived or maybe just sent home, who knows. Perhaps I could pretend to faint? I consider it but the cobbles under our feet are hard and I am fairly sure that my ungainly height and rough hands, my too-short robe and oddly pale-grey eyes will rule me out as a concubine anyway, so it's just a matter of waiting some more before I'm dismissed. Who'd want to live here, with this endless formality? I'd rather stay in Chengde and marry someone local one day, stay close to my family and familiar surroundings.

I glance at the girl to my right. She, too, is perfectly poised, with a superior lift to her chin, which is meant to let the rest of us know that she comes from a high-ranking family, that she has been born and bred for this moment, that she will settle for nothing less than becoming a concubine to the Emperor himself, no matter how old he is now. Not for her the lesser status of marriage to one of the sixteen grown princes, each of them a possible heir to the throne. The odds are stacked against any woman foolish enough to believe she'd be chosen by the right prince and become consort to a future, younger Emperor. Better pin your hopes on the old Emperor now than end up married to some nobody of a prince, living in a house no better than the one you came from, the only difference being the addition of more rules and protocols to your life.

I shift my feet again but now there are footsteps coming and suddenly every girl stands a little straighter. A whole crowd of eunuchs, officials, guards... and amongst them, the Emperor. I catch a quick glimpse of an old but upright man, a skinny frame bulked out with magnificent yellow robes before we all sink to our knees and I'm face down on the cobbles.

There's a lot of noise as everyone arranges themselves. I can't see anything except the cobbles, which are cold against my forehead. Slowly I twist my neck so that my left cheek lies against the hard stone and look up as far as I can. I can see yellow boots, surrounded by many other feet. I can see some of the girls. Now we can only wait.

We are not required to stand. The selection for the Emperor has clearly already taken place long before this moment. Girls are named, they raise their faces, there is perhaps – since we can hardly see anything – a nod from the Emperor, some sign that he finds them to his liking. Their names are called again more loudly, along with the rank they have been given. The girl to my right is quickly chosen as a mid-rank concubine to the Emperor and I catch a glimpse of the satisfaction on her face as she rises. She has fulfilled her destiny. She will be an imperial concubine to the Emperor of China. I can't help thinking that he is old, he may even die soon. If he does, she will live in the Forbidden City for the rest of her days as a dowager concubine. She will never see or be touched by another man, even if she lives to a ripe old age. She will never leave the embrace of the endless vermillion walls. She will live only through the past glory of this moment when, as a girl of only perhaps fifteen years old, she was chosen. I shudder at the thought.

More girls are picked out of the crowd. They are supposed to be pleased to be chosen quickly, for their beauty and grace to have been noted. Even the nervous ones smile when their names are called, although their lips tremble when they think of their new lives. All those chosen are led away. They will return to their parents for just a few short days before they enter the Forbidden City for the rest of their lives.

I am not chosen, of course. I don't feel relief, because I wasn't afraid of being selected. I only hope the next selection will also be quick and I will be free to leave, to pass back through the great red gates and be met by my mother and father who are waiting outside. I can tell them everything I saw today and when we get home I will regale my younger brothers with how I saw the Emperor himself. I doubt anyone will be disappointed that I am not to enter the Forbidden City, since none of us expected me to be chosen. The Imperial Daughters' Draft cannot be ignored of course, every girl from the Eight Banners must be presented at the court between the ages of thirteen and sixteen, before she can be married, so that the Emperor and his sons have the first choice of any woman in the country. But for families like ours, whose daughters are not blessed with extraordinary beauty or grace, whose fathers are only mid-ranking officials, the Draft is simply an excuse for a visit to the capital. The journey from our home in Chengde to Beijing has been an adventure, a chance to wander the bustling streets, so much bigger and noisier than our own town, to be impressed by the majesty of the Forbidden City and to partake in a ritual that acknowledges our rightful place in the Banners, however minor my father's official post is. To belong to the one of the Banners is to be part of the Manchu elite, the ruling class, setting us above the general Han Chinese population.

The yellow boots move as the Emperor stands and there's a great clatter as he leaves. Slowly, we rise to our feet, our knees stiff and cold. I look about me. There's the odd girl in a huff, annoyed at not having been chosen for the Emperor. The worried girl, I notice, has been led away, avoiding any dishonour to her family despite her red-rimmed eyes.

We recompose ourselves for the next selection. More noise. Eunuchs and guards accompany a small woman, perhaps in her late thirties. She too is magnificently dressed, but not in imperial yellow, rather a slightly darker shade akin to apricot. Her hair is dressed with pearls and flowers. On several of her fingers are nail shields almost as long as her digits, worn only by the very rich, made of finely beaten gold, studded with jewels. She has a long thin face and highly arched brows. The overall effect is rather like a horse that has stuck its head through a flower bush.

"Imperial Noble Consort Que Hui," announces the eunuch who is managing the proceedings. "As chief consort of the Emperor, her ladyship will now select the consorts and concubines for their Royal Highnesses, the sons of the Emperor."

We sink to our knees again and prostrate ourselves, but once this is done we are told to stand. Apparently the consort wants to view us for herself. I wonder briefly why she's not been made Empress but then remember that this Emperor is rather tardy about appointing his Empresses. After the first one died, he only seemed to bestow the honour too late, when each of the subsequent chief consorts was near to death, when he would offer the title. Perhaps he hoped it would cheer them sufficiently to recover from their illness, but it never worked. There have been three dead empresses so far in his long reign, so perhaps for the sake of one's health it's an honour best not hoped for.

Lady Que Hui settles herself on a throne and regards us all in silence. She tilts her head minutely and at once a eunuch is by her side, consulting various folded papers and whispering to her, presumably indicating the more superior girls: noting their families, their beauty, how well they did in the preliminary selections. He will have little to say about me. A few lucky others and I were spared the first rounds of selections since we had to travel from further afield. Late in arriving to the capital, we were sent straight to the Forbidden City for the final choice of girls. Those who arrived in good time or resided in Beijing will have undergone the full examinations of the Draft. Stripped naked so their bodies can clearly be seen, they have had their teeth examined, their tongues scraped and their breath smelt, their height and weight recorded, their toenails scrutinized and even (though I can hardly believe this and suspect other girls of telling tall tales) their armpits and even more intimate areas swabbed and smelt for bad odours which might offend an imperial nose. I'm glad the horse pulling our wagon went lame, delaying us so that I have been spared these humiliations.

At last the selection begins. The Kangxi Emperor has over thirty living sons. Sixteen are old enough to require consorts and concubines. The Crown Prince is of course the most desirable as a future husband. If all goes well, he will one day become Emperor himself. But we have already heard the whispers about his sexual propriety or lack thereof. The girls who are chosen for his household look doubtful rather than excited. The rest of us watch those who are chosen with pity rather than jealousy. Of course being chosen for a lesser prince is not as impressive, but then one will still be part of the imperial family and perhaps have less to fear when summoned to the imperial bedchamber.

The naming goes on and on. The First Prince seems to be very fond of women, for a great many are sent to his household. Women are chosen for the Third Prince, the Fifth Prince, the Eighth Prince, the Ninth Prince. I stop listening and hope it will be over soon.

There's a silence. Lady Que Hui seems to have finished. She casts her eye over our depleted numbers and purses her lips. She seems about to rise, when the eunuch whispers to her again.

"Ah yes," she says. "The Fourth Prince. He has not requested a new concubine, but his household is small and a new lady would be appropriate." Her eyes flicker over us and when they rest on me she frowns. "Very tall," she comments.

I try not to move. It's unsettling to have her eyes rest on me. No one has glanced at me twice since I arrived here. I've been passed over so often during this process that I find it hard to meet her gaze.

I lower my eyes. When I raise them again she is still looking at me. Suddenly I find my throat is very dry, even when I swallow.

I swallow again.

The eunuch bows, somehow managing to convey his dismissal of me. "The girl is named..." he has to check his document again to be certain, "... Niuhuru. From Chengde, near the hunting grounds. She was late in arriving, madam," he says. "She was admitted because she will be too old at the next Draft but she has not been through the preliminary rounds. Of the Manchu Niuhuru clan, of the Bordered Yellow Banner."

"Father?"

"Only a fourth-ranked *Dianyi* in the military, madam."

There's a pause. Lady Que Hui's mouth twists a little in something approaching a smile. "Fourth Prince Yong is known for his dislike of corruption in the higher ranks of officials, both in civilian life and the military. He believes that the lower ranked men are often unfairly overlooked," she says, as though repeating an amusing anecdote. "Perhaps he would like a concubine from a more lowly background so that he can be quite certain that it is not her family connections that have brought her here."

Her small smile reassures me that she is joking. This Prince Yong doesn't want another concubine. Besides, everyone knows that it's the girls from the well-to-do families that get chosen. I'm too tall, as she has already remarked, and she's not close enough to see that my eyes are a strange pale grey, which no-one finds attractive, just odd. No imperial prince would consider me a suitable bride when they can choose from the most beautiful women in the empire. No doubt the Emperor's chief consort enjoys making a little joke during this tedious process. I give a faint smile, to acknowledge that I understand that she is joking, that I am about to be sent home and that I am not expecting anything else – Prince Yong may or may not be given another concubine, but certainly it won't be me.

I'm right. She stands, brushes down her heavy robe, taps the paper with one glittering gold fingernail and nods her head, satisfied, to the eunuch, then turns and walks away as the eunuch calls out:

"Lady Niuhuru, chosen as *gege*, concubine, to the Fourth Prince, Yong!"

I spend the following days in shock. I have to repeat what happened over and over again – first to my incredulous father and mother, standing outside the gates of the Forbidden City, then to our relations, with whom we are lodging during our stay in Beijing, then to more and more people – distant relatives I've never met before, the neighbours, local girls not yet of Draft age who want to hear all about what it is like to be chosen. By the time my brothers arrive, hastily summoned from our family home in Chengde, the words have been said so often that they come out of my mouth easily, although I still cannot believe what I am saying.

"Then she tapped the paper where my name was and walked away. I thought I would be sent home but the eunuch called out my name. I'm to be *gege* to the Fourth Prince. His birth name is Yinzhen but he is known as Prince Yong."

My brothers are impressed. Here's their older sister, a beanpole and a tomboy, whom no-one has ever praised for her looks, and she's going to marry a prince! "Is he very important?" they ask eagerly.

I shake my head. "Not really," I say. "He won't be Emperor, because there's already a Crown Prince. He's just a prince. The Emperor has more than thirty sons."

"But he's a *prince*," says my youngest brother. "So you will be a princess."

I shrug in agreement. Yes, I'll be a princess, but really I will just be a concubine, to a prince who is not very important. It's a strange match – full of honour and prestige and yet at the same time oddly lacklustre. I am not marrying the Emperor, only one of his many sons whom no-one has heard of.

When I am not reciting and re-reciting my story, I spend hours sitting in the garden or at the window in silence and stillness. I might as well be a monk meditating, for my mind is blank. Occasionally thoughts drift across my mind – relief that I have heard no strange rumours concerning Prince Yong – wondering what my days will be like – trying to recall my family home in Chengde which I will never see again and which already seems to have a mist drawn over it so that I struggle to recall anything about it even though I was there only a handful of days ago. But mostly my mind seems empty. I cannot imagine my future. I cannot go back to my past. There is only now.

Already the decision made by the horse-faced Lady Que Hui has changed what I can do. I am not to leave the house and grounds until I join Prince Yong's household. I protest. In Chengde I ran our family's errands, walked freely through the streets with my mother to buy food for our household, even went with my younger brothers to catch hares in the woods. Now I am told that I may not walk through Beijing's markets and down its alleyways. Already the red walls of the Forbidden City hold me prisoner. My protests mean nothing. So I sit and look out of the window or wander without purpose in the garden. There is nothing else to do.

The neighbouring house and gardens belong to an elderly scholar, who has a pet gibbon. Its fur is a snowy white, and when released into the garden it climbs up into a peach tree and grabs for the sweet fruit, munching it and dribbling sticky juice onto the servants below, who try to prevent it finishing the whole crop but despairingly admit to me that they are forbidden to administer any punishment, on the orders of its master. The gibbon, having understood this, takes pleasure in cramming each peach into its mouth, taking one or perhaps two bites only, then letting the spoiled fruit drop to the ground, sometimes hitting a servant on the head.

I lean against our garden wall looking up and call out to it, laughing. "Such naughtiness! You should finish each fruit, not spoil them. Or at least pass me one, why don't you, before they're all gone?" The gibbon grins at me, baring his teeth when I hold out my hand, holding the peach close to his chest before biting it and letting the rest drop to the ground. I tut at him but he only makes contented noises and climbs still higher in the tree.

"Why do you keep him when he's such a nuisance?" I ask the scholar, who has hobbled out to the garden and is standing beneath the tree.

"I like his mischief," he says, chuckling. "The gibbon is a symbol of growing wisdom throughout life, as well as good fortune and nobility."

I nod. I'd rather listen to this old man talk about the symbolic beauty of his wicked pet gibbon than the hubbub of the household in which I'm sitting. Today my dowry will arrive. My father will not be providing a dowry, as would be customary were I marrying a commoner. Instead the Palace will provide one for me, thus eliminating any need for gratitude to my family or opportunity for us to claim favours because of our generosity. From the moment when the Emperor's consort flicked a golden nail shield against my name on a scroll, I belonged to the Imperial Household. It is only a question of time before I am claimed. The passing days are taken up with rituals, with decisions made on my behalf, with symbolism and protocol. I would rather hear about the gibbon.

"I hear you have had good fortune yourself," smiles the old man, peering across at me. "And are to join the Imperial Family."

I sigh. Does the whole of Beijing know my fate? It seems so. "I shall have to hope for the growing wisdom of old age to understand why I was chosen," I say, trying to be polite.

He looks at me, my head probably all he can see appearing over the wall that separates us, his smile gone. He seems sad for me, the only person to have expressed anything other than congratulations and wonderment. "It must seem like a strange future," he says. "Although all futures seem strange to us until they become our past and then it is as though they had always been so and could not have been any other way."

I force a smile onto my face. He's being kind but his words are designed to soothe an anxious mind full of worries about the future. I don't have any worries. I have only a strange numbness, a mind filled with fog.

Through the fog comes more noise, a clattering of feet. "I have to go," I say. "I hope you manage to eat at least one peach this summer."

The old man nods and waves to me. Reluctantly, I make my way back into the house.

Bolts of silk, taels of silver, new robes, gifts for family members and all manner of household goods, from dishes to furniture, flood into the house. My family marvel at our good fortune, at my changed destiny. I am surrounded by compliments, by blessings. Suddenly my beanpole height is 'willowy', my odd grey eyes are 'jade-coloured', although that could encompass almost any shade from white to brown via green. If the Imperial Household has chosen me, then clearly I must be beautiful. I think back to Lady Que Hui's half smile and wonder what Prince Yong will say when he discovers I have been chosen to tease him for his beliefs. I step out of the way of more Palace eunuchs, struggling to carry heavy household furniture.

My attention is drawn by a palanquin, decorated in red and gold, which is being manoeuvred with difficulty into a place where it will be at least partly out of the way of the many people trying to enter and leave the house. I make my way to it and peer inside. It's a small space, a dark red cocoon in which I, a wriggling caterpillar, will be taken to the Palace, to emerge, one presumes, a glorious butterfly at the other end of my journey. I smooth down the flat front of my new robe, hurriedly made for me in a delicate pink silk, and wonder how such a transformation will occur. How do I become elegant and beautiful, like some of the girls I saw? How do I learn to walk and carry myself with grace? How do I know... what... well, what is – what is *expected* of me when I meet the Prince? My family seems far too caught up in celebrations and expectations for anyone to have thought of this. I try to catch my mother's sleeve as she hurries by.

"Not *now*, Niuhuru," she says, pointing a maid towards a pile of silk cloth ready for cutting and indicating where it ought to be taken.

I follow after her. "Aunty said that I might see you all again if the Imperial Household go to Chengde for the hunting season." I hope that my mother will agree that yes, of course I will see my family again, that she might even pause to embrace me. I have allowed myself to think of the future, to wonder what it will be like, to be without my family, in a strange place where I know no-one at all. There are probably girls who have prepared their whole lives for this opportunity, who have been schooled in what to expect and how to behave. I have not. No-one thought I would marry a prince. If my family had been asked about my marriage prospects there would probably been vague mutterings about a few local boys in my hometown, from good families, similar to our own; officials, industrious but not exalted.

But my mother has not heard the tremble in my voice, or if she has she is choosing to ignore it. "Niuhuru," she says, her tone one of slightly impatient reassurance, "you are going to be married. A woman does not go running back to her family at every moment. You will have your own home and you will be used to it soon enough."

"I didn't mean all the time," I say, still trailing after her like a lost puppy. "But once a year…" But it is too late. My mother has spotted a maid who seems to be less than overworked and is issuing a stream of orders.

I retreat to the garden and practice walking gracefully in my new silken cloud-climbing shoes. They oblige me to take odd, swaying steps and I cannot stop or start abruptly without holding out a hand to steady myself. They say that noble Manchu women wear these shoes to give their unbound feet the illusion of being bound, the same swaying walk and delicacy of a Chinese girl. I've never worn them before and I dislike them. After a while I take them off and lie on the grass, heedless of the pink silk that only a few days before I would have been terrified to get dirty. I listen to the gibbon's screeches and stare up at the sky. I watch the peach tree's leaves swaying in the breeze and wonder how my life will be in the Forbidden City. I cannot really imagine it. I have been used to some degree of freedom, running about the hunting ground forests with my brothers and cousins, with little thought of what my future might hold for me. I thought Chengde would be my whole world and now it seems I am to disappear from my family's life, closed up behind the vast red walls of the imperial palace, never heard from again. Everything I have been until now will be irrelevant, for the Imperial Family will mould me into their own shape.

When the day finally comes the fog surrounds me, wrapped more thickly about me than the red silk robes and veils chosen to adorn me. I eat breakfast without tasting what is in my mouth. I don't hear the shouts and clattering of the guards and officials. I don't see my family's faces for the last time. I totter out of the house on my too-high shoes and step into the red palanquin, clutching at its sides to stop myself stumbling. Once inside I don't feel the lurching lift as the bearers raise me up. I sit and wait to enter the high red walls of the Forbidden City.

But the swaying goes on and on. My stomach churns and at last I put up one hand to the curtains and pull them back to see how close we are to our final destination. I blink. I cannot see the Forbidden City at all. I pull the curtain back further, lean my head out and see it at last – to my right and almost behind me, its northernmost wall slowly receding.

"Wait!" I cry out and the palanquin comes to a shuddering stop. The most senior eunuch's anxious face appears at the window.

"My lady?"

"Where are we going?" My voice comes out too high, it trembles as though I am about to cry.

"To the Garden, my lady." The eunuch is puzzled.

"Garden?"

The eunuch frowns. "The Garden of Perfect Brightness, your ladyship. The Yuan Ming Yuan. Residence of Prince Yong."

The red walls of my expected future are crumbling. "Not – not the Forbidden City?"

"The only man who may reside in the Forbidden City is the Emperor," the eunuch reminds me. "Prince Yong has a household in Beijing but prefers his country estate. That is where his consorts live."

I try to nod as though I know this. "Of course," I mumble. "I only thought… it doesn't matter."

The eunuch bows. "Is that all, your ladyship?"

I nod and he disappears as I let the curtains fall. The palanquin lurches again and we continue on our way.

I sit back on the padded seat. I know nothing. I am thirteen years old and I know nothing. I do not even know where my own husband lives. I do not know what other wives he has, nor have I heard of this place, this Yuan Ming Yuan, this Garden of Perfect Brightness. I know nothing of what goes on between a man and his concubines.

The numbing fog that has protected me so far begins to lift. Fat tears slide slowly down my face. I feel like a child, and I am afraid.

The rocking palanquin finally draws to a halt. We left in the morning and it is now late in the day. When I step out of the chair my knees shake from lack of use as much as nerves. I try to steady myself on my high-soled shoes and look about me, breathing in the cooling air. Slowly the churning in my stomach, which has threatened to disgrace me for many hours, fades.

I am standing on the edge of a large lake, surrounded by small islets linked together by bridges. On each islet are one or more palaces. There are flowers everywhere. Planted in great profusion, they trail over and around every part of the scene before me. Wisteria hangs heavy while roses reach upward, twining through branches of trees and across windows. Peonies in every shade burst out of their green foliage. The lake is full of lotus flowers reaching up towards weeping willow trees. It is a private paradise, a hidden world far from the stone courtyards and high walls of the Forbidden City. I wonder what kind of man I have married, who chose this secret flowering place as his home.

"Your ladyship?" The eunuch hovering by my side has already tried and failed to get my attention.

"Yes?"

"Welcome to the Nine Continents Clear and Calm, your home within the Garden, my lady." He gestures forwards and I follow him, still unsteady on my little shoes, the pebbled mosaic path along the lakeside doing nothing to help my balance. I focus so hard on my feet and where I am placing them that I almost bump into the eunuch when he stops. I throw out an arm for balance, then hastily try to regain some poise as he turns to me.

"This will be your palace," he says.

The building before me is larger than any I have ever lived in, but I can see that it is small by the standards of the Imperial Household. There are larger palaces further along the lake path, but a smile spreads over my face when I see it. It is so heavily weighed down with clinging wisteria that it almost seems as though it is made out of it. It is a flower-palace, something from a fairytale.

"It is lovely," I say.

The eunuch looks a little surprised at my compliment, but then he smiles and his formal demeanour softens. "It is very beautiful, my lady," he agrees. "I wish you much happiness here."

His good wishes make me nervous again. I nod, my smile fading.

Inside, he shows me round the rooms. Although they are comfortable and large, there is no ostentation, rather a quiet restraint. Unlike the glimpses of the Forbidden City I saw, here there is no ornate gilding or lavish scattering of precious objects. All the extravagance seems to be in the flowers surrounding the palace and in the elaborate floral arrangements in multiple vases within the rooms. I'm so busy looking at them that I almost trip over a small figure in a pale blue robe, doubled up on the floor.

"Your personal maid," says the eunuch, without paying much attention to her. "There are of course household maids who will provide for your meals, clothing and so on. Yan is just for your own personal needs. Get up, girl," he adds, almost as an afterthought.

The little figure unfolds herself and stands. She is considerably shorter than I am, but probably my own age. She looks terrified. "My lady," she all but whispers. Her robe is stiff with newness.

I smile at her. I'm glad someone else is scared and that I have not been given some dragon of an older maid, someone who might judge me and find me lacking against other court ladies she has known. "What was your name again?"

"Yan, your ladyship."

My nerves make me want to giggle. Her name means Swallow, it seems very apt in this country retreat for my maid to be named after a bird. I smile and nod to her and she bows, then follows about behind me as I move, hovering like a shadow, as though worried that if she does not do so I will make some request of which she will fail to be aware.

"It is late," says the eunuch. "You will visit Lady Nara tomorrow to present your compliments."

I feel like an idiot. "Lady Nara?" I ask, wondering if this is perhaps my husband's mother.

"Prince Yong's Primary Consort," says the eunuch, bowing as he takes his leave of me. I stand in the doorway, watching him disappear, along with the guards and the bobbing red palanquin, now empty.

When I turn back into the room, Yan almost leaps out of my way, then stands trembling, waiting for an order like a terrified puppy who has been beaten too often.

"How long have you been here?" I ask.

"Only since this morning," she admits.

"Where were you before that?"

"The Forbidden City, your ladyship. For my training. Then I was told that a new lady was arriving in Prince Yong's household and that I would be sent here."

I nod. It is a mark of my low status, I suppose, that I have been given a newly-trained maid, and only one at that. But it's a relief to me not to have to manage some grand household and for my only servant to be a girl my own age. "We will have to explore our new home together then," I suggest and watch her eyes widen.

53

"Yes, your ladyship," she says uncertainly.

We make our way through all the rooms. I am not sure how I am expected to use them all, the size of this tiny palace is twice the size of my family home in Chengde. I daren't wander outside, for fear of losing my way or bumping into someone unexpected.

"Do you know when I will meet the Prince?" I ask Yan.

She shakes her head. "I was told he is very busy," she says. "They said at the palace that he was very hard-working and did not like to be disturbed."

I take this in. A hard-working husband should be a good thing, I suppose, better than a man who thinks of nothing but his own pleasures, like the Crown Prince. But it doesn't tell me when I'll be called for. I have to assume that it will not be tonight, since no instructions have been left for me.

We both startle at a loud knocking, but Yan hurries to answer the door. Two maids and a eunuch appear. They bow to me but don't speak, only scurry past towards the dining room, carrying several baskets. Yan rushes after them. A few moments later they emerge, bow again and depart.

Yan hovers in the doorway. "Your dinner is ready, your ladyship," she says.

I follow her.

The table is very large and there are a lot of dishes on it – Yan quickly uncovers the little lids, and good smells emerge, making my empty stomach rumble. I sit and Yan pours water for me to wash my hands. I eat. The food is good and very plentiful. There is plenty left when I leave the table. Yan serves me tea in a sitting room, then disappears. I hope that the leftovers from my meal will nourish her skinny little frame into something more substantial.

I wake early. The soft bed and silken covers lulled me into a quick sleep. I woke only once and was comforted by the small rasping snores of Yan, sleeping by the door. When I wake, though, she is already gone and when I call out for her she comes quickly, holding a little bowl of tea in which float rose petals.

"I have to meet Lady Nara today," I tell her and she nods, serious at the challenge. She has already chosen the clothes I will wear, green silk with delicately embroidered peonies. My cloud-climbing shoes today are lower than yesterday's, for which I'm grateful. My triple-pearl earrings are inserted. Gently, Yan brushes my hair, then pins it up into coils, topped with fresh peonies from the gardens outside and some little dangling golden tassels. The effect is very pretty and I tell her so. Her anxious face breaks into a beaming smile.

Now that I see the lake and the islets again I realise that the name of this area, Nine Continents Clear and Calm, refers to the number of the islets surrounding the lake. The streams separating each one are tiny, one could almost jump across them, although certainly not in the clothes and shoes I am currently wearing. Instead Yan and I make our way across one little bridge after another to reach the islet where Lady Nara lives, almost opposite to my own, close to Prince Yong's. I'm a little nervous in case I should accidentally meet my husband nearby and not know who he is, since I have never seen him.

Lady Nara's palace is far larger than my own. It is surrounded by pink roses in full bloom, the scent is overwhelming. Her household is of course also larger, with several eunuchs and many maids in attendance. I am shown into a sitting room, where I am offered a seat and tea while Yan waits in an adjoining room. A rustling announces Lady Nara. I hastily rise and when she arrives in the room I prostrate myself, murmuring respectful greetings due to a senior wife. When I've finished she waves me to a seat, turning to take her own bowl of tea from a maid. I take the opportunity to look at her without being caught staring.

Her face is pleasant and slightly plump. She must be thirty years old but she looks well for her age, only perhaps a little tired. Her clothes are sombre and her hair is arranged simply. I feel a little overdressed.

"You are welcome here," she says, looking me over. "You are very young," she adds.

"I am thirteen, your ladyship," I say.

She nods. "We have not had a new lady join our household for many years," she says. Later I'm to find this is true. All the other women in Prince Yong's household are in their late twenties. I am considerably younger than all of them. "We did not know the Prince had requested a new concubine," she adds, but her tone is not angry or jealous. She gives me a weary smile. "As I say, you are welcome here," she says. "You will find us very quiet. I hope you will not be bored."

I try to nod my head and shake it at the same time, uncertain of the right answer. She rises and I understand that my audience is over. "You may always come to me if there is something you need," she says.

I stammer my thanks before I am shown out.

Walking back through the heavy scent of roses Yan whispers to me that Lady Nara is in mourning. Her only child, eldest son of the Prince, died a year ago, aged seven. The maids have told her that since then their mistress, once a happy woman, is now slow and sad, that she takes little pleasure in her life. We return to my own palace in silence.

Lady Nara is right about it being quiet here. It's late morning and I venture out of the palace again, Yan following behind me, but we see few people. An official rides by, eunuchs go about their work here and there, the odd maid hurries past on an errand. We make our way towards a cluster of women inside a pavilion. With them are two small girls. I feel a sudden shyness and hover for a moment, then force myself to approach them.

There are three women. They are dressed well in good quality silks but their robes are everyday wear, not formal court dress. Their hair is pinned simply, with only fresh flowers, no jewels. They are sipping tea and playing mah-jong. The fourth player is one of the two young girls, but she keeps breaking off to play with her younger sister.

"Pay attention!" scolds one of the women and the older girl consults the board, makes a move and returns to the lakeside and her sister. The women sigh at her lack of skill and interest.

The two girls are dabbling their hands in the lake's edge and dangling improvised fishing rods made of branches into the water. But now the younger girl has noticed me.

"Hello!" she says. "Who are you?"

All heads turn towards me. I can feel myself flushing. "I – I am Niuhuru," I stammer.

There's a bewildered pause and then one of the women stands up. "Oh!" she says. "The new concubine?"

I nod.

She comes closer and pulls at my arm to make me join the women at the table. "I am Mao. The girls are my daughters," she adds, not bothering to name them. She gestures at the other two women. "Lady Ning, Lady Zhang," she says by way of introduction. They nod and smile while Lady Mao continues. "We are concubines to the Prince. We knew you were coming but were not told when to expect you."

I try to bow to them all but they wave my manners away, staring at me with frank curiosity.

"You're very *young*," says Lady Zhang and the others nod.

"I am thirteen," I say. They nod. It's a reasonable age to be married, but still I feel very young, standing in front of these women, so at ease in their surroundings, so much older than me that they have daughters who in a few short years will be marriageable themselves.

"Sit, sit!" urges Lady Mao. "Can you play mah-jong?" she adds hopefully.

"Badly," I confess. It's a game my mother and aunts were fond of. I was too busy running through the woods with my brothers.

"Oh, we'll teach you," says Lady Ning. "We play every day."

I take the place of the elder daughter, who seems pleased to be set free, disappearing off along the lakeside path with her sister. I do the best I can, but clearly the women do play every day, for all of them are far better than I am, even with their attention only partly on the game. I'm quizzed about my family, my background, my hometown.

"Oh, Chengde," says Lady Zhang. "The hunting grounds. The whole court goes there every autumn. Of course the Prince does not really like to hunt," she adds, "so he usually stays as little as possible." The other ladies make faces. "It's a shame," she adds. "It's the only time we get to see everyone. The Prince is not a very sociable person."

"Have you met him yet?" asks Lady Mao.

I shake my head.

"He'll call for you soon, I expect," says Lady Mao. "But don't expect to be called for very often."

I wait for some warning to know my place, some sign of jealousy, but her face is open. "Prince Yong is not really the sort of man to indulge much in the pleasures of the bedchamber," she says, a little despondently. "He works very hard and has little time for pastimes," she adds, suddenly laughing. "You're the first new concubine here in years!"

The others chuckle.

I feel a wave of relief. The stories I've always heard of households full of warring concubines appear not to be the case here. Lady Nara was pleasant if sad, these women seem friendly and I detect no warring feuds, no jealousies. It seems they've all resigned themselves to a husband who is not that interested in any of them, and perhaps his lack of interest has softened what rivalries might have arisen. I can feel my shoulders relax. "Are we the only concubines?" I ask.

"No," says Lady Ning. "There are three others. There's Lady Dunsu, a sweet woman – but she is in mourning. You may not see her for a while."

"Why is she in mourning?" I ask.

Lady Mao looks sad. "She has been unlucky," she says. "She has borne three sons and a daughter, but none of them have survived. She was the Prince's favourite, but lately she has grown withdrawn."

I'm a little unnerved by all these stories of dead children and their sad mothers. Is the Prince's house unlucky? "How many living children does the Prince have?" I ask.

"Two sons and two daughters," says Lady Mao.

I'm a little taken aback. Only four living children is very few. The Prince has a fair number of women in his household. Doesn't he have any interest in them at all?

"Who are the other concubines?"

"There's Lady Chunque – a lovely woman. And Lady Qi."

I wait for a comment to be made on Lady Qi's character but nothing is forthcoming, so I don't enquire further.

An hour or two passes in friendly conversation and playing mahjong, before we break up and make our way back along the lakeside to our own palaces. At the door of my own palace stands a eunuch, waiting for me.

"His Highness requests your company this evening," he announces and leaves before I have a chance to ask any questions. I turn to look at Yan, standing wide-eyed behind me.

"Does he mean...?" I begin, but Yan is already pulling me inside.

"You are going to meet your husband!" she says excitedly. "Quick, I must prepare you."

Bathed and dressed in my finest robe, a shimmering blue decorated with flying cranes and drifting clouds, I sit and wait. Yan and I have been too anxious to be ready on time and despite eating and bathing, followed by dressing and having my hair done, there is still a while to go before the appointed hour. I take off my shoes and try to ease my aching neck, where Yan has pulled my hair too tight and weighed me down with so many decorations that my head is twice its usual size.

I follow the eunuch who has been sent to accompany me. As I reach the gate I look back at Yan, standing in the doorway, shoulders hunched, her little face pinched with worry. When she sees me looking back she forces a too-bright smile onto her face.

We make our way in silence along the lakeside path towards the Prince's islet, crossing two bridges, one a simple thing made of painted wood, the other from blocks of carved stone. Along the way we pass a few palaces. I wonder whether the other ladies can see me from their rooms, if they see my overdressed hair and smile to themselves or laugh at me. I can see the largest palace looming ahead of us, where the Prince resides. Just before it we pass a palace that sits right on the lake's edge. Standing on a little jetty by the water's edge is a woman, dressed in a floating green robe. Her hair is pinned with pink lotus flowers and she stands absolutely still, watching me as I pass by. She is only twenty paces from me, yet she does not acknowledge me when I nod to her, only watches me, her face blank of any expression. I feel a coldness settle on me. This must be one of the women whom I have not yet met and her manner towards me is very different to the mah-jong-playing friendly group I met earlier. As soon as we have safely passed out of earshot I whisper to the eunuch, "Who was that lady?"

He does not break stride nor ask to whom I am referring. "Lady Qi," he says.

I look over my shoulder. Lady Qi is still standing there, still watching me as I near the Prince's palace, its swooping rooftops towering above the other palaces on the islets.

The late summer day is slowly fading away. I am surrounded by unfamiliar faces: the eunuchs and maids of the Prince. They undress me, which I suppose I must get used to, although my whole body grows goose-fleshed with embarrassment. My heavy robes, which had given me courage, are stripped away. My hair is unbound and falls down my back, unadorned. I wonder what the purpose was in Yan's careful preparation of me, since the Prince will see none of my adornments. So far the only person of note who has seen me in my splendour is Lady Qi. If I had known she would be my only witness, I would have worn a maid's robe.

At last the servants step away and I am left alone in the Prince's bedchamber. I'm not sure where I should put myself. I sit on the very edge of the heavy carved wooden bed, which is set into a niche, as is usual, although it's far larger than any other bed I've ever seen. I try not to pull my sleeping robe around me for comfort. My feet are cold on the floor, although the bed itself is heated with a kang underneath it. I consider pulling my feet up onto the bed but I am too nervous to make myself comfortable.

At last I hear footsteps and spring to my feet. I forget about elegance and clutch the sleeping robe to me, although it is made of such sheer silk that it is hardly going to shield my modesty.

The door opens.

The man who enters is of a good height. His robes are surprisingly plain for a prince. They are woven in a pale green silk, fastened with a simple belt. His long hair is neatly plaited in a queue. I know because Yan has told me that he is twenty-seven years old.

He pauses in the doorway, regards me in silence and then closes the door behind him. I stand facing him, only a few paces away. I don't know what to do or say.

"Lady Niuhuru," he says at last. "Welcome. Have you been well cared for here? Do you have everything you need? Are your rooms to your satisfaction?"

He sounds as though he is checking off questions against a list, not solicitously enquiring after his new wife's comforts. I nod and then try to speak, although my voice cracks.

"Yes, Your Highness. Th-thank you."

He nods, satisfied. There is warm wine and two small bowls waiting on a table and he pours each of us some. He holds out my bowl and I take it with one hand, the other still clutching my robe. I have only tasted wine once or twice at great occasions and I did not much like it. I take only a tiny sip and then stand holding the bowl, uncertain of where to place it. The Prince drinks his own bowl dry, then turns back to me. He holds out his hand and I place the still-full bowl in his palm. His hands are warm. He puts it back on the table and then comes close to me. I swallow. I am a tall girl, but he stands a good head taller than me. I have never stood so close to a man for so long.

Gently, he pulls at my sleeping robe. I unclench my fingers so that he can remove it and he lets it fall to the floor, heedless of the fine silk. I try to stop my cold hands balling into fists by my side and lower my eyes so that I do not have to meet his gaze. I will follow his lead, I tell myself. Whatever he wishes me to do, I will try to do it and be a good wife, even though I know little of what is about to happen.

But he does not move again. I can see his hands hanging loosely by his side. At last I look up at him and find that he is looking over my body with a frown on his face.

Shame burns through me. I wish now that I had been through the preliminary selection rounds during the Draft. Whatever he is displeased with now, they would surely have noticed it then. They would have declared that I was unfit for the Draft and sent me home. Instead I slipped through the net and now I am humiliated before a

Prince to whom I am already married. What will he do, I wonder. Will he send me home in disgrace? Will he keep me here but only as a maid or simply leave me to sit all alone in my palace, year after year, forgotten and humbled?

At last he speaks. "You are very young," he says.

I look down at my flat chest, the white goose-fleshed skin shrinking further under his gaze, my narrow hips cold, the tiny hairless place between my pale thighs. "I am thirteen," I say. "I am of marriageable age." My voice is very small.

He lifts his gaze from my trembling cold body to my eyes, which much to my shame are now brimming with tears. In one swift movement he kneels and lifts up my discarded sleeping robe, which he places with care about my shoulders, helping me to put my arms back into the sleeves. Then he speaks softly. "I did not mean to shame you. I simply meant that you are not yet…" he pauses and then goes on. "You are not yet a woman. I am not – I would not wish to lie with you when you are still so young."

I am mortified. The Prince finds me a child. He is dismissing me. A hot tear trickles down my cheek.

He shakes his head and wipes away the tear with the back of his hand. "You must stop crying," he says a little gruffly. "I am not sending you away. You are welcome in my household. But you are too young and I will not lie with you until you are older. You will live here and I hope you will be happy. Later, when you are…" he gestures awkwardly, "… older, I will send for you again. There is no need to cry."

I nod because I know he expects it.

His face clears at once, as though I had offered a dazzling smile rather than a small and miserable nod. "Very well," he says, more cheerfully. "I will call for the servants and they will return you to your rooms."

"Can't I – can't I stay here a little while?" I ask. The thought of walking back to my rooms, along the little pathways where every other woman will be able to see me, when I have barely been in this room long enough to be undressed and dressed again is humiliating. Everyone will know that I have been found wanting.

He seems puzzled by my request. "You would have nothing to do," he says. "I must attend to some papers." He turns away, satisfied that the matter has been dealt with.

The servants gather round me and I am dressed in my robes once more. They leave my hair unbound, so that as I walk back towards my rooms, the evening wind catches it. It whips across my face and I have to hold it back with one hand so that I will not be blinded. As I do so I look across to the lakeside palace and see Lady Qi still standing there, observing me as I make my way back to my rooms. Her face twists into something resembling a smile.

Castiglione: A greyhound at his toilet

"**C**AN YOU DRAW A BIRD?"

I was not expecting to be tested at once, although I had of course brought with me certain paintings I had already completed, so that the Emperor might see my work. I fumbled in my bag and extracted the tools of my trade. My hands shook a little. I tried not to notice as the courtiers and eunuchs drew closer while the Emperor leaned forward. Quickly I drew a bird, of the kind I had seen in the streets of Beijing on our hurried way to the Palace. It sat in its cage, dangling from a long pole slung over the hunched back of an elderly man. I had remarked on them as we passed and was told that pet birds were taken for 'walks' each day in their cages, so that they might benefit from the exercise. I am not entirely sure even now how they can be said to benefit from the exercise of their master's legs rather than their own wings. Perhaps a change of scenery sufficed them. I did not have my colours with me, so it was only a sketch, but when I turned it towards His Majesty he started back and smiled, then held out his hand, into which I placed the image.

"Astonishing," he said, examining it very closely. "It seems as though it is swaying on the end of its pole!" He looked at me with some kindliness, his wrinkled face cracking in a smile. "You can draw a bird, I see. What else can you draw?"

I hesitated. I did not wish to seem too humble and of insufficient prowess, nor to make a poor first impression which might damage my relationship with my new patron. I had, after all, been chosen for this task and sent across the wide seas for this very undertaking, to act as court painter to the Emperor of China. I was nervous of suggesting that I painted portraits, although of course I was able to do so, for fear that he would immediately ask me to portray his own physiognomy. As I did not yet know his likes and dislikes in this regard, and I had already found that all sitters had very particular desires when it came to their own portrayal, I cast about me for some other object that I could illustrate for him.

In a corner of the great receiving hall was a greyhound, fiercely engaged in removing himself of lice, by means of his teeth, drawn up in a grimace as he twisted his neck round to his own hind leg. A greyhound being a good shape for this kind of quick drawing, all long lines and movement, I did not reply to the Emperor, only began to sketch again. He leaned forwards and within a few strokes he had recognised the shape and looked about him, following my eyes. He chuckled at the sight of the greyhound's efforts and then waited while I completed his likeness.

"I can almost see his fleas," he said, looking down at the sketch and then back at the dog, surprised. Later I was to learn that it was rare for a painter here to show an animal as I had done, in movement and in such a bestial pose. Their horses and dogs are much portrayed but they are shown with nobility and grace, posed as their masters might be for a formal portrait, not grimacing to rid themselves of crawling pests. Perhaps the Emperor had never seen such a sketch, of an animal caught in the midst of its own toilet. At any rate he seemed pleased with my work and spoke with his Chief Eunuch, a most magnificently dressed fellow, who nodded at his sovereign's commands. With much bowing and scraping and the never-ending kowtow which I had already practiced more than once, we were dismissed from the imperial presence and waited in an antechamber along with Brother Matteo Ripa, our interpreter for the meeting. The Chief Eunuch followed us there and addressed me rapidly. I struggled to catch his meaning and he became irate, until Brother Ripa interceded. Pacified, the Chief Eunuch spoke with him for some time, issuing a stream of instructions. Ripa nodded as though all was clear, while I cursed my slow learning of the language. Despite the years of study since I had first agreed to come here my Mandarin was still poor and I made a note to myself that I must continue to engage a native speaker to improve my pronunciation skills, for I knew I would not advance in my career if my patron could not speak with me.

The Chief Eunuch indicated we might depart.

"He thought you were me and could not understand why your Mandarin was not better," explained Brother Ripa.

"How could he have mistaken us for one another?" I asked. "We bear no resemblance at all."

"They say they cannot tell most of us apart," he replied unperturbed. "They say our faces are too similar."

I pondered this.

"You have been given a new name," added Brother Ripa, as though it were a matter of no importance.

"A new *name*? Why?"

"The Emperor finds your name hard to pronounce. You will be known as Lang Shining. Shining is the first name, Lang is the family name. It is pronounced Shur-ning," he emphasised. "You had better practice it."

I muttered it to myself.

"You will work under the auspices of the Palace Board of Works in the two Imperial Painting Studios," he continued as we walked back through the noisy streets of Beijing to the church of St Joseph's, my new home. "One is called the Painting Academy Office and is based within the Forbidden City. The other is located in the Hall of Fulfilled Wishes. It is situated within a country estate close to Beijing."

I was distracted by both my new name and my surroundings and did not enquire further into my future place of work. All around me were new sights and I was elated by the Emperor's praise of my skills. I would surely amaze him once I could work with my oils and canvas, a large quantity of which had accompanied me on this long journey to my new destiny and which even now was following me to Beijing from Macau.

Amidst the curved rooftops and single-storey height of the local Chinese architecture my new home, St Joseph's, stood out, the classical style from home that ought to have been familiar to me looking oddly out of place here. It was built in a grey stone two storeys high, finished off with three dome-topped towers, one of which housed the bells to summon us to Mass. The interior of the chapel was fairly plain by the standards of home, with little in the way of gilding or stained glass, but otherwise pleasant enough. Behind it were located both the living quarters and refectory of the Brothers, as well as a small garden for contemplation, somewhat in the Chinese style, with decorative black rocks from the South, small areas of grass and some simple flowers.

The names of the various Brothers of the Mission rushed past me at that first meeting, with only a few making a firm first impression. An elderly Father Friedel was our Superior, Brother Matteo Ripa who had acted as our interpreter was an engraver of copper and an ardent missionary. He was much pleased to welcome Brother Costa, since they both hailed from Naples. Meanwhile a Brother Michele Arailza, a Venetian by birth, was a fellow painter, but he seemed ill-disposed towards me from the very beginning. I wondered if he disliked the idea of two new painters, of having competition in serving the Emperor.

The Brothers might have been a little taken aback by Laura's presence, but most of them welcomed us warmly enough.

Our first few weeks as we settled into St Joseph's offered nothing but boredom, for the endless cycle of prayers that made up our days was of limited interest to me. I viewed Brother Arailza's paintings and privately felt that he would indeed have something to fear from my arrival at court, for his work was mediocre at best. I could see Laura felt the same, although neither of us made anything but polite comments on the subject matter. The food was not what I had expected, consisting mostly of plain fare such as steamed breads and stewed fruits or foods prepared to our own homelands' recipes. Brother Arailza screwed up his face when I asked about the local food and said that many of the Brothers did not care for it.

"They have good enough fruits, I suppose," he allowed. "Apples and pears, quinces, tolerably good plums. You will find the nuts here are similar to our own although the cherries are wild and therefore too sharp. And they do not make wine from grapes, but from rice: it is passable."

I tried the rice wine and found it very pleasant, certainly better than the poor quality sour grape-wine made by the Brothers to use at Mass. When certain dishes were sent to us from the Emperor's own table, which was, we were informed, to be seen as a gesture of benevolence, the Brothers ate from them only sparingly and somewhat unwillingly, although myself and Laura tasted meat-filled buns, an oddly sour soup and some honeyed sweetmeats and thought them all good.

I chafed a little under Father Friedel's constant worried reminders that I must eventually take my vows. Autumn was already upon us but he seemed unwilling to let me start work, as though he thought I might disappear into the Forbidden City and never come out again.

"Gherardini," he would repeat often, returning to my predecessor's time here as though it haunted him, "Gherardini never really took to the Mission life. He did not take his vows, you see, and grew too accustomed to the local way of life, eating their food and following some of their customs. Eventually he refused to live within the Mission at all and the Emperor gave him lodging with one of his trusted officials." The thought of this almost made him shudder. "Therefore you must understand how important it is that you yourself will take vows and live as we do. And your work must be pleasing to His Majesty, for as you know at this time he has forbidden us from even preaching and we must find a way to soften his heart in this matter."

I nodded and promised more than once that I had every intention of taking my vows in due course. I waited impatiently to begin my work and was relieved when I was finally taken to my new place of work in the Forbidden City, late in the autumn, with sharply cold days already predicting winter's arrival. I was informed that my working hours would henceforth be from seven in the morning until five in the afternoon and therefore I must present myself at my place of work at an appropriate hour to begin my painting for the day.

"You will find that some of the eunuchs are jealous of the praise and attention we receive," muttered Brother Arailza. "They often keep us waiting before allowing us entry, perhaps they think to cause trouble for us."

My first impression of the Imperial Studios was of both speed and silence. Large rooms led one into another, each with a different focus. Ceramics were worked on elsewhere, as well as enamel and glasswork studios. Here, where I was to work, were primarily paintings and calligraphy used for decorative purposes. The more senior artists worked in frowning silence, their assistants and apprentices scurried about them on cloth soles, which led to a constant soft pattering sound. Scrolls of paper were being made up, laid out, painted on, rolled up and despatched elsewhere. There were racks for drying and wide tables for works to be completed on. Saucers containing paints were kept warm on a tiny stove, to prevent them freezing on cold days. The eunuch showing me around whispered softly about all that we saw and finally led me to an area which had been set aside against my coming, where I was grateful to see many of my materials had already been transported and set out for my use. A variety of young men bowed deeply to me and I was told more names than I could remember. Many of my assistants and apprentices were eunuchs, I was to realise over time, for eunuchs performed most of the tasks within the Forbidden City, from the very lowliest even up to the great offices of state. Those who showed artistic talent might hope to work here, in the Studios. In other parts of the complex, I was informed, there were also dressmakers and perfumiers, jewellery-makers and designers of such small ornaments as might please the Emperor and his family: board games, vases, carvings of jade and wood, scented furniture and much more. Altogether there must have been many hundreds of artisans and artists at work, each of us dedicated only to the Emperor's pleasure and the beautification of his surroundings. The Brothers had seen fit to provide him not only with myself and other painters, but clock-makers, astronomers, medical men such as Brother Costa and even engineers. Our purpose here was daily made clear to us: to enchant the Emperor with the wonders of our Western skills, that he might, in time, consider our God also worthy of devotion.

That winter was a time of frustration for me, attempting to recall people's names and observing the work of those around me, mostly eunuchs trained as painters, who laboured over various imperial commissions, from portraits to landscapes and still lifes. Some were on scrolls of paper, others on stretched silk, a few were made into screens and other such ornaments. I admired their ability to paint with inks on silk, for it was fast work that must be perfect the first time, there was no room for error. It reminded me of fresco work, each stroke quick and light, the brush lifted away between each touch to avoid drips or inadvertent contamination. I tried using the inks myself and spent many hours experimenting with their colours and shades. They used rice paper which was stronger than I expected, as well as mulberry bark paper which came in vast sheets the size of blankets and which could not be torn by a man's bare hands. My tools had all been delivered and I spent time arranging them for my work: metal styluses, pencils and pens, inks, white and black chalks, pastels, watercolours and of course my oils.

"The Emperor prefers watercolours," said Brother Arailza gloomily. "I have tried to persuade him of the quality of oils but he has stubborn tastes."

I nodded, finding Arailza's constant complaints about his work here somewhat tiresome. I was eager for a commission of my own. But I was made to wait. Nian Xiyao, a court official, had been assigned to me as a tutor for my first few months, to explain my duties, guide me in the meanings of local symbols and suchlike. He seemed to consider learning by rote the best way to educate me, and so I was made to repeat back the symbolism of bats, hedgehogs, persimmons, dragons and other such things until I thought I would go mad with boredom.

"I will learn best if I am commissioned," I tried suggesting, but Xiyao only shook his head and continued unperturbed with his instruction until the first warmer days made their welcome reappearance.

"You are given the task of painting a view of the Garden," he informed me at last.

I thought of the so-called 'gardens' I had seen in the Forbidden City so far. They were not what I would have called a garden, myself, being primarily composed of stone: not only the cobbles beneath one's feet but also strange, twisted, dark rocks taller than a man. They were brought here from the South of the empire and apparently much admired for their natural beauty. There might be one or two trees, some pots of flowers, but they seemed almost out of place, surrounded by stone. Nevertheless I smiled, pleased at last to have work of my own to do. "Which garden is it?" I asked, hoping it might be the Emperor's own.

"The Garden of Perfect Brightness," said Xiyao.

I was beginning to grow accustomed to their lavish names for even the simplest of places. "Certainly," I said. "Where is it?"

"A day's travel to the northwest," he said.

I stared at him. "What?"

"It was once the Emperor's hunting ground," he explained. "It is now the residence of Prince Yong, one of the Emperor's sons."

"And I am to paint it?"

"The Emperor wishes to commission a particular view of the Garden," said Xiyao. "A view of the Prince's own palace, seen from across the lake."

Clearly the garden in question was not some little courtyard after all. I was given an escort and a mule-cart, which was loaded up with my materials. I was advised that once there I was to join the painting studio located within the estate and to familiarise myself with the surroundings before carrying out my commission. There was no hurry, the commission was seen as part of my training in this, my new world.

Laura was jealous. "I have not even met the Emperor, only one of his senior ladies and she knew nothing about painting, she only played with her lapdog," she complained when I told her. "And I have no commission."

"You are an apprentice," I reminded her.

"I am not," she retorted. "I have completed my apprenticeship."

"Well, you are still learning," I amended. "Sketch the people

73

who come to Mass. It will be practice for you in their costumes and physiognomy, as well as their customs. "

"I want to come with you," she said.

I shook my head. "We are in the Emperor's employ," I reminded her. "It is not for us to countermand his orders. Sketch the parishioners and await my return."

She pouted but was there to wave me off when I departed Beijing for the country estate.

The roads were bumpy and I was glad towards the end of the day when we reached large gates set within a long wall of rose and cream-coloured rocks. Evidently the site was large, for I could not see the end of the wall as it stretched away into the distance. My mounted escort left me at the Eastern Gate, where a guard admitted me and guided me towards a cluster of studio buildings in a pleasingly green setting: a large area of grass with trees here and there in blossom. This, I was informed, was the studio where various artists were based when work was commissioned. In a small village named Hai-Tien some way distant from the estate was a house the Brothers had purchased where those of us working in the Garden were to sleep, for it would be impractical to return to Beijing every day. I was weary enough not to wish to explore that evening and instead viewed the studio and then retreated to the house, which had stables for the mules that we were to ride to the Garden each day. A serving girl gave me food. I ate and slept.

I woke early and rode a docile if slow mule back to the Eastern Gate to request entry. Once in, I determined to walk across the entire estate, to familiarise myself with it if I was to be based here for a while.

Making my way along the edge of a small lake I came across a gardener kneeling by a tree, adding new flowering primroses to those already in bud.

"My name is Lang Shining," I said, remembering just in time that I must offer my surname first, in the local fashion. "I am His Majesty's painter. What is your name?"

The gardener stood and bowed with a smile. "My name is Kun," he said.

I smiled back at him, he seemed a pleasant fellow. "I am seeking the Garden of Perfect Brightness," I told him.

He spread his hands. "This is the Yuan Ming Yuan, the Garden of Perfect Brightness," he said.

I frowned. "It is the name for the whole estate?"

"Yes."

"I am to paint a view of Prince Yong's palace," I clarified.

"Nine Continents Clear and Calm," he said, nodding. "It is a lake around which are set nine islets, on which the Prince and his ladies live."

"Ah, I see," I said. "And where is it?"

He gave me directions and I set off at a brisk walk.

But it was hard to walk swiftly for long. Kun's directions took me along a tiny winding path which worked its way around a larger lake where willow trees dipped down to the water and an early-morning light mist drifted at its far side. The pale blue sky was filled with scudding clouds and everywhere I looked were the first signs of spring: tiny buds of pastel colours, a haze of green from the newly-leafed trees. The very air smelt of spring, a fresh wet scent of the earth while the early sun lit up everything around me with a delicate glow. I wished that I had my paints with me here and now and thought that I must paint my commission in this early light, no matter how many dawn risings it would take.

After some time I realised that I had perhaps misremembered or misunderstood Kun's directions, for I had expected to see the lake he had mentioned, ringed with the palaces of the Prince and his ladies and yet still I found myself walking, beginning to see for myself just how large the estate must be. I reminded myself that after all there was no hurry and began to explore the tiny paths I found here and there, each temptingly hiding another view of the Garden. Unlike the formal gardens of a grand house at home or even the grounds of a monastery such as those where the Jesuits had offered me training for my mission, here I found it impossible to locate a standpoint offering a view of the entirety. Low hills surrounded me. Many of them I suspected to be manmade, deliberately restricting my view to the immediate surroundings, before a few steps would take me beyond them and into another small area. Tiny streams were everywhere, linking up one lake after another until I began to think of the visit I had made years before to Venice. Here was the same delicacy of a water-rich landscape surrounded with both natural and man-made beauty: temples, circular ponds filled with large multicoloured fish and artfully clustered trees that reached out their blossom-laden branches. Coming to a far larger lake than those I had seen so far I found jetties at which were moored little rowing boats awaiting use.

At one of these I paused and then unhooked a mooring rope to free a small craft. Awkwardly, I climbed aboard and took up the oars. It took me a few moments to coordinate my strokes, so that the little boat bobbed this way and that before it steadied. Slowly I rowed across the large lake, circling around a building set in its very centre, perhaps a temple or simply a viewing point. It was surrounded by lanterns, now spent, their golden hues reflected in the stillness of the lake's waters. Two black swans glided by, their crimson beaks dipping to one another.

I stopped rowing then and allowed the oars to rest within the boat. A slight breeze meant that the boat drifted slowly on the water but I paid it no mind. Something in me gave way. It seemed in that moment that all the tension of the past years: the waiting, the journey, making my way in a strange new world, the summons to court, the desire for a commission to prove my worth – that all of this was gone and instead I was simply here, in the place I had long dreamed of, fulfilling my ambitions. It was a strange place to have such a revelation, for in my ambitious daydreams I had imagined such a moment coming when I delivered to the Emperor a portrait or other commission that he would praise. And yet this place, this Garden of Perfect Brightness, seemed suddenly very aptly named to me, for I felt that I was surrounded by some strange clarity and happiness. I lay down in the boat and watched the clouds in the sky, their ever-changing nature suggesting first one form and then another, my mind content to watch as each shape came and went.

I must have lain there for some time, for the sun began to feel warm on my face. At last I sat up and looked about me. The boat had drifted close to the far shore and it was the work of only a few moments to row to a nearby jetty and fasten its moorings. I clambered to the top of one of the small hills and saw another, smaller lake, which might be the one I sought, though by now I was certain that I was thoroughly lost. No matter. I set off along the lakeside and passed one or two palaces, which made me believe that I might indeed be close to the Nine Islets, although the path I was on began to grow smaller and led away from the main lake. Ahead of me was a tiny path lined in bamboo, casting a dim green light over the way ahead, the dirt path leading somewhere further on. I turned back and paused for a moment, uncertain whether to return the way I had come back to the larger, cobbled path or press on. But the little pathway, framed in the delicate green of fresh bamboo towering above my head, was too tempting. I turned to face it again, ready to explore further.

In the brief moment while I had paused with my back to the bamboo, a figure in green silk had come into my view.

The Emperor's greyhound still guards the threshold of my memory palace. I am old enough to know better but still I pretend to myself that I pause here so that I may caress him. In truth I pause so that I may take a deep breath. Even now, I need to take a deep breath before I see her.

Forty Views of the Yuan Ming Yuan

I HAVE NO-ONE ELSE TO CONFIDE in so, stumblingly, I tell Yan of my disastrous first meeting with my new husband and she, already fiercely loyal to me as her sole charge in her first official post, is indignant. "You're taller than any of the ladies," she declares.

I look down at my body as she bathes me. "I am not womanly," I say sadly. I think of my mother and a few unbidden tears come.

Yan tuts. "I will feed you up."

I can't help but giggle but Yan takes her new task seriously. She begins by ordering larger portions of food to be served at every meal and plies me with sweet cakes at any opportunity between meals.

"He didn't say I should be *fatter*," I remonstrate.

"You're too skinny anyway," retorts Yan, certain of the path she is following. "You need to eat more and then your womanliness will come for sure."

She spends hours sitting re-stitching my robes so that they are just that little more fitted, giving the illusion of curves where I have none, and I am touched by her efforts. Her mission gives her a new-found confidence and the ample food I am unable to finish adds some much-needed flesh to her own undernourished frame although she is still a head shorter than me.

But I quickly grow tired of this new life. The unending bathing, the dressing, the elaborately arranged hair which is only dismantled again each evening, the too-much food and sitting about bores me. I see the other ladies from time to time and they are always pleasant but their own lives are as sedate as mine. I find daily mah-jong tiresome and sitting with them makes me feel older than I really am, yet I do not feel I can roam about with their daughters, for fear of being thought childish.

"Let's go out," I say to Yan one day, already bored when I have only just finished breakfast.

"To the ladies?" asks Yan, obediently setting down her sewing.

"No," I say.

"Where to, then?"

"I don't know," I confess. "Just out, before I go mad."

Yan follows me, confused. I stand outside my home, gazing one way and another, before setting off along a path I have never followed before. It leads away from the lake, through an avenue of tall bamboos and softly waving pink and white anemone flowers. I totter along in my high shoes, occasionally stumbling. Yan has to catch me twice and in the end I hold her hand as though we were friends and her sturdy clasp gives me better balance.

"Where are we going?" asks Yan after we have passed a tiny temple, its swooping golden roof and scarlet paint hidden amongst the tall bamboos.

"I want to see where we are," I say.

Yan is bewildered. "In the Yuan Ming Yuan," she says, as though I have lost my senses and need to be reminded of my new home's name. "The Garden of Perfect Brightness."

"I know that," I pant irritably. We are walking up a small hill now. It's a hill I would have run up a few months ago but it's hot, my shoes are impossible and it's been a long time since I did more than saunter fifty paces down to the lake's edge. "But how big is it? What other buildings does it have in it? Do we have neighbours?"

Yan shakes her head. "I don't know," she says.

"Didn't you walk through the whole estate when you arrived?" I ask.

"No," says Yan. "I came through a side gate and the eunuch who brought me here led me along a little path through a grove of trees to the large lake, to your palace."

I pause for breath. Yan waits while I gulp in air, her little face worried. She must be wondering what has possessed me, after months of barely setting foot outside my own rooms, to suddenly be wandering down hidden paths and panting up hills. I am beginning to wonder the same. What am I trying to find?

But a few moments later I have my answer, for we reach the top of the hill. We stand in silence, looking about us and then turn to stare at one another.

"It's *huge*," I breathe.

The Yuan Ming Yuan is no large garden or even multiple gardens. Instead it stretches as far as I can see in all directions. Yan and I turn about ourselves and gape at its size. The lake onto which my own palace faces, which I had considered large, is dwarfed by another, far off in the distance. There are rivers and canals entwined across the whole landscape. I can see a few buildings dotted about, some nestled delicately into the embrace of trees and flowers, almost hidden from view, others in clusters bigger than any of the palaces by our lake, almost tiny towns. I look at Yan and she looks back at me, open-mouthed.

"I thought the lake and our palaces was all there was," I say.

Yan nods, dumbstruck. It is as though we have lived in one tiny room for the past few months and suddenly opened a door to find that we live in a city.

"Can we go anywhere?" I ask.

Yan is looking about. "There's a wall," she says, pointing. I peer at where she is indicating, a cream and rose stone wall higher than a man, which stretches out into the distance. Slowly we make out that there is a grand entrance to the Garden, sitting at the southernmost wall. After that there are a number of official looking buildings, which follow on to the lake and our palaces. But this makes up only a third of the first part of the estate, somewhat square-shaped. To the east of this part sits another, far larger square of land, the centre of which is a huge lake. Even further along, we can just make out another square, perhaps the size of our own plot. And finally, sitting below that, a smaller, less neatly-shaped area. We assume from what we can see that there is a perimeter wall surrounding the entirety of the Garden.

"We should explore all of it," I say, excited. "We can go to a new part every day!"

"Off again?" calls Lady Mao.

I nod and she waves, laughing. I think she finds my explorations amusing. I am sure she thinks I am turning back into the country girl from the hunting grounds I was before marriage rather than the overly-daintily-dressed concubine she first met by the lakeside. We spend most of our days outdoors. My cloud-climbing shoes are left back at the palace and instead I wear sturdy boots and fur-lined coats as the autumn descends on us. Behind me tramps Yan, bundled up against the cold. The brisk wind turns our cheeks pink even as the leaves turn red. We stride through waving golden chrysanthemums as big as our outstretched hands and scramble up the small but steep man-made hills surrounding us. Our hair blows every which way, pins falling as quickly as the leaves from the trees. When we are worn out we descend to the level of the lakes and follow canals and rivers to find our way home, where Yan pours cup after cup of hot tea and stokes up the kangs to warm us. Every day we find new sights. We pass temples and offices, the kitchens and even a vegetable garden, immaculately hoed and ready for the new sowing season to come. We find orchards of fruit trees, scattered with artful care across sloping fields as though each tree had planted its own children.

"What will it be like in spring?" murmurs Yan.

"Beautiful," I say, imagining clouds of blossom.

Snow falls like petals and we look out of the windows at the frozen lake. Yan hums lullabies and I drink hot tea until the drifts are deep enough, then I drag her outside and throw snowballs at her. At first she does not retaliate but then, quick fingered, she shapes a small ball and knocks off my little fur cap. After that, the snowballs fly fast between us and I know that my once-shy maid has become a friend.

My first year passes. The wisps of hair between my legs turn into a soft down. My hips, once so narrow, become curved. My breasts ache and then grow from tiny buds to rounded cups, causing Yan to beam each time she bathes me.

"Prince Yong will call for you now," she promises me, when my first bleeding comes. She is proud of her work, as though she had moulded my new body herself.

I blush. "Don't be silly, Yan," I say. "He will have forgotten all about me." But secretly I hope that he will remember me and that when I am summoned he will note with approval that I am no longer a child. I lift my chin as I think of being a real woman, desired by her husband, perhaps even favoured above the older ladies. I don't want to be part of a jealous war but still, it would be nice to be singled out. Perhaps I could be noticed for my beauty or elegance or some such trait, like the women in the romantic stories my mother and aunts were fond of. I might be known as the Prince's favourite. I cannot help making up little daydreams in which I am such a favourite, although my imagination fails at the thought of what would actually happen between the Prince and myself behind closed doors.

But he does not call for me. We hear that he is sent by the Emperor to manage a flooding along the Yellow River and does well, is praised for his hard work and diligence. More papers arrive for him to work on, he is often gone from the Yuan Ming Yuan. When he does reside there, the women of his household are not called for very often. Those that are do not even boast, only tell me with a resigned shrug that he does not linger with them. He is known for his kindness and gentleness towards us all, but shows little interest in our lives. He sends gifts to all of us without favouring one or another, and the nature of his gifts are such that I suspect that he appoints this task to one of the eunuchs and that our names are simply ticked off a list – conventional gifts of fruits, of flowers, perhaps hairpins or other delicate jewellery for our birthdays, a fan, game or other trinket for important occasions. Sometimes I wonder if he has forgotten me entirely, although when I see him at the celebrations for the New Year, which come just after my own birthday he at least seems to be aware of when I was born.

"Happy birthday," he says politely.

"Thank you for your gift," I reply, as though to a kindly aunt.

He smiles and nods without replying.

In the summer of my fourteenth year I take up archery. I used to play with my brothers' bows and thinking of them now I have my own bow made and arrows tipped with colourful feathers. Yan sets my targets and retrieves my arrows, and in return I teach her to shoot as well as I do. We become accomplished, but there is no one to praise our efforts excepting ourselves. I wonder whether my brothers would still beat me or whether I would shame them with my accuracy. In the heat of the summer I request a boat and we row – at first badly, then with greater confidence – on the lakes and explore every part of the

Garden, from the great lake in the centre, which I now know is called the Sea of Blessings, across ever smaller lakes and down canals and tiny rivers which sometimes end up as minor streams or springs and from which we have to drift backwards to return to a place where our boat can turn round. No-one knows this place as well as we do. The servants only hurry from one designated spot to another. The Prince's other women prefer to follow well-worn paths – from one palace to another, from the boating lake to the shrines, from their mah-jong tiles to their own quarters: they do not venture further afield. The Garden is a quiet place, Yan and I can wander a whole day and see only the odd servant pass by or a guard in the distance if we venture close to the perimeter walls.

New Year comes round again. The Prince wishes me a happy fifteenth birthday, I thank him for his gift. He nods and smiles.

I grow bolder. The Garden is my home now. I may ask for anything and it will be done. I may dress how I please, for no-one of note will see me. Who is to care how I behave or how I appear? The autumn rains fall and after days of staying indoors I take an old robe of Yan's and we venture outside, where we make little streams and dams out of mud and twigs, stones and flowers.

"You're not five!" Yan yelps.

I laugh and reach out a filthy finger to paint her nose with mud. She slaps her hand in a puddle to splash my face and by the time we return home it is almost dark and our clothes will probably make the laundry maids weep.

It is New Year and there are fireworks. I pass Prince Yong who wishes me a happy sixteenth birthday. I thank him for his gift. I have almost forgotten that he is my husband. It is more like being a younger daughter to an often-absent father.

"Happy birthday, my dear," says Lady Mao a few days later. The other ladies join in wishing me long life and happiness. Today I have dressed elegantly and joined them in Lady Mao's palace. I make an effort to play mah-jong and listen to their conversation. They give me little trinkets – a string of prayer beads, silk flowers for my hair. Only Lady Qi is absent. She does not join the other women when we sit. I take the opportunity of perhaps being considered old enough for gossip to ask about her and at once their voices drop lower.

"She is ambitious," says Lady Mao.

"Ambitious for what?" I ask.

"She has two living sons. She wants one of them to be the Prince's heir."

It seems a small ambition. There are no other living sons, so her ambition would appear to be already achieved. I shrug. "If she has the only living sons…" I say.

Lady Mao makes a face. "She would also like Prince Yong to be made Crown Prince."

"But there is already a Crown Prince."

Lady Mao nods and lowers her voice. "Of course. But there are rumours that the Emperor is displeased with his conduct. The Kangxi Emperor has more than thirty sons and at least twelve could be considered for the position of heir. He could demote the Crown Prince and appoint another son in his place, should he so wish. This is what Lady Qi dreams of."

I grimace. "She has a lot of dreams."

The others giggle and we play on. Only as I return to my own place do I catch a rare glimpse of Lady Qi outside her own home. Even after three years here I have only seen her a handful of times. I change my course a little to avoid her, for I do not like her cold eyes and her fixed stare. But she seems uneasy to see me herself and disappears promptly into her own rooms. I wonder about her behaviour but later I see a male figure leaving her palace as dusk falls. I wonder who it is and where Lady Qi's loyalties lie. I tell Yan and she, curious after the gossip I passed on to her, makes it her mission to spy on Lady Qi. It does not take long before we realise that she often has visitors, men in sumptuous robes who, however, appear quietly and without an entourage, who visit with her for a short period only before quickly making their way out of the Yuan Ming Yuan and heading back towards Beijing.

"Is she being unfaithful to Prince Yong, do you think?" asks Yan.

I shake my head. "I don't know, but surely if she is ambitious for her sons she would not want to be discovered being unfaithful? She would be dishonoured, maybe even sentenced to death and they might be set aside rather than being heirs."

"There's no-one to take their place," points out Yan. "Unless one of you ladies has a child."

"Not much chance of that," I tell her and she makes a face that shows what she thinks of Prince Yong for ignoring me all this time, something she takes as a personal affront.

"Perhaps we could plant blossoming trees on the island in the Sea of Blessings," I say. "Think how pretty it would be."

Yan nods.

"I need one of the gardeners," I say. "Can you arrange for one?"

Yan makes enquiries and on a bright late winter's day a young eunuch presents himself at my palace. He is my own height, with a pleasant face burnt brown by the sun and a ready smile. He bows before pointing to a boat by the water's edge, which is filled with young saplings, ready to be planted.

"Cherries," he says, when I ask.

Yan and I row ahead of him to our favourite place, the tiny island on the Sea of Blessings lake and I tell him where I want him to place the trees. Yan busies herself with making hot tea and I indicate that she should offer him some as well.

"Rose petals," says Yan, passing him the tea with a superior air. "I dried them myself."

He bows to me and takes the tea, smiling at Yan. He has done a good day's work and I wave him goodbye when we part. But the next time we visit the island to check on the trees he is there again, although I have not summoned him. We are used to having the island to ourselves.

"What are you doing here?" asks Yan, none too politely.

"Planting roses for you," he says, looking directly at her as though it was the most natural thing in the world. I have to stifle a laugh at Yan's expression.

"What is your name?" I ask, for I know she will not ask and something tells me she will want to know.

"Kun," he says.

I think perhaps they are well suited, this man of the earth who has dreamt up an island of roses for an insignificant little maid and my swallow Yan who is so practical and hardworking but inside has a soft little heart. I sigh as we leave the island.

"What's wrong?" asks Yan.

"It's a shame he is a eunuch," I say, unable to keep my thoughts to myself.

"What do I care what he is?" splutters Yan and I know her thoughts matched mine.

But now that we have met him Kun seems to be everywhere. We go rowing and he is on the lake, clearing away dead lotus leaves. We walk along secluded paths and there he is, sweeping away old leaves or planting new bulbs for springtime. He does not speak to us unless I speak first, for that would be presumptuous, but he bows to me and smiles at Yan and I smile back, while she looks this way and that and does not know how to respond at all. So she scowls.

Yan has a headache and is being grumpy, so I set out alone, along a tiny path thickly planted with primroses. The early spring day is marked with strange cloud formations that keep my eyes on the sky rather than what is in front of me. I startle when a dark shape appears on the path ahead of me.

"I beg your pardon," says a man's voice in stumbling Mandarin. I step back, alarmed.

The man before me is dressed in a scholar's dark robes but he is not Manchu, nor Chinese. He is a Westerner. His eyes and hair are a dark brown and his skin is coloured by the sun. I have only ever seen two such before, at the hunting grounds. They were elderly Jesuit priests, in service to the Emperor. This man is young. Their beards were long and grey whereas his is short. The old men I saw years ago were stooped and pale, their skin sheltered but their backs warped by years of study in cloistered rooms. I saw them only briefly and at some distance, for we were not permitted to approach the imperial party. This man is tall and is standing only ten paces away from me. He is staring at me as though I were a ghost. I am probably doing the same. I close my mouth and try to regain my composure.

"Who are you?" I ask and it comes out too haughty.

He makes a bow that must be how they bow in his country, one foot behind the other, both legs bent, one arm out to his side. He does it smoothly, but it looks strange in the robes he is wearing and as he finishes it I see him recall that this is not how to present himself here. He tries instead to bow as we do and does it badly, unsure of how low he should go and where his hands should be.

His double bow makes me bow in return, although I am not quite sure whether I should be bowing at all.

"My name is Giuseppe Castiglione, I am here to serve with the Jesuits as a painter," he says and at the frown on my face he amends what he has said. "You may wish to call me Lang Shining," he says, pronouncing it with excessive care, the 'Shining' emerging almost correctly as 'shur-ning'. "The Emperor has been so kind as to bestow a new name on me, for he says that my name is hard for people here to speak."

"Cast-eel…" I begin, but see that he wants to laugh. Something stubborn in me makes me shake my head. "I do not need you to have a new name," I say. "Say your real name again."

He says it more slowly. "Joo-se-pe," he says. "Castiglione is my family name."

I struggle but finally I say his name and he nods, smiling as though relieved that he is able to converse with someone here, even in his poor Mandarin.

"And your name?" he asks.

"Niuhuru," I say. I do not say who I am. I am not even sure why. Surely I should have told him that I am Prince Yong's concubine? But it is too late. He is already trying to pronounce my name, which he manages better. I smile. But now I am unsure of what to do next. We stand on the path in silence and at last I gesture awkwardly at the path beyond him. "I… go that way," I manage, wondering why I am simplifying my speech as though to a child.

He moves out of my way at once, stepping aside and bowing again as I pass, this time remembering to bow as we do.

I walk away. I don't look back, because that would be to show an unseemly amount of interest in a strange man, but when I come to a little hill I climb it more quickly than usual and scan the landscape below me to see where the Jesuit was headed. But he is gone. When I reach my own home I am about to tell Yan about my strange encounter with the Jesuit but find myself remaining silent, as though I am unable to summon up the right words to describe him, although the image of him is bright before my eyes when I close them.

The next day and the day after that I am up early and fretting to be out and about, striding through the Yuan Ming Yuan's vast expanse as though searching for something lost. Yan mutters something about household chores but she is willing to follow me on my explorations, although she does insist on at least having something to eat and some hot tea first. "It's still winter," she chides.

I laugh. "It's springtime," I tell her, standing in my doorway and looking out across the lake, turning my head this way and that. There is a pale green haze spreading across the trees as their new leaves emerge and everywhere I smell wet earth. There is a freshness in the air that makes me fidget.

"What's the hurry?" asks Yan, after we have rushed along the little path I took the day before, climbed the highest hill I can find, hurried back down and gone to find a boat. "Where are you trying to go? What are you looking for?"

Who, I think. *Who am I looking for?*

We row down one canal and then another. Yan is getting annoyed by my distracted air. "Go to the little island," she commands at last, as though I were her maid and she my mistress. "Let's see if any of the trees have blossomed or whether that eunuch has killed them all."

"His name is Kun," I remind her, although I know she needs no reminding.

She shrugs as though his name is of no interest but her cheeks are already pink. I can see her leaning forward a little as we approach the island and look over my shoulder to see that the first cherry trees are indeed flowering, some white, some pink. And there is a figure on the island already, a man in a blue robe. I smile to myself. Kun must be looking after the saplings, he has an uncanny knack for being wherever we are. I would almost say he was spying on our movements. My back to the island, I pull harder on the oars and smile as I watch Yan pretend not to look at our destination. It is only when she gets out of the boat that I hear her gasp as though she has stubbed her toe. I finish tying up the boat and turn, to find her folded up on the rough gravel of the shore. Standing over her is Prince Yong. My husband.

My mouth opens but nothing comes out. I am suddenly, horribly, conscious of the informality of my robes and hair, of having ordered the planting of these trees without my husband's permission, of having rowed here as though I were a servant rowing my maid, of… of… most dreadfully of secretly having been looking for a man, a stranger, a Jesuit Westerner that I have met only once, whom I have been seeking without even knowing why. I am sure it is written all over my face. I am very aware of my husband standing closer to me than he has done since the first time I met him in his bedchamber, of being almost alone with him rather than in a crowd.

"Highness," I half-whisper.

Yan quickly rises to her feet and creeps a little way off, pretending she is out of earshot.

I manage something like a bow, possibly the worst and most inelegant bow ever performed by a concubine to her lord. When I straighten I find I have grown more than I realised since coming here. I am almost as tall as the Prince.

Yong looks at me with his head on one side. "Niuhuru," he says. He says it as though he has dredged my name up out of some far-off memory.

I nod, unsure whether he is simply naming me or whether he is asking a question, possibly 'what on earth are you doing here, looking like that?'.

He is silent for a moment. Then he turns and gestures at the trees. "You ordered them planted?"

"Yes," I mutter. I wonder whether I should apologise at once, to save being reprimanded.

His face is still turned away from me. "Why?"

"I – I thought it would look beautiful in the springtime with flowering trees. I thought the falling petals would look like snow." What a stupid thing to say, I think. *Why* did I not ask for his permission? I swallow, feeling cold and small. I wish Yan was closer to me, so that I could clasp her hand for courage.

He turns back and looks at me in silence. I wait. Then he smiles. A full, warm smile, such as I have never seen from him before. Suddenly he looks younger. His usual expression, of serious attention to duty, is lightened. He actually looks happy. "They are perfect," he says.

I don't know how to respond, so I only smile back. It is hard not to respond to this new smile of his.

"Plant whatever you wish," he says. "It seems we are of one mind, you and I. You see this place as I see it. It is a refuge, a taste of the gardens of the Immortals. A place to have one's worries taken away. A place to fortify the soul. A place to be happy and free, unshackled by the expectations of others. It is unlike anywhere else in the empire."

I almost say that I don't know what he's talking about. The Yuan Ming Yuan is just a large country estate, however pretty it is. It is simply my home, now that I have lived here for some time. But I catch myself before I speak. Here we are, I in a violet robe that, although made of silk, is about as simple a robe as one could have made, especially when paired with my sturdy, muddied boots. He is so plainly dressed that I mistook him for a eunuch from a distance. And this is the first real conversation together we have had in three years and he is speaking to me as though I were a friend, someone who understands his thoughts and feelings. Slowly, I nod.

He nods back as though we have settled on something. "I must return to my work," he says. He looks about him at the trees and then turns back to me. "Beautiful," he says and smiles again, before walking briskly away, towards the eastern shore where his boat must be moored.

Yan hurries back to my side. I give her a surprised smile at what has just occurred. "He said the trees were beautiful!" I say, pleased with his praise and hugely relieved at how well this unexpected meeting has gone.

Yan is grinning a mischievous grin, her eyes alight with pride. "He was looking at you when he said 'beautiful'," she points out. "He wasn't looking at the trees."

The Screen of Twelve Beauties

HER EYES WERE GREY.

I clung to this certainty, for everything else in my life had changed.

Even at mass, which I had to attend more frequently than was my natural inclination, the music and liturgy that should have been comfortingly familiar was strange to my ears. They had their own instruments here unlike those to which I had been used and the brothers, wishing to make their devotions seem more familiar to their new converts, allowed their use in the church, as well as some songs to be sung in Mandarin. The unmelodic wailing combined with the sudden crashing of gongs and strange cymbals in the full midst of the service startled me the first time I heard it, turning sounds known to me from childhood into something strange and unknown, my own faith, such as it was, into a strange ritual devoid of meaning.

Most of all I struggled with the very thing that should have been my saving grace, my anchor in this strange sea: my skills and talent as a painter. After my initial success with the Kangxi Emperor, I had expected that my skills would be much admired and rewarded, that I would be master to grateful apprentices. Instead I received a rude awakening when my work arrived and I unpacked some of it to show the painters here, intending to instruct them in the techniques used by Western masters.

Xiyao, my assistants and the other painters stood around me, curious. But despite showing them numerous sketches and paintings, I was met only with puzzlement regarding the correct use of perspective, for they had only the most rudimentary grasp of how we Western artists used it, their own work using an oddly different approach.

Xiyao intervened, interrupting an explanation. "Shining, you must learn to use our own watercolours and inks rather than your oils. And also to paint onto rice paper or silk."

"Why?"

"Supplies of your own materials will be harder to obtain here. And also, the Emperor and the court prefer local materials to be used."

In vain I tried to explain that oils might bring a greater depth of texture, that the canvasses seemed to my mind more robust than rice paper. I was met only with stubborn silence followed by an insistence on their own ways. Silently, I determined that I would paint a full portrait in my own style, so that they might see once and for all how superior the technique was.

Her eyes were grey.

The very straight black hair and pale ivory skin of the women I had seen here I had already grown used to in only a few months here. The shape of the eyes, also. All brown of course, but that was hardly a novelty to me, since most of my countrymen also had dark eyes, myself included.

But her eyes were grey. Startled as I wandered, I had almost thought her a spirit of the Garden: the pale skin and eyes, the long loose hair whipped about her face, a lone woman in the deserted landscape. I tried to recollect the colour of her robe, what exactly she had said to me, how she had moved, the faint scent of her as she passed by me. All of it gone, details that I would usually notice and commit to memory to enable me to reproduce them faithfully with my paints. Gone. I was left with a confused feeling, something like desperation but I did not know what for. I had only her name, which I mouthed silently to myself, afraid of forgetting it amidst the too-many new things surrounding me daily. And her eyes. Strange, yet compelling in their difference. I could not stop thinking of them.

I picked up my brush and mixed a colour, which was wrong. Too blue. The next, too brown. The third, too dark. My trusted skills, dismissed and failing me in this cursed place.

"I need to see her again," I muttered.

"Master?"

An assistant, standing by too eagerly, noticing my mutterings and failed attempts too closely. "Do you need something?"

I shook my head, hoping he would leave me be, then closed my eyes and tried to see the colour once more.

"You are summoned."

I turned. Xiyao. "What?"

"You are summoned."

"The Emperor?" I asked, already moving towards the door, knowing that such a summons required an immediate response.

"His son."

"Son?"

"Prince Yong. Fourth prince."

"Are there many?" I asked, following dutifully. I had been briefed on the Emperor's family but could not recall all the details. A fourth prince did not sound very high-ranking and I knew he had not been named the Crown Prince. So he would not be his father's heir, only a lesser prince, bound to serve a future emperor-brother. Then again, he had been given this estate, the Yuan Ming Yuan, by his father the Emperor and so perhaps had been somehow singled out for praise and honours.

"More than thirty," said Xiyao. He walked swiftly, across a small bridge and onwards, as I hurried to keep pace, shaking my head at the thought of thirty princes, all vying for one throne, for I had been informed that they did not follow primogeniture as we would have done at home. Surely, I found myself reflecting, making the first son heir would prove the simplest solution when faced with such a multitude of offspring? Did these people not wish to learn anything from us?

We followed the curve of a lake's edge. Ancient willows dipped the tips of their tumbling branches into the shore-ripples of the water, while further into the lake the buds and first flowers of lotuses rose up from their fresh green pads. Winding paths led away from the water's edge and up towards small palaces, which ringed the lake. One was entwined with an ancient wisteria, its bare branches encasing the palace like a bird's nest. I thought that soon it would create a glorious frame of tumbling purple flowers. Still I looked about me, conscious that the path I had followed had led here, that the woman I had met must have passed by this place before she met me. I wondered if she was a maid, although I had been told that all the maids wore blue robes with red hair ribbons to tie their neat plaits. The woman – *Niuhuru* – she was not dressed as a maid, but neither did she wear the elaborate hair of a court lady or concubine. Perhaps she really was a spirit?

"Prince Yong's residence," announced Xiyao and I found myself ushered into the receiving hall of a lakeside palace far larger than those we had passed until now.

"Shining." A clear voice, quiet but purposeful.

I found myself before the Prince, a man perhaps my own age, of a similar stature. He was dressed less ostentatiously than two of the other princes whom I had met so far in my time here but there was something in the way he carried himself that reminded me of his father the Emperor: a regal bearing.

"Highness." I bowed.

He gestured to me to follow him. "How is your Mandarin? Do you still have need of an interpreter?"

I shook my head. "I manage better, Your Highness. I have daily lessons and hope I am improving. Although I am sure there is still much to learn."

"There is always something to learn," the Prince said, almost wearily. We had reached a room that appeared to be his study. There were so very many papers on and about his desk that most people would have allowed them to become a jumble of confusion, but it was clear even from a distance that they were laid out in a strict order. The prince took a chair and indicated that I should be seated.

"You have a most beautiful estate," I said. "It is a pleasure to be based here, in the studio."

He gave a brief smile and nodded. His serious face was much lightened by the smile and I thought that this was a man who should smile more and take his duties a little less seriously.

"I wish to commission an artwork," he said.

I made a small bow in my seat. "I would be most honoured," I said. I found myself hoping it would be a large piece of work including the portrait I had in mind, for until now I felt that I had only made small sketches here and there and mostly been instructed on how *not* to paint. I longed to show something of the skills I believed I possessed, the skills for which, after all, I had been selected by the Brothers. I believed that if I could show what I was capable and the prince were to be pleased, I might yet change the painting conventions used and find my place here.

"A decorative screen," specified the Prince. "It will be used to adorn this room and it should be titled *The Screen of Twelve Beauties*."

I found myself wondering whether this seemingly severe and dutiful man was asking me to paint for him the kind of images of a woman that in my own country might be concealed within snuff boxes and other trinkets, for a man's personal viewing pleasures. Surely the Prince was not asking me to paint such images on a large screen to decorate his study?

"I would like each lady to be viewed within a setting of nature," the Prince continued. "And to show her perhaps undertaking a task to indicate her breeding and cultured mind. Reading, or perhaps studying a work of art… You can bring me the first preparatory sketch to approve within a month, along with your ideas for the others."

I nodded, still uncertain of what exactly the Prince was asking of me. I did not dare to ask for clarification, even as I bowed on leaving his presence.

"A classical idea," said Xiyao, when I recounted the commission. "Each lady should symbolise an ideal of beauty. I can show you some examples."

"Please do," I said. I felt my shoulders drop with relief as he showed me various examples, all of them fully-clothed. "Of course," I said, with enthusiasm. "I shall begin at once."

I wandered through the Garden, noting particular settings or plants that would provide suitable backdrops. I thought that with their being twelve beauties, it would be suitable to have them posed in the twelve months of the year and asked whether a gardener could be assigned to me for a day to describe the plants of each season, as I had not yet been here long enough to observe them all. Xiyao sent me the pleasant young eunuch Kun, whom I had encountered on my first day in the Garden. He walked alongside me and described what would be in flower or fruit in different seasons. He also pointed out structures that might be suitable, owing to their being covered with flowers: a lotus-framed palace, one wrapped in climbing roses.

"That one is the most beautiful," he said, pointing to the wisteria-entwined palace I had already noted. I could see the first buds of the purple flowers beginning to emerge. Seeing their first haze of growth I closed my eyes and in a rush saw the woman again, standing before me as I had first seen her. I dismissed Kun and all but ran back to the studio, to paint her before she disappeared again.

A frame of endless tumbling wisteria flowers, their rich purple almost like the dark bunches of grapes from home. Standing within it, the shape of a woman. Her robe a pale green, almost as though she herself was the stem holding up the multitude of flowers. Her hands should have been reaching up to touch the petals in a classical pose but were instead held up in a startled gasp. Long and black, set loose about her shoulders, her hair was unkempt from the wind's strength. Her eyes were grey and open wide as she met an unseen man, a stranger. I ignored the warnings I had been given and instead painted her as I would have painted her at home, oil on canvas, the shade falling across her face.

I called for Xiyao, wanting to show him the painting. I was confident that he would acknowledge, now that he could see a completed painting, the impact of the techniques I used.

His eyes lit up with recognition when he saw the image before him. "Lady Niuhuru," he said at once and I felt something in me turn over. I looked at him without speaking and he frowned and pointed more clearly at the painting, as though speaking to a fool.

"Lady Niuhuru," he said again. "Her eyes are like that. And the wisteria palace is her home," he added.

There was a sudden moment when I wanted to strike him for having noticed her strange grey eyes. A madness gone in an instant, since anyone not half-blind would observe her eyes at once. And then a sense of falling as I heard, after they were spoken, his other words. "Her home?"

Xiyao nodded. "Lady Niuhuru lives there," he said.

"Who is Lady Niuhuru?" I asked and even as I asked him the

question I wanted to stop up his mouth, to unask the question because something told me that her title meant something I did not wish to hear.

"She is *Gege* to the fourth Prince," said Xiyao.

"*Gege*?" I asked, still hoping for some other word, some reprieve. My Mandarin was not good enough for this specific title and yet I knew the meaning of the word he had proffered before I had to ask him to translate it.

"Concubine."

I wanted to ask something else but my mind was a confusion of thoughts that I could not even name.

Xiyao, meanwhile, was shaking his head. "Lady Niuhuru is not a suitable subject for the screen," he told me briskly, as a housewife might discard a bruised fruit.

"Why not?"

"Images of Beauties should be idealised examples of beauty. They are not intended to portray real people." He paused. "And Lady Niuhuru... is anyway not really a true beauty," he added, lowering his voice as though to avoid causing offence to an absent Prince Yong. "Her eyes are rather odd and she is extremely tall. They say she was chosen as something of a joke by Lady Que Hui, because her father was a lowly official and Prince Yong likes to think that any man may rise through diligence and hard work. So Lady Que Hui thought he should have a concubine from a modest background. Usually the concubines are chosen from more high-ranking families."

I did not want to hear more about her, to hear details of how she was seen by others.

"But you can see what I mean about the technique," I said, almost curtly. "It is far superior to that used here."

Xiyao was still shaking his head. "This..." he began, indicating the heavy shading, "this... it looks like dirt."

I smiled, feeling myself on safer ground. "It is shading," I explained, adopting the kindly tone my master had used with me when I was still a boy. "We call it *chiaroscuro*. It means 'light and dark' and through its use in a painting, especially of a person as you can see here, can be used to give depth and the illusion of the body's contours being present, rather than flattened onto canvas." I paused, waiting for him to acknowledge that I was right, but he was already shaking his head again. I almost wanted to slap him to make him stop.

"The effect is inauspicious. It appears as dirt and would be entirely unsuitable for painting most subjects and particularly portraits." He almost shuddered as a thought crossed his mind. "Most *certainly* not of the Emperor or his family." He nodded at my bemused expression. "Your predecessors here also had to learn to paint without using this method, in our own style. Did the Brothers not tell you? Allow me to show you some examples." He hurried away.

I stood alone, feeling like a fool. I tried to imagine painting without the techniques that I had used ever since I was apprenticed to my master's studio. Now approaching my thirtieth year, I had spent close to two decades painting in this way. I could not help feeling irritated. What had I been brought here for? What had I promised my life to? Had the brothers lied to me, promised me that I might share my skills with devoted disciples whilst knowing full well that I would be obliged to become the student, rather than the master I had envisioned?

Xiyao returned. "Coronation portraits of previous Emperors," he said, gesturing to two minor eunuchs to help him roll out a variety of scrolls. On each appeared a past monarch, glorious in imperial yellow, bedecked with precious stones, magnificent on their carved thrones.

They looked like a child's paper dolls, flat and lifeless, gaudy but inert. No painter worthy of the name in Europe would consider painting like this. I nodded, wordlessly, as portrait after portrait was displayed before me. Emperors, lesser nobility, even animals: all lifeless. I felt my excitement for this post drain away and with it came the weight of knowing I was trapped here.

Time passed and still I struggled. The screen was completed with input from the other painters of the imperial studios, so much so that I barely recognised it as my own work, despite a half-hearted attempt to introduce a linear Western perspective, which they found unusual, although Xiyao seemed to have at least some interest in it. I found little pride in the finished screen when it was delivered to the prince, who nevertheless seemed pleased with it. I was not allowed the use of *chiaroscuro* and without it the non-existent women portrayed seemed devoid of life to me. The unusual symbols used around them, which I had dutifully tried to memorise (*bats mean fertility, mushrooms promise good luck, a calabash augers many sons*), seemed only a meaningless jumble of objects.

Laura, meanwhile, pestered me endlessly to look at her work.

"Very well," I said at last, exasperated at the failure of my own attempts. "Show me what you have been working on, then."

She put a sheaf of papers in front of me and I began to leaf through them. She was accomplished at sketching, she caught the quick small details that made an image come alive: a design on a sleeve, the turn of a head, the weight of a heavy burden being carried past.

"You will have to learn to do without *chiaroscuro*," I said, explaining what I had been told.

"How?" she asked, echoing my own thoughts.

"I don't know," I said honestly, for once unable to play the part of all-knowing master to her apprentice. "We will have to find a new way. Perhaps lighter shading, but I have tried it and it does not work: they will still see it as 'inauspicious dirt' – I snorted at the idea – and we will see it as inadequate to convey the depth that we must strive for. Show me the parishioners you have sketched."

She hesitated, but brought me another sheaf of papers. I looked at the first image, a woman caught looking over her shoulder as she entered the church, her gaze direct at the viewer, curious and yet bold. Even in a rough sketch Laura had caught the sunlight touching her hair, the flowers in it, the expression on her face.

"Very nice," I said without looking up. "Who is she, do you know?"

"A Madam Guo," said Laura. She did not elaborate.

I turned to the next image. The same woman, this time at prayer, her hands clasped in front of her, her head bowed.

The next, her gaze uplifted towards the altar.

Then her mouth open, the rest of her face only hinted at, as she sang a hymn.

Another, as she stood, one hand on the pew for balance, her fingertips spread out.

And again, this time passing Laura again as she left the church, her face closer, lips half-parted, eyes fully wide, fixed on the viewer, on Laura.

I looked up from the images at Laura. Her cheeks were flushed, a delicate stain of pink on her collarbones.

"They are very good," I said slowly.

She said nothing.

"We are in such a different place," I said to her gently. "We find ourselves enchanted by what is new to us, do we not? How strange it all is here, how we long to pin down what it is that makes it so. We think our skills must be able to do this for us, for they have never failed us yet, and yet they fail us. We try again and again and yet we cannot grasp what it is that we see. But perhaps it is ourselves who must change, who must grow used to what we see. Perhaps the magic will fade a little, perhaps it will become commonplace and then we will depict what we see with our accustomed ease."

She nodded quickly, her cheeks still pink and did not reply, only took back the sheaf of papers and hurried away. I let her go, thinking that this was a lesson to myself as much as Laura. I must learn to see this place as it really was. It was different, no more nor less.

The portrait of Niuhuru I rolled up and put away in a corner of the studio, telling myself that I had learned many valuable lessons in undertaking the screen commission, not least that I must set to and learn the many different symbols of my new home and that I had to find a way to share my own skills in a way that would be acceptable. I did not look at it again.

Once inside my memory palace there is a hidden winding path lined with bamboo. Within it she stands, surrounded by flowers. Her hands raised as I startle her in her wanderings, her grey eyes wide. It was the last time I painted the way I had been taught. I never saw the portrait again and perhaps after many years it was destroyed, yet as I walk in my mind along the lake's edge of the Yuan Ming Yuan she is always there, her image bright as the first moment I saw her, when a madness took hold of me.

It has not left me yet.

Lilies Tangled by Peonies

THE WISTERIA BLOOMS, INDICATING THE fourth anniversary of my arrival here. My palace is covered in the purple flowers and the Yuan Ming Yuan bursts into late spring: no longer a delicate blossom in a high-up branch or a hidden primrose here and there but great swathes of every-coloured petals rising up from fresh green growth and all around the sounds of ducks and songbirds returning from their winter homes. The lakes and streams come alive with butterflies and kingfishers. Tiny turtles crawl out from their winter sleep and sit on the sun-warmed rocks.

I tell Yan that since I am now seventeen I really should take more care in my appearance, even though I do still want to continue my walks across the Garden's vistas. Yan smiles a secret smile and shakes out robes decorated with skimming dragonflies and rising reeds, then binds up my hair with fresh flowers. So that I can walk easily she orders flat-soled shoes, decorated with tiny gemstones and embroidered crickets.

"Now if you should happen to meet the Prince on your wanderings you will not have to worry that you are not elegant enough," she says, as though the thought has only just occurred to her. I know that she takes it as a personal slight that I have still not been summoned as a companion, despite being a grown woman, not the half-child I was when I first came here. I have heard her muttering about it sometimes, how Prince Yong must be an idiot not to want me as a companion, where are his eyes?

The early summer heat begins to rise and the gardens of the Yuan Ming Yuan become busier. Eunuchs and maids trot back and forth along the tiny paths, each busy with their workloads. It takes a lot of work to keep such an estate in good order and I know that my husband has requested more gardeners: to plant over a thousand peonies, his favourite flowers, across a terraced field on one of the islets; to create new tiny streams linking up rivers already criss-crossing the meadows. He asks for ponds to be filled with carp. Yan and I follow the eunuchs carrying buckets full of slippery burdens and watch as the golden bodies are poured into the water. They soon learn to rise to the surface and beg for crumbs of cake that we throw in. Tiny fauns peep at us from behind trees, wide-eyed and curious.

The other ladies become more active in the summer, we see them boating and gossiping, collecting fruits and flowers, their maids wandering behind them with baskets, glad to have a pleasant task to fulfil rather than anything more onerous. I join them on a day when their gossiping seems to have taken on an ominous tone.

"They said he bought children from the South," says Lady Nara, lowering her voice.

"Who?" I ask.

Her voice lowers even more until she's barely speaking above a whisper. The others don't bother craning their necks, they know full well who she is talking about. "The Crown Prince."

I frown. "What did he buy children for?"

She looks at me.

"And then he had that man killed for questioning him."

The other ladies shake their heads. "Such a violent man," murmurs Lady Mao. "What will the empire be, in his hands?"

Lady Zhang looks about her. "They say that there are factions developing," she says, and all the ladies drift towards her, as though by accident. She nods at their interest. "They say that the Emperor may change his heir and that there are those who support the Eighth Prince Lian, those who support the Fourteenth Prince Xun and…" she pauses as though unsure of how far to go with this information. "Those who support Prince Yong," she ends in a rush.

We are silent for a moment. The notion of our own husband being appointed Crown Prince is a little overwhelming. Lady Nara looks thoughtful. As Primary Consort to Yong, such a move would one day see her crowned Empress.

"And Third Prince Cheng and First Prince Zhi?" asks Lady Mao, who clearly has a better grasp than I do of which princes are most likely to be considered for such an honour.

Lady Zhang shrugs. "Prince Cheng is wrapped up in his studies," she says. "He has no interest in becoming Emperor. Prince Zhi…"

"The Immortals protect us from Prince Zhi becoming the Crown Prince," shudders Lady Nara. "The man is a sorcerer. And seeks only after his own pleasures. *How* many concubines does he have now?"

Walking back with Yan I tell her I don't much care for the ladies' gossip. "It all sounds a little frightening," I confess. "I'm glad we live here and not closer to the Forbidden City."

The heat rises until even our woodland walks are too hot. I sleep badly, plagued either by heat or the hum of mosquitoes who enter my rooms at once if the windows are left open to cool me. I can only hope autumn will come quickly but the heat drags on.

One particularly bad night I don't fall asleep until several hours after going to bed. I'm woken what feels like moments later by Yan's face barely a hand's breadth from my own and yelp. "What?!"

Yan keeps her face where it is, her voice low and scared. "The Prince is ill."

I am still half asleep despite the rude awakening. "What Prince?"

"The Prince. *Your* Prince. Prince Yong."

I struggle to a sitting position. "Ill?"

Yan nods.

"What with?"

Yan shakes her head. "No-one knows. A fever. The physicians came in the night and now they have all gone away, they say it is sorcery and they can do nothing for him."

I look blearily about me. "Is it still night?"

Yan shakes her head. "Dawn."

"What are his servants doing?"

Yan whispers. "They have run away."

"They can't do that," I tell her. I have never heard of such a thing.

"They have," says Yan. Her little face is scared. "The ladies have all locked themselves in their own palaces and the servants of His Highness' personal household have run away even though they will be beaten for it. Everyone is scared."

"But who is looking after him?"

"No-one."

I think back to the times I have had fevers, the restless tossing, heat burning through me and all that kept me from fear was the soothing hand of my mother or the anxious ministrations of Yan. To be all alone and ill… "Help me get dressed," I tell Yan.

"Are we running away?"

"We are going to look after the Prince."

Yan shakes her head violently. "You can't go to his palace! You might be struck down by the sorcerer."

"I can't leave him on his own," I tell her.

"He's barely looked at you!" snaps Yan. "He hasn't even called for you! What do you owe him?"

I am getting dressed as fast as I can, without much help from Yan. I don't have a proper answer to give her, only that I still remember the warmth of his smile on the Sea of Blessings' island. He cannot be left alone with no-one to care for him. "Are you with me?" I ask her.

The Garden is silent. There are no maids or eunuchs to be seen, no officials. No gardeners. The little paths along the lakeside are empty in the grey light of dawn. It makes me nervous. At first I keep looking around for other people but eventually I fix my eyes on Yong's palace so that I will not be entirely unnerved by the quiet around me.

Once in his courtyard I call out, for I still cannot believe that Yan is right. For all she knows, the servants ran for help, not away. "Hello? Hello?" But no-one answers. I stand before the doors to his apartments and hesitate. What if the sorcerer-brother really is here, what if, as I enter, he calls on his powers and causes me to fall ill? Beside me, Yan makes a small whimpering sound of dissent.

In a fit of courage I push open the doors more violently than I meant to, so that they bang against the walls and Yan lets out a tiny scream.

"Stop that," I hiss at her. "You have to be brave. You have to help me."

"We shouldn't be here at all," she hisses back. "All the other ladies have stayed in their palaces where they are safe. So should you."

Standing in the empty receiving hall, I ignore her. I think back to the dim memory of being brought here four years ago. Tentatively, I make my way to the Prince's bedchamber.

The room is quite dark. The windows have not been opened and I hesitate on the threshold, one hand still on the door. In the silence around me I can now hear ragged breathing. I am almost ready to turn back, to run along the lakeside path and lock myself into my own rooms, safe with Yan by my side until someone tells me what to do. A touch on my hand makes me jump but it is only Yan, her small hand gripping mine. Together we step into the darkness.

"Highness?" I whisper. There is no reply, only the breathing, which seems to grow faster as I listen. I try again, raising my voice to something approaching my usual speaking voice. "Highness?" I am horribly afraid that the breathing will stop, even as I stand here, helpless in the dark.

Yan lets go of my hand and I nearly call her back to me but in a fit of boldness, she is already wrestling with a window shutter. At last the weak light of early morning filters through and I can see the room.

I have correctly recalled that this was my husband's bedchamber. It has not changed much. At the far end is his bed and a figure lies across it, coverlets crumpled to the floor in disarray. I make my way towards him as tentatively as though playing a game, hoping he may suddenly sit up and laugh at me, call his unseen servants and tell me he is well and that I am a foolish girl. I would rather be laughed at than find what I have been told is true: my husband is very sick and it seems everyone but Yan and I has run away.

But when I reach the edge of the bed and see my husband it is clear that he is not about to laugh at me. His skin is flushed and his eyes closed, each breath is closer to a pant and when I reach out a tentative finger his skin nearly burns me.

I turn to Yan, truly afraid. "What do I do?" I ask and I am ashamed of the tears trembling in my voice. "I have never looked after someone so ill," I add, although I know that this is not why I am so fearful. My own destiny is hanging in the balance with my husband's, for his fortunes are inevitably mine. If he dies, what will I be? A widow when I have barely even been a wife?

Yan looks as though she would rather be elsewhere, but being asked for advice seems to make her practical side come out. "Take off all the coverlets," she says.

"He will be cold," I say without thinking and then realise that this is a stupid thing to say about a man whose skin is on fire. I take one corner of the topmost coverlet and pull at it with very little effect. Beside me Yan tuts at my tentative effort and gives it a firm yank. The coverlet slips to the floor and my husband's body, entirely naked, is revealed to us both. I gasp and try to look elsewhere.

Yan glares at me. "He's your husband," she says. "It's not your fault if you've never seen him naked, you ought to have done by now. He needs something cooler over him." She busies herself removing all the heavy covers and then stalks away, muttering. I can hear her rifling through chests, presumably in search of something lighter to cover him with.

I look down on Yong. I have never seen him like this. Always, he has been in command of the situation during our brief meetings. It has been his place to speak, to command, to decide. It has been my place to listen and to obey, to reply when spoken to and to hope throughout that I do not displease him. I feel a sudden rush of tenderness for him, of pity. I sit on the edge of his bed and take out a little fan from my robe. I fan his face. He does not respond, but I think perhaps the deep crease in his forehead lessens a little, as though he senses that someone is at least trying to care for him, that he is not alone.

Yan takes charge. She orders me to grip my husband's ankles so that she can place fresh sheets under him and covers him with a light silk cover, which redresses his dignity. She has me bathe his face with a wet cloth while she cleans the room.

"How could the servants have left him?" I ask her. "When they know they will be whipped and dismissed for this?"

Yan struggles to open more windows, letting out the sour air of illness. The room is filled with a fresh morning breeze carrying the scent of blossom on it. She utters various choice words on what she thinks of Prince Yong's servants and what she thinks will happen to them. "Has he even been fed or given a drink?" she demands.

I look at him. He was a thin man anyway, but even under the

cover I can see his ribs. Now that I can see better, his lips are cracked and his skin seems dried out, stretched across his cheekbones. "I don't think so," I say. "He must be thirsty."

Yan finds and brings fresh water. I try to hold a little bowl to his lips but he does not swallow properly and water dribbles down his chin. I look to Yan and she dips a clean cloth in the water and shows me how to drip water into his mouth drop by drop.

"I will find a kitchen maid and make her bring food," she says, stamping away.

"Find Kun," I say. "He will not run away, Yan. We need more help." I am not sure what I mean by help. I think I am just afraid to be here, alone and unsure of what to do. I need people around me whom I trust. Kun's cheerful face would be a blessing right now.

Yan hesitates, then she nods her head and hurries away.

The water drip drips into Yong's mouth and does not come back out again. Pleased, I try talking to him. Perhaps this is all it will take? A spring breeze scented with blossom, some water and he will be well again?

"Do – do you feel better, Highness?"

He does not reply.

"The flowers are out," I say, not knowing what else to speak of. I think for a moment how strange it is to be married to this man and to know nothing about him, nor even to have ever seen his naked body. All I know is that he loves the Garden. I do not know if he can hear me. But if he can, surely he would be pleased to hear of the Garden. "I went down to the river and the turtles have woken from their winter sleep. They lie on the logs and rocks and bask in the sun. If you were there, the cool water would take away the heat you feel." I can hear the pleading in my voice. "If you recover a little, Highness, I will take you there to watch the dragonflies."

"How romantic."

I leap to my feet, upsetting the bowl of drinking water balanced on the bedclothes, which falls to the floor and breaks into shards. In the doorway stands a man. Broader in the chest and waist than Yong, he is dressed magnificently in robes only a tone darker than imperial yellow. I stand, unsure of what to do. By his clothing, he must be one of the imperial princes. But which one?

"You should kowtow," he informs me. "Don't you know what the Crown Prince looks like?"

Slowly, I kneel. A shard of broken bowl sticks into my knee and cuts me through my silken robe, but I bow forward without flinching into a kowtow. I only raise my head a little for each of the three obeisances and when I raise my head fully I find the man has crossed the room and is standing in front of me. My face is now too close to his groin. I lean back on my heels and turn my face a little away as I rise to my feet. I have always been told I am too tall for a girl but at this moment I wish I were taller still, for the Crown Prince towers over me.

"Ah, the young concubine," he says, looking me over. "I was annoyed they did not send you to me. I heard you were barely *formed* enough to be wed." The tip of his tongue comes out of his mouth and wets his lips. "And I also heard that my brother wasted the chance to bed you at once. Fool."

I back away, half-sitting on the edge of the bed and taking up Yong's limp hand in mine, as though seeking his protection. The Crown Prince only laughs.

"You can't expect him to come to your aid, girl. He's as good as dead. Anyone can see it. He was a little too dutiful, you know. A little *too* helpful to our father. All that efficiently done paperwork. All those trips to ensure works were being done to the correct quality: roads, dams, canals. A little too much praise was spoken of him. It made the rest of us look bad. And we can't have that, can we?"

"He will be well again soon," I say, my voice cracking mid-sentence.

The Crown Prince looks at me and smiles. It is a slow smile, a pitying smile. "Afraid of him dying?" he asks. "Afraid of being a dowager concubine, an untouched widow for the rest of your days?"

I don't answer but my eyes blink without my will. He knows only too well the true source of the fear I feel at Yong being ill. I barely know my husband. He is almost a stranger. What should it matter to me if a stranger dies? And yet. And yet if he dies the Yuan Ming Yuan will be given to some other prince, whilst we, the little-used (or in my case not used at all) concubines will be packed off to some discreet but lowly household to live out our days. We will not have a palace each. We will not be free to wander through the Garden. We will all live together, perhaps on a quiet side street in Beijing, with just enough servants to satisfy imperial protocol. Our names will be forgotten on some dusty old bit of paper that once named us as consorts to an imperial prince, now long dead. I swallow.

"I would not wish you to go to your grave untouched," says the Crown Prince.

I hold Yong's hand tighter and press his fingers. *Wake up*, I think. *Wake up*.

"Come here," says the Crown Prince.

I don't move.

"Do as you're told," he says.

My grip on Yong's hand is so tight that he should be in pain, should open his eyes and speak, should send his brother away, heir or no heir. Slowly I release my grip and his hand falls back on the covers, as though lifeless. I stand. I wonder whether I can run, whether if I move fast, without warning, I can make my way out of this room. In my mind I see the receiving hall, the doorway, the courtyard garden, the tiny lakeside path, my own palace and the wisteria flowers that cover it. I stand before the Crown Prince, keeping my eyes on the floor.

His hands are large and suddenly all over me. One hand grips my behind, one hand roughly fondles my breast through my robe. "Undress," he says and his voice is hoarse.

"My lady," says Yan's voice, loud and clear, no hint of a tremble. "I have found the servants. His Highness' head eunuch will also be here in a moment."

His hands leave my body as he turns to see Yan and Kun at the far end of the room. Without a word he leaves, pushing past them as though they do not exist. Behind him, Kun quickly shuts the door and drops a bar across it, so that no-one else can enter. Yan crosses to me and looks at my face before kneeling to collect the broken shards. I sit back down on the bed and try to still my trembling hands.

"Have you really found the servants?" I ask.

Yan shakes her head.

A hot tear makes its way down my face. "What will we do?" I ask Kun, as though he were able to do something.

Kun's voice is soft. "I will remain with you night and day," he says. "We found the kitchen staff. They will bring food to the gates. Yan and I will collect it. They will not come to the palace. They are afraid of sorcery."

"He is ill, not ill-wished!" I say, although I know no such thing.

Kun is serious. "The servants are afraid either way," he says. "If it is illness then they have never seen such a strong fever. He has been ill for days, with no sign of recovery. He is likely to die if it continues. If it is ill-wishing then they are still scared, for who knows on whom a sorcerer may cast his eye next."

"Who is this sorcerer they are talking about?" I ask.

"Prince Zhi," says Kun, and as he says it I remember the gossip of the other women.

"Where are the Prince's other ladies?" I ask. "Shouldn't they be here too?"

Yan snorts. "They are afraid," she says. "There's loyalty for you."

The sun sets and food is brought to the door. I make Yan and Kun eat with me. I do not care if it is improper, I am too afraid of being left alone again. I try to feed Yong with broth, but I am not sure that he takes in much. When we have left the dishes back outside the gates I have Kun bar the door and Yan close the window shutters. We spread silk coverlets on the floor and Yan sleeps by me, with Kun by the door.

All night I wake, then sleep and wake again. Yan and Kun sleep, but Yong mutters and turns. I rise and go to him, hoping he may be waking, but his eyes are shut. I hold his hand again and think perhaps he returns my clasp. At last, my eyes aching with tiredness, I lie down on the bed by his side and sleep.

Morning comes. The three of us stand together, looking down on Yong.

"He isn't getting better," I say to Yan. My eyes ache from tiredness, I'm so weary I could sleep on my feet and my shoulders are slumped in defeat. He will surely die. What chance do we have of curing him if his doctors have deserted him?

Kun ignores our pale faces. He goes to the kitchens and returns with food and fresh water, he takes a broom to sweep the courtyard garden and then the rooms of the palace, one after another, methodical, calm, as though nothing at all is wrong. His practicality is the only thing stopping me from crying.

I sit, still dripping water into Yong's mouth, while Yan searches for stores of medicine, though none of us would know what to do with them.

"Enough," I say suddenly. "I am going to the other ladies' palaces. We cannot do this alone. They have as much to lose as I do."

But the palaces are all closed up, doors and shutters barred. I cannot tell if there is anyone is inside each one, I hammer on the doors with my fists and call out the names of each lady but no-one replies. I half-run from one islet to the next across the tiny bridges, only one thought in my mind. I am afraid the Crown Prince will return and find that we fooled him, that we are alone. He will not care for a maid and a eunuch, he will dismiss them and do whatever he wishes with me. I shudder at the thought.

I try Lady Qi's palace last, although it is one of the closest. I have never spoken to her directly but I no longer care for niceties. My fists already feel bruised from the other doors but I pound harder than ever and when the door suddenly opens I am so surprised I nearly fall onto Lady Qi.

She stands framed in the doorway, dressed in dark plum, her hair pinned up with green jade pins and decorated with dangling golden threads as though it were an ordinary day. I am well aware my own hair is a mess and that my clothes are crumpled. I have never seen her this close before, she always stood apart at events. Not tall, not short, of average build and beauty, there is nothing much to set her apart except her eyes, which are large but hooded, giving her a secretive look, as though she knows something precious and guards it with her life. I feel my heart sink, remembering the smile she gave when she saw me dismissed from Yong's bedchamber too quickly, knowing I had been found wanting in some way. But I have no choice.

"The Prince – please help me," I blurt. "No-one will help me." I can hear my voice shaking, can feel the tears building up.

She doesn't answer, only steps out of her palace and follows me. I am so out of breath that I do not even try to speak with her, only walk as quickly as possible.

When we arrive Yan and Kun look shocked to see Lady Qi. They do not know I had no choice. She walks past them as though they do not exist. Crossing the room, she looks down at Yong. She takes his pulse as though she were a doctor, feeling at different points, before inserting a golden nail shield between his lips and pulling his mouth open to inspect his tongue.

"Poison," she says.

I hear Yan make a hissing sound behind me, know that she will be making signs to warn off evil.

"How do you know?" I ask.

"His tongue is discoloured," she says, as though everyone knows the signs of poisoning. "And the twelve pulses are very weak. The poison may have damaged his vital forces beyond repair. Has he been like this all the time you have been here?"

I nod.

"Why are *you* here?" she asks, her dark eyes fixed on me.

"I felt sorry for him," I say.

Her eyes bore into me.

"And I... do not want him to die," I say. "If he dies, I..." I stop. It sounds selfish.

"All of us," she says, finishing my thought. "Some dreary back palace, squabbling amongst ourselves, our destinies warped and broken and no chance of changing them."

I drop my eyes. She knows full well what we have to lose.

"We will do our best," she says, her tone more practical than I expected. "My own servants will help us."

"Aren't they afraid?" I ask.

"They are more afraid of me," she says. I believe her.

The days that follow blur into one another. Lady Qi sends two serving girls whom Yan takes to commanding.

"Don't you know how to make a bed?" she chastises them. "Hurry up and serve tea for their ladyships."

In this way the palace is kept clean and everyone is fed. Between them they wash Yong's body and change his sheets, make up a bed for me on the floor in his bedchamber while Kun, quiet as ever, tends to the gardens and the indoor flowers. He lies by the door at night and I am grateful for his presence. There is no sign of the Crown Prince and after her first visit Lady Qi does not spend much time in the palace.

"I am going to Beijing," she tells me after a few days.

"Why?"

"I must speak with someone," she says.

"Who?"

"No-one for you to worry about," she replies.

"I need to know what you are doing," I say, more boldly that I thought I was capable of. I am so tired from broken nights that my mouth speaks the words I think out loud rather than holding back.

"The court is gathering around the princes," she says. "There are factions growing in favour for one or another, this is why someone will have struck out at Yong, he was growing to be a favourite to replace the Crown Prince. They have written him off as dead already. It is my job to ensure he is remembered, that his supporters do not give way to fear of Prince Zhi's poisons nor the Crown Prince's position. They must stand by him or the Crown Prince will be left as heir."

"Don't leave me here alone," I say. I have not told her of the Crown Prince and his everywhere-grasping hands.

"There is no use in him being kept alive if he is not remembered," she says and leaves without a backward glance.

I am alone with Yong and after days of caring for him with no response, I want to cry. I look down on him. He has not once opened his eyes, not once spoken. Sometimes he groans, or pants, as though the pain inside him or the heat burning up his skin is too much to bear, but mostly he lies still and quiet, a corpse in all but name. I put a hand on his shoulder and shake him a little, raise my voice. "Wake up, Highness."

He does not move, of course, he does not respond and suddenly I am angry, beating first my hands and then my fists against his bare skin, screaming at him. "Wake up! Wake up! How dare you lie here like this? How dare you leave me alone without protection? How dare you – how dare you – " and I am sobbing as I fall to my knees by his bedside, burying my face in the coverlet.

"Ladyship?"

I stand quickly, wiping my eyes with the back of my hand, trying to pat my hair into place although I cannot see what it looks like. I know that my eyes are red, that my skin is blotched.

"Enter," I say, turning. "Oh."

It is the Jesuit painter. He steps forwards and his eyes glance behind me to Yong. "It is true, then? The Prince is ill?"

"Yes," I say, wishing that I did not look so dishevelled.

"Will he recover?"

"Yes," I say. "Yes, he will."

His dark eyes meet mine and I know he sees the fear in my red-rimmed eyes that are now brimming with tears again.

"How can I be of service to you?" he asks. "To the Prince," he amends too quickly.

I am about to shake my head. What can he do that is useful to me? But if I shake my head he will go away and I know that I want him nearby, that I need people I can trust about me and that without even knowing this man, I trust him, for his level gaze and because he asked what he could do for me before he remembered that he serves the Emperor and Yong, not me. "You may paint a picture for him," I say, naming the only thing I know for sure he can do. "The Prince loves paintings and he loves the Garden. You must paint some flowers to please him when he wakes."

He bows his head. "I will do so and return to you as soon as possible," he says, turning to go.

"No!" I say, too loudly. He turns back to me. "You misunderstand me," I say. "You must paint here."

"Here?"

"In this room," I say. "I wish you to work in this room." I struggle to meet his gaze but I force myself to do so, to tell him what I cannot say. *I am afraid. Stay with me. Keep me safe.*

He looks at me for a long moment, then nods. "Kun will fetch my materials," he says. "And my subject matter."

Kun brings flowers and a vase and Giuseppe spends time arranging them. I sit by Yong's side and watch as first one stem and then another is placed and then re-placed. For the first time in many days I feel safe. There is something calming about him, he is so focused on his work that it leaves no space for other worries.

"Are you happy with the composition?" he asks me.

I nod. I do not care what he paints. I only care that if he is here I am not left alone. Watching him work soothes me, I can feel my shoulders lose their tightness and my face lose its worried frown. I feel my eyelids droop and I do not try to fight my tiredness. I can sleep while he works and I will be safe. I have such need of sleep.

Lady Qi returns from Beijing and frowns when she sees Giuseppe, ignoring his bow to her. "The Crown Prince is all but unseated," she tells me. "He went too far. First his proclivities, the scandals. Now his name has been linked to Yong's illness. His father is more than displeased, he is angry. It requires only a reminder that there are better princes to choose from for him to change his heir. But Yong needs to awaken or it will all have been for nothing. Has he stirred?"

I shake my head.

"I found a doctor who will treat him," she says.

"I thought the doctors said it was sorcery," I say.

"Silver changes minds," she says.

The doctor she has brought back with her is a wizened little man who mutters and shakes his head and spends an age looking over Yong, before beginning to grind up who-knows-what to give to him.

"He could be a sorcerer himself, for all I know," I say to Giuseppe.

He pauses in his work to watch the physician. "Lady Qi has much to lose if he is," he points out. "If your husband is made heir then one of her sons may be an Emperor one day. She would be the Empress Dowager, a great and powerful lady."

"I cannot think why she would want any such thing," I sigh.

He looks me over. "You do not wish to be…" he stumbles over the word concubine, "…married to an Emperor?"

"I want to stay here where it is peaceful," I tell him. "Or it was."

He smiles. "You like the Garden more than the Forbidden City?"

"I've barely seen the Forbidden City," I tell him. "I know it is grander. But the Garden is so lovely. And I do not like all this fighting over who is to be heir. Look at what it has done to – to the Prince." I am not sure why I do not just call him my husband.

He looks back at his painting, where bold orange-hued lilies stretch out their dark stamens above delicate white-pink peonies. "I hope the choice of heir falls on someone who can bear such a burden," he says quietly.

Night falls. Lady Qi and her doctor leave us. I see Giuseppe packing up his things and badly want to ask him to stay within the palace so that he will be close by, but that is an unthinkable request, so instead I try to engage him in conversation to keep him with me as long as possible.

"Have you spent much time in the Garden?" I ask. "Or is most of your work in the Forbidden City?"

"A little of both," he says.

"Which do you prefer?"

"The Garden," he says smiling. "It is so beautiful. Although I am frequently lost here. It is so large and each little part invites you to explore further rather than sticking to your own path."

I can't help but laugh, acknowledging the number of times Yan and I got lost when I first came here. "You need Kun with you," I tell him. "Kun knows every tiny part of the Garden. You should ask him to show you the fireflies one evening, they are magical."

"They sound enchanting," he says.

I have to let him go, with Kun accompanying him to carry his tools. After Yan and I have eaten I stand looking down on Yong. I sigh at the thought of another night of heat and worry.

"You should go and see the fireflies yourself," Yan says.

"I have to stay here," I say.

Yan shakes her head. "You need to get out," she says. "You've been indoors for days, you'll fall ill yourself. Go and watch the fireflies, dip your toes in the water. Breathe some cool air. He'll still be here when you get back," she adds gloomily.

I chew my lip. But Yan is right. I crave cool air and to be free of this sickroom. It's making me feel ill myself. "I will be back soon," I promise her and she waves me away.

The night air helps me breathe more deeply. I can feel my shoulders relax a little after days of anxious watching over Yong. I make my way towards one of the little streams that leads to the wider lake.

Remembering that the riverbank is slippery, I take off my shoes and creep softly along its edge, disturbing the frogs who stop croaking for a few moments and then carry on with their usual night chorus, accompanied by crickets. I make my way along the twisting bank, knowing that there is a large rock further ahead on which I can sit and keep watch. The fireflies should emerge soon.

"Is that you, Kun?"

I gasp at the unexpected voice emerging from the darkness ahead and nearly lose my footing.

"Kun?"

"I am not Kun," I say. I recognised the voice at once. It is Giuseppe. No-one else speaks Mandarin with his odd accent, the tones in the wrong places, the vowels at the end of words where there are none.

He is silent. I am not even sure where he is, except that Kun has probably led him to the same rock that I was going to sit on.

"I have disturbed your evening, I will go," he says and I can hear that he has stood up.

"No, no," I say quickly. "If you are here to see the fireflies you should stay. They are beautiful. I will go."

"Please," he says. "Stay."

I think of what Yan would have to say about such a suggestion. "Where is Kun?" I ask, still hovering at the edge of the river, hoping that he might reappear. I try to peer about me but the darkness is made up of nothing but shadowy shapes which could be anything.

"Ladyship?"

I breathe out in relief at Kun's voice. All is well. I have a eunuch by my side. Decorum is preserved. "We are watching for fireflies," I inform him, as though this is a well-known pastime shared by foreign priests and concubines. "You will wait with me."

Faintly, I see his dark shape bow by my side. "Ladyship." His voice is calm, no surprise, no questioning. A good servant does not question.

I sit down on the grass. The ground is still warm from the day's sun. Kun squats down nearby. I hear a faint rustle, indicating that Giuseppe has also seated himself. We wait in silence.

They come so slowly that at first you cannot be sure you have seen them at all. A tiny spark. I twist my head and already it is gone. But there was another just there, but now it too is gone. And suddenly we are surrounded by tiny lights, as though the stars have come down to earth, twinkling all around us.

"Do you have fireflies where you come from?" I ask the darkness.

"I used to try and catch them when I was a little boy in my grandmother's garden," says his voice. "With my brother."

I hear something in his voice. "How long did it take you to travel here?" I ask.

"More than a year," he says.

I think of the distance, of how everyone he knows and holds dear is so far away that he cannot know how they are, what they are doing, even if they are alive. "When will you return to your home and family?" I ask.

There is a slight pause. Then, "I cannot return," he says. "The Emperor asked for a painter who would stay here. I accepted the post on this condition, that I will never return home." He is silent for a moment and then adds, "I will never see my family again." He almost sounds surprised, as though it has taken him this long to realise what he has agreed to.

"Are you homesick?" I ask.

He is silent and then, "Yes," he replies, and his voice is too steady, so calm that I know even in the darkness that my question caused pain, which he has covered up before replying. I am sorry for it. I think that I should stay silent, that I should think more carefully before I ask such stupid questions.

"Does your family live nearby?" he asks me, as though hoping to lighten the mood.

I hesitate. He does not know how my life is ruled. "I am a c-concubine," I say, stumbling over the word. "We do not see our families again once we marry into the Imperial Family."

He is surprised. "Ever?"

"Ever."

And then we are silent while the Garden twinkles and its night sounds surround us. The moon has risen very high by the time I tug at Kun's sleeve and tell him to escort me home. Giuseppe's voice is soft as he says goodbye.

"Thank you, Niuhuru," he says. "It was beautiful."

In the morning Yan looks me over. "You came back late but you look better than yesterday," she says.

"I needed to be outside in the Garden," I say.

"Did you see the fireflies?"

"Yes," I say. Now is the moment when I should tell her that I watched them with Giuseppe but I can't quite think how to frame the words.

Yan is anyway uninterested in me. "The Prince's skin seems cooler," she says.

I hurry to his side. "Is he awake?"

Yan shakes her head.

I look down on Yong. "Highness?" I say gently. But he does not stir.

"Perhaps the poison is leaving him," I suggest.

"Perhaps it was not poison, only an illness," says Yan, although she sounds doubtful. "Some of the servants have come creeping back," she adds disdainfully.

I see a few of them tentatively taking up their tasks again, although they all look afraid. The same thing must be going through all their minds: what is worse – to be infected or ill-wished, or beaten for desertion?

When Giuseppe arrives I am unsure whether I should refer to our evening together, but he surprises me by laying a small piece of paper on my table.

"What is this?" I ask, expecting perhaps a rough sketch for his floral composition.

"Something I painted last night when I could not sleep," he says.

I look down. A strangely-formed building made of stone clad with tumbling roses. A garden, neatly tended. Between the rows of vegetables, two little boys, their arms outstretched while tiny pinpoints in the air elude their grasp. I stare. The painting is not like any I have ever seen, it seems alive, as though it were a model rather than a flat painting.

"You and your brother catching fireflies in your grandmother's garden," I murmur and he smiles when he meets my gaze, although his eyes glisten for a moment.

"I think I have found a way to paint which may be accepted here," he says, and I can hear excitement in his voice. "Instead of dark shading I am using tonal shading: you see, here, the darker green against the lighter green which gives the depth. It is a question of the light source being more diffused and coming more from the front than the side, so that the shading is not as dark. Do you think it will be accepted?"

"It looks as though it is real," I say. "It is beautiful." I am about to ask him more, to ask him to draw me another such building, another moment from his unknown life before here, when Yan exclaims behind me and I turn to see Yong's eyes opening, his gaze fixed on me.

"Niuhuru," he croaks and I run to his side.

Atlas of Blossoms in an Everlasting Spring

I CONFESS IT: THERE WAS SOME part of me that hoped the Prince might die. There: I am not a good man, not a holy man who would never have allowed his mind to wander where it should not. There was some part of my mind filled with fireflies, where a woman's voice spoke to me of home in the darkness and she was mine, not another's.

I confessed it, of course. Kneeling in the stifling confessional beneath the high arches of St Joseph's criss-crossed ceiling I whispered my baser thoughts and received absolution, in return for who knows how many Hail Marys and Our Fathers, as well as a well-meaning reminder that I must set my thoughts to higher things, that I would find the years of service ahead less onerous were I truly dedicated to the missionary cause that had brought me here rather than continuing to think of myself as a free man.

I confess it: I even tried on a hair shirt beneath my robes, feeling foolish as I did so, as though I were self-aggrandising my thoughts, for what man has not had such thoughts after all? They were only thoughts with no possible conclusion, no possibility of a reality. What, the Prince would die and his concubine would run away with me to Milan? Of course not. I wore the shirt for a few days before I chastised myself for my own pride in imagining myself a holy man beset with doubt. Instead I lit candles and knelt to give thanks for the recovery of Prince Yong and, safely ensconced within the painting studio, hurried to complete my floral commission using the tonal shading I had at last found as a means of bridging the two styles of East and West together. First the eunuchs in the studio and then Prince Yong declared themselves delighted with the work. Yong set me to work on a portfolio of images, which he wished to name *Atlas of Blossoms in an Everlasting Spring*.

"Roam wherever you wish in the Garden," he told me, smiling, his skin still pale. He gestured across the view of the lake from his study window. "You must capture its beauty for me. I wish it to be a gift for one of my concubines, Lady Niuhuru."

Her name must have changed my expression for he nodded. "You know her, of course. She commissioned your painting for me."

I bowed, unsure of how to reply but the Prince was already speaking again.

"She is very young, but she has an eye for beauty in nature," he said. "She spoke to me of the Garden and I heard her, only for a moment. It is all I recall from my illness. She spoke of the river, the lakes. Of turtles and kingfishers. The Atlas will be a gift for her, in recognition of her loyalty to me."

I bowed again. "As you command, Your Highness. I shall ensure the Garden's beauty is captured."

Laura had heard gossip. "They say many of Prince Yong's ladies are in disgrace for hiding away."

"The servants were beaten and some turned out for their cowardice in the face of his illness," I said. "Although I cannot entirely fault them."

"You have met Lady Niuhuru?" asked Laura.

"Yes," I said. I was pleased that my voice remained steady.

"It seems the Prince is quite taken with her. He says she was the only lady truly loyal to him."

"I am to paint her a portfolio of images of the Garden as a gift," I said.

"And I thought he was such a stern and dutiful man," said Laura laughing. "Perhaps he has romantic side to him after all."

"Perhaps," I said, and turned away.

I was true to my word, spending my days roaming about every part of the Garden. The Atlas grew under my brushes, sixteen images to capture the unending landscape around us. Peonies in every shade opened their fat buds while poppies unfurled their fragile petals and then disappeared within days. Fresh green bamboo stalks soared heavenwards while morning glories wrapped their delicate stems about them and turned their faces to the morning sun. I recalled the pure white magnolias of early spring and captured the ripening cherries of summer. Every part of the Atlas celebrated the beauty of the Garden.

Frequently I came across Kun while I worked and he would greet me. Sometimes from afar, adrift in a small boat as he cleared the lakes of weeds, one hand raised in wordless salute. Sometimes close to, when I would settle down to paint a particular detail and he worked close by. I had never liked to have people watching me while I worked, but strangely I found Kun's presence soothing, for he did not speak overmuch, only continued his work, his rough hands tender with the flowers and shoots in his care. We often spent much of the day working side by side in silence. He would nod when he saw the fruits of my labour, not with admiration but in simple recognition, which somehow pleased me more, for to Kun each plant was an individual, not merely *a* peony but *this* peony, no other like it in the Garden.

"I am to be married," he told me one day.

I looked up, startled as much by his voice as by his news. "Married?"

He nodded and I saw from the happiness in his face that this was something much-longed for.

"I – " I paused. I did not want to hurt his feelings but then again I felt that there was honesty between us and so I spoke again, but carefully, choosing my words one by one. "I did not know eunuchs were permitted to marry," I said.

He nodded, acknowledging the question I had not asked. "Not all eunuchs marry," he said. "But it is permitted, if their masters allow it. And Lady Niuhuru is very good to Yan."

Yan, of course. I smiled. "Did Yan ask for permission then?"

His smile was so wide that it made my eyes fill up a little. "She asked her mistress before I asked her myself," he said.

I had to laugh out loud at the thought of fierce little Yan, always scowling, going to Niuhuru and then all but telling Kun he was to marry her, like it or not. Kun joined me in laughter, acknowledging that my thoughts were true.

"But will Yan have to leave Niuhuru?" I asked. "I was told the maids had to work a certain number of years before they were set free to be married."

"Lady Niuhuru permitted her to marry me only if she continues to serve," said Kun. "All will be as before."

For a few days afterward I avoided Kun. When I sought him out it was with a gift.

"For your marriage," I said, holding out a scroll.

I had painted tumbling climbing pale pink flowers, wrapped about a tree. He held the gift and did not speak, only nodded, recognising with his gentle smile the roses he had planted for Yan after the first time he had met her, on the island of cherry trees.

"Show me what you have been working on," I said to Laura and she brought me new sketches and some initial paintings using the refined version of the *chiaroscuro* technique I had developed, using the new direction of light and tones of colours rather than the darker shading we were both trained in.

"These are very good," I told her. If anything she had understood the new refinement required quicker than I, she had applied herself diligently to practising it and now she executed it perfectly, bringing her Chinese subjects to life with a delicacy that I admired. Secretly I was also relieved that I could not see any more sketches of Madam Guo and supposed that Laura had taken my words to heart and was striving to be less enchanted by the new world in which we found ourselves. I praised her for her work and she was pleased. I saw her set to such commissions as we now began to receive with greater confidence and enthusiasm and I congratulated myself on having managed her still-young emotions well. She had proven herself first as a worthy apprentice and then assistant and I was glad to have her working by my side.

But my own feelings neither left me nor could be hidden within my work, for over and over again amongst the flowers pairs of songbirds appeared, their tiny wings and flashes of colour fluttering within the branches of my trees and the petals of my flowers. They gazed at one another, sat so close together their feathers touched, sang for each other's pleasure. I was helpless in the face of their devotion.

I sought out Father Friedel, hoping that his customary fretting over my time here would remind me of my chosen path. I submitted to his lengthy reminders of my obligations to the Mission and his reminders of my as yet untaken vows.

"You will find spiritual guidance in the chapel, my son," he said kindly. "I have seen you little at prayers, of late."

At his urging I retreated from the imperial studios to the church, hoping to commit myself to a greater cause. As the final words of Mass were spoken and the final 'amens' resounded from the congregation, I raised my eyes and caught, for only a brief moment, Laura ahead of me as she rose and left. Before she reached the outer door, however, she turned and her eyes sought out Madam Guo, who in turn gazed after Laura with an expression of such love that I caught my breath at what was so obviously laid before me.

Afterwards I stood alone in the church, wondering what to do. Should I speak with Laura again or even take my concerns to one of the senior Brothers and ask for his advice in guiding Laura's soul away from this temptation? Yet the longer I stood there, trying to feel concern, the more I realised that all I felt was jealousy. Not for Laura's sake, for I had never regarded her as anything but my pupil, but for the gaze between her and Guo. It came to me suddenly that what I most desired but could not have was that same gaze between Niuhuru and I, the same certainty that what I desired was desired also by her.

Within my palace of memories, in a sheltered corner of the Garden, there is a peach tree where pink blossom bursts into flower while two swallows regard one another, their bodies entwined. Only in the moment of knowing I could not have Niuhuru did I come to know I loved her.

Flying Bats Filling the Sky

A s Yong recovers, the Garden returns to life. The beaten servants hurry back to their neglected tasks. Gardeners pull up weeds, sweep the pathways, skim the lakes for algae. Maids see to the laundry that has built up, clean rooms with extra diligence. The kitchen staff send out elegantly presented dishes, anxious to make up for their failings. The disgraced ladies slowly re-emerge from their homes and sit quietly together by the lakeside, chastised but relieved. Lady Qi nods to me when she sees me now; I am an ally in her quest and she takes to updating me on the political machinations of the court, of which I understand little and wish to know less.

"The Crown Prince has been demoted," she tells me. "A new heir has not yet been announced. It's possible the Emperor will delay choosing a new heir for some time. He was not impressed with all the rivalry between his sons, the factions that developed. But he could well choose Yong. He is everything the Crown Prince was not. He is devoted, filial, accomplished in his work and mindful of the people of the empire."

I think of the Crown Prince, of his hands on me. I shudder.

Qi mistakes my reaction. "You would be consort to an Emperor," she reminds me. "A greater destiny by far than our current path. We are still young and could be promoted many times. Our children would be princes of the first rank."

Or made Emperor, I think, knowing this is her ultimate goal for her own sons. "I am not as ambitious as you, Qi," I tell her. "But I am glad the Prince is well again."

She smiles at me and pats me, as though I am an amiable daughter, one content to allow her mother to lead the way. I know that my lack of ambition must endear me to her, since no woman seeking power is likely to want a rival. "One step at a time," she says. "The first step is taken. Others will follow."

I am called to Yong's palace only a few days after his recovery and formally escorted to his bedchamber as though I do not know where it is. He is lying in bed but he sits up when he sees me. His face is deathly pale.

I kowtow. "I wish you all health and happiness," I say. I sit back on my knees and look up at him. "Are you well, Highness?"

His voice is hoarse. "I am not dead," he says. "Because of you."

I shake my head. "Lady Qi," I begin.

"You were the first to come to my aid?" he asks.

"Yes," I say.

"And I have been told you stayed with me until I awoke, night and day?"

"Yes," I say.

"Then I am in your debt," he says.

"No," I say. "I am grateful you were spared."

Yong gestures and his head eunuch comes forwards.

"Lady Niuhuru is granted an additional maid and her own personal gardener in recognition of her service to the Prince," he announces formally.

I kowtow, but the eunuch continues to read out additional gifts. My household allowance is increased by many bolts of silk, taels of silver and I am to receive gifts of jade and other precious gems. I am not sure when to stop kowtowing. When the announcement is over

Yong smiles at me, but he looks exhausted by even this brief meeting and I am quickly led away. I do not see him for another month.

Yan is shining. "You are summoned."

"Summoned where?"

She is too busy to answer me. Kun is now attached to my palace as my own personal gardener and I have a second maid, as promised. Yan is making the poor girl traipse back and forth with armfuls of clothing. Every robe I have is on display, silk in every colour draped all over the room. Yan is examining each with the air of a general inspecting troops.

"Yan? Summoned where?"

"To the Prince."

"What does he want?"

Yan looks at me in disbelief. "You," she says. "He wants you. At last."

Something in my stomach turns over. I feel heat rise up my neck and into my cheeks. I swallow. "Tonight?"

"Tonight."

I sit down. Yan continues her inspections. I try to think. All those foolish daydreams I made up, where I was summoned by the Prince and he… he… he what? What? I never got beyond the summons; beyond knowing I was desired at last. All my imaginings ended somewhere out on the lakeside path, as an image of me – a more beautiful, infinitely glamorous and elegant version of me, of course, in my mind – tottered along the tiny pathways in my highest shoes, my most elegant robes, on my way to… to what? To being important, to being beautiful and a favourite, whatever that might mean. That was enough for me when I was thirteen, fourteen. I nod wordlessly at Yan's final choice: palest rose silk, jade pins to hold tiny rosebuds mixed with giant peonies in my hair. Shoes so high I have forgotten how to walk in them, sewn all over with gems. I stand in the doorway of my home and have to wait for Yan's small hand in mine to step forwards. She keeps me steady along the pebbled lake pathway, each tiny stone making up mosaic images of birds, flowers, even fish. We make our way over one bridge and then another, onwards towards the wide curved rooftops of Yong's palace, set amongst trees. At the gateway, Yan pulls her hand away and I must take the last tremulous steps alone. When I reach the doorway, where a eunuch stands waiting to receive me, I look back, but she is already gone.

His bedchamber should be familiar enough to me by now. I have slept by Yong's side for many nights, have given orders in this room. But now it feels different. It is no longer a sick room. Fresh flowers adorn niches in the walls, lanterns glow softly. The large wooden alcove of the bed has been adorned with fresh hangings in a deep red silk, something like a bridal chamber. I stand alone and try to keep my head erect, my hands from trembling. I wonder when the servants will arrive to undress me and unpin my hair. I wonder if the sleeping robe they will give me will be as sheer as the one I remember from the first time I was summoned, aged only thirteen.

"Niuhuru."

I turn to face Yong. He looks a great deal better than the last time I saw him. In my highest shoes I am now the same height as he is, our eyes level with one another. His eyes are bright, his skin has resumed its normal colour, his voice is clear.

"Your Highness is so well recovered," I say.

"Thanks to you," he replies.

I bob my head in some sort of acknowledgement. He steps to a small table and picks up the two small bowls of warmed wine and passes me one, as he did before. This time I sip it, thinking that its warmth will give me courage. When I pass it back to him I hope he does not notice my hand tremble.

He smiles and indicates the bed. "Come."

I follow him and perch on the edge of it, unsure of what to do about my shoes. Noticing my glance downwards he reaches out and indicates I should lift my feet onto the silken coverlet. I do so and he takes each bejewelled shoe and removes them, dropping them uncaring to the floor, their carved wooden soles clattering as they hit the stone.

"You don't look comfortable," he observes. He himself is cross-legged on the bed, at ease, while I am sat so close to the edge I am in danger of falling to the floor myself. "Sit beside me. I have a gift for you."

Awkwardly, I half-crawl to his side, my robes hampering my movements. I settle next to him, my back against the carved wood, unsure whether or not our bodies should touch.

He has picked up a package wrapped in silk. It is large but light and I unwrap it with care. It lands upside down on my lap and I see it is an album of paintings. I wonder for a brief moment if it is a pillow book and feel my cheeks flush, but as I turn it over I see its subject matter is not what I expected.

"It is called *Atlas of Blossoms in an Everlasting Spring*," says Yong. "I had it made for you by the Jesuit painter."

I had already recognised Giuseppe's work. His way of painting is not like the paintings I have seen all my life. There is something about it that is alive, that lifts each petal from the paper as though it might be touched, as though, plucked, it might fall from the page to the silken coverlet on which I am sitting. Entranced, I turn the sheets and see parts of the Garden held within delicate brushstrokes. The flowers, the trees, the butterflies and birds that I see every day around me are captured here, beneath my fingertips. I touch the petals and feathers, where his brushes have been before me. Beside me, I slowly become aware that Yong is watching, not the pages, but my face. His hand lifts to caress my cheek and I, unsure of how to respond, keep my eyes on the pictures and feel his caresses on my skin even as a breeze blows through the branches of a peach tree and two swallows incline their necks so that each caresses the other, their feathers intertwined.

He is very gentle with me. My silken robes are taken from me one by one and he does not hurry his task. My hair he leaves bound. He lifts my hands and guides them, he holds me in a tender embrace and even when there is pain I am not afraid, for he murmurs to me that I am his flower, his songbird, his Garden of Perfect Brightness.

When he opens his eyes he observes the petals loosened from my hair, now strewn across the bed and chuckles. "You are indeed a garden," he says. "See, you leave petals wherever you go."

I blush at receiving endearments with his eyes on me, unsure of what to say in return.

"You will come to me again," he says.

"Yes, Highness," I whisper.

Yan is delighted. "About time," she says.

"He said I must go to him again," I tell her.

"Of course," agrees Yan confidently and I cannot help but laugh at her conviction.

Her faith in me is rewarded. Yong calls for me nightly unless Yan informs his household that it is my time of bleeding. Each evening I walk the lakeside path to his palace. The moon grows round over and again. Each night I am welcomed with a warm smile. Sometimes he reads me poems, sometimes he will show me paintings he admires. A few times we stand by the lakeside and admire tiny lanterns he orders to have floated across the dark waters. I catch a glimpse of his study and see it piled high with unread papers. Each night I am taken into the scarlet hangings of his bed and gradually I learn for myself where my hands might be placed, to give as well as to receive tenderness.

"Where shall I put this?" asks Yan, holding up the silk-wrapped package containing the *Atlas*.

I shrug, holding first one autumn chrysanthemum and then another to my hair, smiling in the mirror. "Somewhere safe, Yan. Do you prefer the red or the orange?"

"The Prince doesn't care what flowers you wear, you should know that by now. You could go to him wrapped in a sack and he would be happy. You lovesick pair."

I giggle and tuck a golden-orange flower into my dark hair.

"Yan," I ask, almost in a whisper.

"Yes?"

"When you... with Kun... how...?" I stop, uncertain of how to continue.

Yan does not answer, only walks away and then returns with a box, lacquered in black. With the air of one confiding a secret, she offers it to me and I open it, then start back in surprise, for I have never seen such an object. Under a red silk cloth lies a porcelain model of a man's member, painted with tumbling roses.

"Kun had it made for us," she murmurs.

I think of Yan, how the frightened child I first met when I came here is now a fierce little woman, whose face shines with love when she sees Kun, who sings to herself when no-one is listening. I place the red silk cloth back over the piece and close the lid with a smile.

"We are both happy, Yan," I say. "We have been blessed."

She takes back the box with a little laugh, her cheeks flushed pink. "So happy," she echoes.

I bask in Yong's attentions throughout that autumn and winter. The first almond blossoms come into bloom, heralding spring.

"Wine?" he offers.

I nod, smiling, and take the little bowl from him, making sure to brush his fingertips with mine, for the simple pleasure of touching his skin. He stands by the window, looking out over the lake and I stand beside him, leaning my head on his shoulder and closing my eyes.

"My flower," he murmurs.

I am about to speak, to say his name when suddenly my stomach roils and I clutch at his arm, the little bowl falling to the floor.

He lifts me before I can even speak, carrying me swiftly to a chair and kneeling before me. "Niuhuru? What is it?"

"I feel sick," I gasp.

A servant manages to hold a bowl before me just before my stomach voids itself. I retch over and over again until, as swiftly as it came upon me, the sickness ends. Yong holds a cloth dipped in perfumed water to my face. I try to gasp my apologies but his face has lost its initial fear.

"I believe you need to rest," he says, a wry smile twisting his mouth. "I will send the physician to you."

"Highness?"

He strokes my cheek. "Farewell, my flower. I will miss you. But all will be well."

Yan might as well be with child herself, she is so pleased. "A son," she tells me. "You must have a son."

I make a face. "I'll have anything you like if you'll stop giving me disgusting drinks."

"The physician prescribed them."

"I don't care. They've vile. And I want to see Yong."

"You won't be seeing him till this child is born," says Yan cheerfully.

"Why not?"

"Oh, you'll see him at festivals or suchlike," says the uncaring

Yan. "But not as a companion. It might harm the baby. Besides, now you are with child he has done his duty by you."

"I was not a duty!" I say angrily.

Yan rolls her eyes. "He has given you a child. What more did you want? A great romance?"

"He said he loved me," I protest. "He said… lots of things."

"I'm sure he did," says Yan, unbothered by my tone, which is growing tearful. "But there are other ladies to call on while you are otherwise occupied."

I throw a hairbrush at her but she only dodges it and tuts at my outburst.

Spring comes and I hear that other ladies are called on. I set my jaw and mope. I make Yan's life difficult, asking for first one dish that I claim to have cravings for and then another, before turning them away uneaten. I refuse to go out. I sit in the palace until Yan is tired of my sulking face and petulant tone. She drops Giuseppe's *Atlas* in my lap.

"If you won't go into the Garden, it will have to come to you."

Once again the petals rise up as though I might touch them. Butterflies hover above lotus flowers and I can almost hear the songbirds. I place the album on my chair and leave my rooms.

I had forgotten the joy of springtime in the Garden. Pale primroses and violets nestle in the shade of great trees, the first blossoms open their petals and everywhere tiny green tips emerge from the bare branches. I find a sunny ledge of rock by the lake's edge and sit myself down on it. I stay still long enough that a frog emerges from the water and sits on a fallen log, basking in the warm sunlight.

"I saw you from a distance."

The frog dives into the water with a splash. I look up at Giuseppe's dark form standing over me. "You walk quietly."

"I did not want to disturb you, only to know if you are well."

"Well enough." It comes out ungracious and I try to make amends. "The *Atlas* you painted of the Garden is beautiful."

He smiles an odd smile, as though I have said something sad but which must be smiled at. "I am glad it brought you pleasure."

I gesture at the rocky ledge. "Sit."

He hesitates, but then settles himself on a rock some little way off from me. He gestures awkwardly towards my hair. "An unusual motif."

I reach up to touch the hairpin I am wearing. A flying bat, its form shaped in kingfisher feathers, a gift from Yong. I grimace. "It symbolises fertility."

He nods. I can tell, from his face, that he has heard the gossip already.

"A reward for my loyalty," I add and hear the bitter note in my own voice. I know I should stop, but the bitterness will not be contained. "He has given me a child and now he ignores me." My voice shakes. "I thought he loved me."

"No-one could not – " says Giuseppe and suddenly he is on his feet. "Forgive me." He turns and strides away, his feet hard on the pebble path.

But he returns. As spring wears on and summer comes, I spend each day in the garden and he finds me again and again. I come to look out for him. I ask him to paint what surrounds me: the golden carp in the pools, the chirping crickets, the plum-red peonies. He does not speak much, unless I engage him in conversation.

"You still use your own paints," I remark. "But on our paper?"

He looks up at me. "I thought the rice paper would wrinkle or curl up when I first used it, as our paper at home would do. But it does not. It surprised me. And canvas is not as easy to find here."

"But you don't use inks and watercolours?"

"I prefer my oils," he admits. "They seem to work well with the rice paper. They seem to have an affinity – the finished texture has something silken to it."

"They always seem alive," I say. "The things you paint. As if they were real." I look down at the carp, who are begging for crumbs, their pursed lips mouthing at the surface of the water and then at his image of them, their bodies swirling through watery depths. "Can you paint people the same way?"

He smiles. "I am practicing with plants and animals first," he admits. "If I can achieve the effect I want I may go on to people."

My rooms fill up with his works. Some are only scraps, sketches or quick swirls of the brush that I beg from him when I see them, for there is something lovely even about his half-finished works, a glimpse of the Garden as it is in motion – a petal falling, grass swaying, the ripples of a turtle's dive. Some are larger works that he gifts to me. He does not give them into my hand, only leaves them where I may find them, on the outer windowsill of my room held in place by a stone, on a smooth rock where I like to sit. He will not let me thank him for them. When I speak of them he shakes his head and says they are nothing, only something half done. But I know better, for each blade of grass is finished and often the scene is something I have remarked on.

My belly grows and grows, a pumpkin swelling in the summer sun. I do not walk as far and find the heat too much. I stay within the sheltering shade of a giant willow and dabble my toes in the water, much to Yan's annoyance.

"You will chill your womb," she admonishes in doomed tones.

"Since when were you appointed Court Physician?" I ask, ungraciously removing my hot feet from the cooling lake. I lie back on the covers Yan has laid out for me but stretch my arms so that I can feel the grass at the edges, tickling my palms.

I am lonely. Yong's sudden withdrawal pained me. I had basked in the glow of his affection and now find myself left in a cold solitude, no matter how bright the summer sun shines on me. He sends me the same dutiful gifts I used to receive and has returned to court business, to long journeys away and hurried returns to the Garden and his study, to his piles of paper and a furrowed brow. I have only Yan, who worries incessantly about my health. So I turn to Giuseppe.

"Tell me about your home town," I ask him.

He describes the daily lives of his family, he draws little sketches for me to show me their strange clothes, their homes. I see his world in miniature, spread across scraps of paper, while in my mind it comes to life. Smoke curls from tall chimneys, beggars hold out their hands for alms, ladies lift heavy skirts out of the dirt of the streets. The summer leaves us and the first cool winds of autumn come. I sit in the Garden and walk the streets of Milan.

The pain is so bad that I cling to Yan and beg her to make it stop. But the midwife only rolls her eyes and tells Yan that I will be better at this next time, that all the ladies make such a fuss the first time, why, we have barely started.

"There will never be another time!" I scream at her, baring my teeth in rage and pain. "Never, you hear me?"

Yan, emboldened by the midwife's calm, shakes her head as though she has seen a hundred births. "Not pining for the Prince anymore then?" she asks cheerily and then yelps when I bite her. "You beast!"

"Beast yourself!" I shriek. "You are supposed to comfort me. Make it *stop*!"

Even Yan is sorry for me soon, as the warm autumn night drags on and I weep and writhe, covered in sweat and tears, sobbing that I will die for sure. She holds me in her arms and allows me to clutch desperately at her while the midwife only hums to herself and waits as though she has all the time in the world. I hate her.

"A boy!" Yan crows as a wriggling, mewling, blue-toned creature struggles in the midwife's expert hands. "A son for the Prince."

He is given the name Hongli and when they place him in my arms his eyes open wide and fix me in a commanding stare. I stroke his silken cheek and wonder what destiny holds for him and for me, his mother.

Long-haired Dog Beneath Blossoms

"**A** FROG! I FOUND A FROG!"

The boy came running towards me, his hands cupped. I held my breath for a moment, thinking he might fall, so intent was he on looking at his treasure, heedless of where his feet might be placed on the uneven lakeside path. But he reached my side safely, arms outstretched to reveal a terrified baby frog, crouching in his muddied palms.

"It is a very nice frog," I said, nodding at it before I dipped the brush back in my paints.

"Paint him for me!"

"I am supposed to be working on a commission for your grandfather," I reminded him. "And as he is the Emperor, I believe his command outranks that of a prince?"

"But you are my *friend*," said Hongli, smiling persuasively.

His room was filled with my paintings. Frogs, dragonflies, fish, turtles, painted on little scraps of paper. A recent and more formal painting, given for his tenth birthday, showed a small, brown, long-haired dog panting beneath a gnarled but blossoming tree: his own pet, now lying lazy in the spring sunshine, already worn out with its young master's endless quests for adventure by the lakeside. Hongli might be confined on a daily basis to a study by his tutors and by all accounts he was an excellent scholar, but as soon as he was let loose each day he roamed the Garden and sought me out to paint images for him.

Ten years had passed since Niuhuru had given Yong a son. I had seen him grow from a wrapped-up bundle in her arms to a waddling infant, enchanted by the waving willows overhead. He had grown fleet of foot as the years went by, racing about the Garden, now become his personal playground. Kun's skilled hands had woven for him a great water-dragon made from reeds, placed so that it rose from the waters of a small lake near Yong's palace, its tongue a bright swatch of red silk begged from Niuhuru's chests of clothes. He poked with sticks in the reeds, startling frogs and herons alike, ignoring Yan's wringing hands and pleas to take care, in part directed at her own daughter, Chu. Adopted by Yan and Kun shortly after their marriage, Chu was the same age as Hongli. She spent her mornings embroidering under Yan's supervision, her afternoons following Hongli about the Garden. She was as tiny as Yan must have been as a girl, quick on her feet and fearless, scrambling up rocks and leaning over the sides of walkways to gaze into the lakes, side by side with Hongli. He had now passed his tenth birthday but he was still a child and full of playfulness. The two children brought me gingko leaves and I painted them so that they looked like butterflies, which they tied to silken threads and ran with, the leaves fluttering like wings. Niuhuru drifted in their wake, carrying her son's many new-found treasures – a golden leaf, a fallen petal, a pebble. These she kept on a tiny altar in her rooms, changing them as he saw fit to gift her with them.

I saw them once when I had visited her to offer up a small sketch of a cricket for Hongli. The boy hopped excitedly about us, before suddenly diving outside, having glimpsed a timid cat peering at the window. Left alone, I moved away from Niuhuru. She had a scent about her, which I had identified as the blossoms of linden trees, a beguiling mix of fresh cut grass and honey. I found it easier to speak to her when I could not smell it.

"Is the Prince well? I have not seen him recently."

She gave a half-shrugged smile. "He is always so busy. Shall we follow the children? I am afraid the poor cat does not much enjoy their company, they frighten it with all their jumping about."

I followed. She never liked to speak of Yong. I remembered the old gossip, that said his short-lived passion for her had been partly his relief in coming back to this world after being so ill, that for once he had forgotten duty and work and obligations and given himself over entirely to love. There was certainly something of the romantic about the Prince: his flowering Garden bore testimony to it but once she had fallen with child he had remembered his duties and thrown himself back into work. His father the Emperor favoured him for it and I could not but reluctantly acknowledge him a brave man in continuing to stand out from his brothers and risking their jealousy, since years had passed and a new Crown Prince had still not been chosen. But his return to duty and his neglect of the romance he had once allowed to flourish must have hurt Niuhuru and now her attention seemed focused only on Hongli, as though she had closed up some part of herself, something I tried and failed to do myself. I had hoped, in giving time and attention to her son, to perhaps have created more of a brotherly kindness towards Niuhuru, but I knew full well that my continuing feelings towards her could not be dismissed as such.

I was not free to spend all my time in the Yuan Ming Yuan, much as it drew me. When Hongli was only five years' old an earthquake had rocked Beijing and while the local wooden buildings had weathered the shaking of the earth, St Joseph's had been irreparably damaged. It had been pulled down and was still being rebuilt, even five years' later. Its outer structure was in the hands of a newly-arrived Brother

Moggi, a Florentine architect of a similar age to myself, a cheerfully enthusiastic man who had begged my time to help create the necessary decorations to the ceiling and walls of the building, now nearing completion.

"I have had flowers carved into the outer walls," he said, showing me round. "But of course it is the interiors for which I will need your help, Giuseppe."

I nodded. "I will do my best to aid you," I said. "Although I have little time these days. The Emperor keeps me busy."

"Whatever time you can spare me I would be grateful for," he replied. "I have in mind that the pillars might be painted to suggest a marble finish. And then there is the ceiling. I have heard you can create painted illusions, would it be possible to paint a false domed roof?"

I looked up the flat ceiling. "A cupola? Yes, it is possible," I said. "And the walls?"

"I leave them to you," he said confidently.

"I am concerned, my son."

I sighed inwardly. This was a topic I was growing tired of and yet I could not fault Father Friedel for raising it again.

"You have been here for many years now and yet you have not yet taken your final vows."

I nodded but did not answer. I applied the paint in tiny brushstrokes, going over the same area again as though there were some fault in it.

"I must remind you that you were chosen not only for your skills, which we acknowledge we are well pleased with – as has His Majesty grown to be – but because you agreed to our requirement: that you must take the vows of the Jesuit priesthood. It would be normal for these to have been taken within two years of you reaching these shores. And yet it is more than ten years that you have been with us now."

I opened my mouth to speak but he held up a hand.

"I know of course that you have told me many times that you have struggled with maintaining pure thoughts, that you have doubts and that you wish to allay such thoughts before you take such serious vows – and they are, of course, very serious. But to be a Jesuit does not mean you have no doubts at all. We all have doubts or we would not be human, vows or no vows. I have heard that you have used hair shirts, even flagellation, in your attempts to be worthy of the priesthood. I believe perhaps you are too harsh on yourself. And so, my son, I urge you now to take this final step. And soon."

I looked at the hand I was even now engaged in painting within the Church of St Joseph while he spoke with me, a rare commission of a Biblical scene which seemed almost strange to me now that I was used only to court commissions. Even this hand was Niuhuru's. I wanted to tell Father Friedel, wanted to turn his face to it and tell him that because I could not paint her face in this scene I painted her hand, because her hands were known to me so intimately that they came first to my mind, because my brush knew how to paint each line of her fingers as though I had held them in my own.

Instead I nodded. "I will pray for guidance, Father," I said.

He nodded. "When we pray for guidance we must also listen for it when it comes from the mouths of those about us," he said and walked away.

Laura was singing, a rare sound, for usually she worked in silence with her eyebrows fiercely drawn together.

"You are happy today," I said.

She looked up from her work. "The Brothers have allowed me to begin work on an altarpiece for the church," she said.

I smiled. An altarpiece was a rare piece of work and given only to those whose skill could withstand the constant scrutiny of the congregation. "Have you chosen your topic?"

"The Madonna and Child," she said.

I nodded. A fitting piece for an altar and also for a woman to paint. "Have you completed the preliminary sketches?"

She hesitated. "Yes."

"May I see them?"

She hesitated again and when she brought me the work I knew already what I would see: Guo's face, lit up with joy, a baby in her arms, the outline of a halo above her head. Laura hovered over me, one hand clenched as though to stop herself from taking back the sketch before I could examine it.

"I am sure it will be important to the congregation to have a local woman depicted as Our Lady," I said.

Laura nodded.

"Has she been delivered of a child?" I asked.

"He is so good-natured," she said. "They have sat for me again and again and he does not cry, not at all."

"Is her husband pleased with the idea of the commission?" I asked.

She took back the sketch. "He does not complain," she said. She returned to her usual, frowning silence and I was sorry to have taken away some of her joy.

"Can I accompany you to Mass on Sunday?" I asked her and she nodded in silence.

When we arrived at the church I watched as Guo arrived with her husband and baby. I saw Laura stand apart as though she could not see them and watched her as she closed her eyes in prayer.

After the service I intercepted Guo and asked to see her child, still tiny, with a growing dark shock of hair above sleepy eyes. I held him awkwardly and thought of Hongli when I had first seen him, the same dark hair but bold eyes, dark and commanding. As Laura passed us, her eyes looking only ahead I caught at her sleeve. "You will have to hold the subject of your painting," I said. "He must grow used to your company for his sittings if your altarpiece is to be a success."

She took him from me and for a moment held him stiffly, her own face held rigidly in a polite smile. But his small hand reached out and touched her face and she could not help herself. A smile spread over her face and she stroked his cheek with her finger, murmuring to him in our own tongue an old lullaby. Guo's husband had wandered away to speak with a friend and for a moment Laura and Guo stood together, their faces lit up with love for the boy until I had to look away as though I had seen something not meant for my eyes.

We walked together through the noisy streets of Beijing, saying nothing until we reached the gates of the Forbidden City.

"Do you regret the life you might have lived?" I asked her, as the guards examined our wooden passes and let us enter.

"What life would that be?" she asked.

"Remaining in your home city. Marriage. Children."

"Do you?" she asked.

I sighed. "Sometimes. I thought my painting would be my life, that I needed nothing else."

"And were you right?"

"Some of the time," I said.

"Do you regret leaving Milan?" she asked.

"No," I said, certain.

"Marriage?"

"I would not have made a good husband, leaving for China," I tried to joke. "And anyway, I was asking you."

"I have found everything I need," she said quietly.

"Everything?"

We paused outside the studios. "It is not how I might wish things to be," she said. "But what I have found here is everything to me."

155

We were silent for a while as we settled to our work, but after a time Laura lifted her head. "And have you found what you need here, Giuseppe?" she asked, and there was something in her tone that told me that she already knew the answer, that where others might have seen only a courtier's care for a young prince over these past years, she had looked beyond Hongli and seen his mother, just as I looked beyond the baby Christ she had painted and saw the face of Guo.

"I could not be elsewhere," I said.

Our eyes met for a moment and she nodded. "I hope that you find happiness," she said. "Even if it is hard, sometimes."

I thought of the moments when I undertook to run races with Hongli and heard Niuhuru's laughter behind us, of her smile each time we met, the scent of her perfume when we passed one another. "I take joy in the small things," I said.

We did not speak often nor directly of such matters, but there was a shared truth between us that no-one else could understand, and it gave me comfort.

The tiny stones I had asked Kun for were hard to work with but when I brushed the dirt off my hands I had to smile. Sheltered close to a rock, by the lakeside there now sat a tiny house, barely a hand's height, something like a fisherman's hut. I waited for Hongli's return from his studies and was rewarded with a beaming smile when he saw what I had made.

"Is this like the houses from your home?" he asked me.

I nodded. "A simple house, not a palace like yours," I told him.

"You could build me a palace from your own country! A big one, that I could live in!"

I let out a laugh. "It would take me years, Hongli. I would need a team of workmen."

"You shall have them," he told me grandly. "When I am a man, I shall give them to you. Then you can build me a palace."

I see him running towards me as a boy, his hands muddied, his eyes bright with the wonders of the Garden that now holds all my memories. By the lake of the Yuan Ming Yuan there runs a child I loved as though he were my own.

Engraved Moon and Unfolding Clouds

THE IMPERIAL HUNT IS THE favourite time of year of the Kangxi Emperor. Yong has never been a great hunting enthusiast, but even he has been unable to resist Hongli's begging to attend. Ever a dutiful father, he has held Hongli to excel at his studies, promising in return that he will be taken to the hunting grounds at Chengde, near my family home, when the Emperor decrees the start of the hunt.

"And I will shoot from horseback, like a real Manchu, while galloping!"

"You will do no such thing," I tell him. "You will stay at the back where it is safe and you will observe the hunt. No more."

"I am very nearly twelve," he tells me, his bottom lip already beginning to pout.

"And I am your mother," I say.

But he must have some freedom. He begins his day before the sun has even risen, he is taught not only Mandarin but Manchu and Mongolian scripts, he must study all aspects of Han culture. He has been studying since he was six, his little head bowed before his stern tutors for most of each day. His afternoons are given over to combat lessons using swords or improving his archery. He runs from his studies each day to target practice, even leaving Giuseppe alone for once. I cannot help but smile when I see his black-robed figure walking along a high ridge, seeking us out, wondering at Hongli's unexpected absence from his side.

"Ah, archery," he says when he sees us. "The hunt, of course, I had forgotten."

"Are you coming?" asks Hongli, eyes fiercely narrowed at his target.

"I go every year," he says.

"To paint the hunt?"

"Yes."

"You could paint me! On horseback! With my bow!"

Giuseppe laughs. "Of course."

"And you can paint me holding a tiger I have killed!"

Giuseppe's eyebrows go up and I see him try to hide a smile. "Of course," he says with great seriousness. "Will there be many tigers?"

"I am sure I will find one," says Hongli and his arrow flies true. "I hit it! I hit it!" he shrieks. Yan blocks her ears at Chu's squeals of excitement.

I exchange a smile with Giuseppe. Sometimes I feel as though he is Hongli's father, for he spends all his time with the boy and it is clear to anyone that he loves him. He paints at his command, he has made all manner of tiny buildings for him, hidden along the rocky edges of the lakeside, his eyes are warm when they rest on him. I remind myself that of course Yong is also proud, that he has chosen great scholars for Hongli's education and that the many hours he holds him to studying are a mark of his esteem. But still, sometimes I wish that Yong would leave behind his endless papers to crouch in the mud by the lake and hold Hongli's hand to steady him while he gathers tadpoles, or run hampered races with him, robes flapping in the wind while my boy easily outstrips him, giggling madly.

Chengde's rooftops seem strange to me now, half-familiar, half-forgotten. I have rarely attended the hunt, for Yong always has some excuse why we should not go, masking his own lack of interest. I think of my mother and father, my brothers. They are so close to me and yet they will not see my son or me. After all these years they seem distant even in my memory. I am almost thirty and I have not seen any of them since I was thirteen.

Our vast procession turns away from the path leading to the city. Instead we take up residence in the forest in a never-ending maze of luxurious tents erected by the thousand servants who have been sent ahead with the baggage carts. The tents are laid out to mimic the Forbidden City, with the various households of princes and other officials enclosing it in an outer ring. My own tent is comfortable enough and Yan is quartered close by.

Hongli is impossible to control. He wants to set off now, at once, at *once,* to catch a tiger or a bear or a deer or even a rabbit – anything to show his prowess with a bow.

"You have to wait," I tell him. "There will be a hunt tomorrow. Tonight your father will want to present you to your Grandfather the Emperor. You must be on your best behaviour."

He succumbs, fretfully, to being dressed in his finest robes and demonstrates, in the privacy of our tent, the correct way to kowtow. He has been well trained in his short life. His manners are flawless when he concentrates, he has a fine bearing and speaks well. I feel a welling-up of pride.

"Are you coming?"

I shake my head.

"Please come," he says, suddenly losing his confidence at the notion of meeting the Emperor alone, with only his quiet father by his side rather than my warm hand in his.

I embrace him. "You will like your grandfather," I say. "He is a great hunter. Talk to him of the hunt. Ask him questions."

Yong nods to me as I push Hongli forwards. "He looks well," he says formally.

I want to tell Yong that Hongli is nervous but I know this would bring a frown to his face, for he believes that his son should have been trained out of such childish thoughts. Instead I smile more broadly than I feel and say loudly that Hongli is very excited to be meeting his Grandfather and looking forward to the hunt.

Hongli is so far ahead of me that at first I can barely see him. He has been given a place of such honour that even Yong's face showed surprise. His still-short legs clasp his horse's sides with such keenness the poor stead is constantly trying to move forwards, mistaking his enthusiasm for a command to gallop. He looks up into his Grandfather's face with eager anticipation. By my side a guard helps me move forwards so that I can see the hunt better from my horse. It is a long time since I rode and I find myself nervous, although the horse has no doubt been chosen for its docility so that a woman may ride it. There are few women on the hunt today, the ladies of the court prefer to remain in the relative comfort of the encampment. I am conscious that just behind me, comfortable on his mount, is Giuseppe. I turn to smile at him.

"He is so excited," I say.

"The Emperor has taken a liking to him," says Giuseppe, smiling back at me.

"Now all he has need of is a tiger," I say and we both laugh. It makes me happy to know what joy this day brings to Hongli and to share that happiness with someone who knows him as well as I do.

Up ahead there are shouts as the beaters and dogs draw closer. The riders tense with anticipation for what will emerge from the dense thicket before us. Deer? Wild boar perhaps? Certainly from the crashing ahead it is a large animal or even several large animals. The men are eager for a first day of good hunting, to put the elderly Emperor in good humour and get the season off to an auspicious start.

It is a bear. Its dark coat pounds through the brush and now arrows fly towards it. The Emperor's bow is at full draw and his own arrows embed themselves in the bear's chest. I see the beast rise onto its legs, standing taller than a man, its great body riddled with sharp arrows, hear it roar in pain. I cannot help but wince. Quickly it is over, for what creature could withstand such an assault? The great body slumps to the ground and a cry of victory goes up. But now Hongli is being called forward by the Emperor, who indicates that he may finish the beast off with his own little bow. Hongli dismounts at speed and steps forwards, his face alight with pride, his arm draws back to let loose the final arrow that will allow him to say he took part in the hunt. I smile a little at his moment of childlike glory, not knowing the creature is already safely dead.

But the bear rears up again, its great claws reaching out to swipe at him, missing by less than a hand's breadth. There are shouts all around me. Men rush forwards while my child stands still, his face a mask of silent terror as a beast plucked from any babe's nightmare roars in his face, before it falls again at his feet and is still.

I open my mouth to call out to him but see my hands go slack on the reins as my body crumples in the saddle. I fall and am caught in a man's arms.

"Hongli," I say, my mouth trembling so that the word comes out badly formed. "Hongli."

"He is safe." Giuseppe's voice is close to my ear, so close his voice is a ragged whisper. "He is safe."

I feel my body go limp again in relief and turn my face towards his chest. My cheek now pressed against his warm body, I become aware that I can hear his heart beating, fast and strong. Unthinking, I put up a hand to press against his cheek before suddenly I recollect myself and struggle in his arms to draw away from him.

"Stay still," he says. "The guards are bringing a palanquin."

Slowly I begin to hear the noise about us, as though my ears had been unable to hear anything but his voice. I see the silk curtains drawn back and the bearers waiting for me. I turn in Giuseppe's arms as he lowers me to the ground and feel for one brief moment his arms grow tight about my waist when he should be releasing me. I look into his face and see all that he has never told me in all the years we have known one another, all he cannot ever tell me. Then his arms are gone and I am inside the darkness of the palanquin. Through the drapes I see the white face of my little son, brought to speak with me. Yong stands by his side, his face an equally pale mask of protocol.

"Hongli – " I say, tears starting in my eyes.

"I am unharmed, Mother," he says, his back too straight, his voice too loud.

I want to clasp him to me but I know he will cry if I do so, know that my embrace will prove his undoing. I look to Yong to help me, but he does not speak and so I look beyond him to Giuseppe.

"How brave you are. A true Manchu!" says Giuseppe loudly.

I smile a great smile, as though he has faced nothing worse than a rabbit. "A true Manchu," I echo, glad to have something I can say that will hold back Hongli's tears.

"He is indeed. I am very proud of him."

The Emperor. All around us, courtiers fall to their faces as he advances. I make to step out of the palanquin but he gestures that I should stay seated.

"Your Majesty," I murmur, bowing my head. He has grown older since the first time I saw him, he is more stooped than the upright old man I remember from the Imperial Daughters' Draft.

"I am impressed with your son, Lady Niuhuru," he says.

"He is honoured by your favour," I say, the meaningless response the only thing I can think to say.

"A brave boy," the Emperor says, patting Hongli's shoulder. He looks at Yong. "This boy is destined to lead a charmed life."

There is a murmur from the courtiers around us. Yong bows without replying.

"We will visit your family," announces the Emperor. "A formal Court visit will be arranged to the Yuan Ming Yuan."

And he is gone in a wave of courtiers and guards. I look out of the palanquin at Yong and he looks back at me.

"What does it mean?" I ask.

Yong shakes his head. "I do not know," he says and now he has finally spoken I hear his voice shake and know that despite his controlled formal manner he felt my own terror when he saw the bear rear up. "Hongli will return to the encampment with you," he orders.

I hold out my hand to Yong. "Return with us," I say. I cannot say more, cannot say that I am afraid of all the emotions I am feeling – the fear from Hongli's encounter with the bear still cold in my belly along with my heart which is beating too fast for a man I should not even think of. I want Yong to take his place by my side, to comfort Hongli, to erase the feelings I should not be feeling.

But he shakes his head. "I must attend my father," he says before walking stiffly away.

I offer my outstretched hand to Hongli and he climbs in beside me. Giuseppe steps forwards and closes the drapes about me and for a brief moment our eyes meet. Within the darkness of the palanquin, hidden from public view, my shaken son lies his head on my lap and sobs as he has not done since he was small. From outside, a hand reaches in and strokes Hongli's head. The bearers lift us but before the hand can be withdrawn I clasp it in my own.

The palanquin sways through the rustling woods while outside Giuseppe keeps pace with us. Exhausted, Hongli falls asleep while I stare down at our entwined hands and wonder how I will ever let go.

"Keep still," snaps Yan, exasperated with her task.

I twist under her hands, fretful. "They will be here soon. I must be there to welcome them."

"Not with your hair unfinished," says Yan.

More than one jade pin falls to the ground and Chu, standing by to help Yan, collects them and returns them to her mother, her little face serious at the gravity of the event.

The now-flourishing Peony Terrace is the location for the Emperor's visit. Set on a small island close to Yong's own palace, over ninety kinds of peonies are in flower, each bloom wider than the span of my hands. There will be seating so that we can admire the flowers, a throne for the Emperor. The peonies Yan has chosen for my hair are a deep pink, with contrasting petals of pure white at their centre. No fewer than six are pinned into my hair, now so full of flowers, tinkling golden strands and white jade pins that I can barely hold my head up. My robes are a delicate green embroidered with grasses and butterflies. I must look like a walking garden. I try to hurry along the path but my shoes are higher than I usually wear and I am forced to take smaller steps. I reach the pavilion on the Peony Terrace just in time to see the imperial party arriving. Beside me, Lady Qi glows with satisfaction.

"A formal visit from His Majesty can only mean favour for the Prince," she says quietly.

I nod, distracted by the sight of Hongli who is so excited he can barely keep still.

"Perhaps he has realised that it is time to choose a new heir at last," Lady Qi continues. "We must do all we can to ensure the Prince is seen to be worthy." She glances towards her eldest son, Hongshi, already an elegant young man. She indicates to him that he should stand further forward, where his grandfather will see him.

"Ladyship," says Hongshi, bowing his head politely to me.

I nod back to him, still half-distracted by Hongli. I am not overly fond of Hongshi, he has a touch of arrogance to him which makes me think of the demoted Crown Prince, an expectation that the world will shape itself to his desires. I am well aware that Lady Qi has high hopes for Hongshi. This meeting is crucial for her and Hongshi. If the Emperor takes to her son it may well move her one step closer to her ultimate goal.

The Emperor is surrounded by courtiers as well as his own ladies and it takes a while for everyone to find their correct positions around his throne. Hongshi, at a nod from his mother, steps forward and makes an elegant obeisance to his grandfather, who nods. I wait for Yong's glance towards me and then make a small gesture to Hongli, so that he may do the same. Hongli rushes forwards but entirely omits to kowtow, instead he perches on the arm of the Emperor's throne and thrusts a scroll into his hands. I see Yong's eyes widen in horror. Lady Qi's mouth twists in amusement.

"I wrote it myself!" Hongli declares. "A poem about the hunting grounds for you, Grandfather!"

"Wonderful," chuckles the Emperor, apparently delighted by my son's breach of protocol. "Read it to me."

Beside me I feel Lady Qi stiffen. Hongshi has lost his elegant composure. He shifts uneasily from one foot to the other, unsure of what to do, his face bewildered as his younger half-brother is embraced by the Emperor as he finishes reading his composition.

"A poet as well as a hunter, eh? The boy is a marvel! Now where is your mother, boy? We will not frighten her with bears this time, I think – peonies are safer!" He gives a hearty laugh and the courtiers hurry to join in.

Hongli looks about him and indicates me. I step forward, kneel and begin my kowtow.

"Enough of that," says the Emperor cheerfully. "Rise, rise."

I rise and stand before him.

"I believe your son will bring you great honour one day, Lady Niuhuru," he says, his tone more serious. He looks at Hongli and then at Yong, then nods, as though making a decision. "You are a lucky woman."

I hear the muted gasp from the crowd around us and see Lady Qi's face freeze over as she takes in the implication of his words.

The moon rises. Lanterns begin to glow throughout the Garden and we make our way to where a banquet has been laid out. Hongli is led to a position of honour at the Emperor's side, with Yong close by. I sit among the ladies and feel all their eyes on me but do not dare to meet their gaze. I cannot bear it if all of them are filled with the same sudden hatred as Qi's. I eat slowly, tasting nothing. I think back to the Imperial Daughters' Draft, the day I was chosen as a minor concubine to an unknown prince. Now the Emperor has implied before half the court that my husband will be made his heir with my own son to follow. There are whispers that he would have liked to skip Yong altogether and give the throne directly to Hongli, but that would not be the proper way of things. But everyone is certain that Yong has been preferred largely because of my own son to come after him. How has this happened?

"I never asked for this," I tell Yan, tugging at the peonies in my hair. They fall to the floor, crushed by my shaking fingers. "I never asked for this. I am happy here, in the Garden. I don't want to live in the Forbidden City, to have the other women hate me because my son is to be Emperor one day. I don't want to have scheming and whispers all around me. I don't want to be stuck inside those red walls and never be able to go out. I want my son safe by my side, I don't want his brothers trying to poison him like the Sorcerer Prince did to Yong. I don't want – "

"Stop pulling!" exclaims Yan. "Half your hair will come out with the flowers if you keep yanking at it like that."

I try to sit still while she dismantles my hair, my eyes brimming up with unshed tears.

"You should rest," she says, when she is done. My hair hangs loose and my high shoes are off. My green robe is still on but I wave her away.

"I will undress myself," I tell her.

"Rest," Yan repeats. "Tomorrow you can think about what the Emperor said. For now, be grateful your husband and son are shown such favour, instead of worrying about the other women. They would not be worrying about you, if they were in your position."

I sit alone for a few moments. I try to think of something else – the peonies, perhaps, the lanterns and how well they looked in the moonlight, but all I can think of is Qi's eyes locked onto mine as I stood with my son in front of the throne while she and her son went unnoticed on the sidelines.

At last I stand up. I cannot sleep like this. Instead I walk out of my room and stand in the entrance of my palace, the door wide open to the cool night air. Down by the lakeside I can see the outline of a man, standing motionless in the soft glow of the fading lanterns. My bare feet hurt as I walk down the rough path but I do not stop until I am standing in front of him, not quite touching and yet close enough to feel the heat of his body.

"I can't," I say and I am not sure what I am talking about. That I cannot bear the future that has suddenly opened up ahead of me or that I cannot reach out and touch him?

"No," he agrees.

We stand in silence and all I can hear is my own breathing and his.

"Why are you here?" I ask.

"Because I saw your face," he says and again I do not know if he means when we first set eyes on one another years ago or if he means the moment this evening when the Emperor spoke and I heard the muted gasp from those around me that meant I had interpreted his meaning correctly.

One of my feet hurts, it is resting on a too-sharp pebble. I shift. The tiny motion allows my robe to touch Giuseppe's and suddenly his lips are on mine, his arms wrapped so tightly about me that I can scarcely breathe. I return his embrace with such desperation that he draws back for a second to look at my face. It takes only that second for me to turn and run.

The summer heat rises and then falls. The months pass and for the first time in all the years I have lived in the Garden I do not venture outside the walls of my own palace during daylight hours. Instead I endure the stifling heat indoors, my fan in constant movement. Yan asks if I am well, frowns at me, even brings me disgusting concoctions from Yong's physician, which I leave untouched to grow cold. She tries to entice me out, makes Kun bring fresh flowers and water reeds to show me, talks of dragonflies and boating trips across the waterways of the Garden. I turn my face away and eventually she grows silent, hurt by my withdrawal from our friendship. I cannot find a way to tell her why I do not trust myself to walk in the Garden and not run to find Giuseppe.

Late each night I walk to the top of the path that leads to the lakeside and look into the shadows, where I can see him standing under the willow tree. Each night I see his outline turn towards me and each night I drop my head and return to my palace and my sleepless bed. The leaves fall from the willow and still his shadow waits for me among the bare branches while the wind turns cold and winter comes upon us.

The snow lies thick across the Garden, so bright it hurts my eyes, icicles sparkling from every rooftop. While my eyes are dazzled, my ears are left abandoned, the whiteness muffling any sound. My days are empty. As the leaves turned red, the high walls of the Forbidden City claimed my son. The Emperor decreed that Hongli's tutors were no longer good enough for such a talented child, that he must continue his schooling within the imperial city, alongside the Emperor's own youngest sons. I have been given an even more generous allowance along with my own eunuchs and additional maids, but my palace is quiet. Hongli is gone from me, Yan maintains her silence and I do not allow myself to speak with Giuseppe, for fear of what either of us may say.

It is the deepest day of winter and the sky is a darkening grey when my ears are assaulted with an unexpected sound of clattering armour and horses' hooves. From the window I see a senior eunuch surrounded by more than thirty imperial guards ride past, their sweating horses headed for Yong's palace. I have little time to wonder at their presence here when they pass my palace again, this time surrounding a mounted figure wrapped in thick furs. Yong.

The winter air almost makes me gasp, I have been indoors so long. I walk through the snow in high boots, a silk wrap clutched about me. I quickly wish I had chosen furs. When I hear footsteps behind me I turn to see Yan following me. I offer her a small smile and she nods at me without smiling, as though reserving judgement.

The eunuch who opens Qi's door regards me without speaking. He does not invite me in and I imagine he has been given orders to that effect. Instead he disappears and after a cold silence Qi herself appears. She looks at me with her eyebrows raised, ignoring any niceties due to a fellow concubine.

"Where is the Prince going?" I ask.

"*You* don't know?" she asks, mocking.

I shake my head.

"The Kangxi Emperor is dying," she says.

I gape at her. "Dying?"

"He has summoned seven of his sons to his bedside. What else do you think he is doing?" she asks me.

I swallow. "Who is the heir?" I ask.

"Yong," she says.

"You can't be sure of that," I say.

She looks at me as though I am an idiot.

"You should be pleased, then," I say, forcing a smile.

"Why would I be pleased?"

"You wanted Yong to be made heir."

"I wanted my son to be Emperor," she corrects me.

I don't want to ill-wish my own son but I do not want this future for him or for myself. "He still might," I say, but my voice trails away.

Qi half-snorts. "Yong has only been chosen for heir because of your son Hongli," she says bluntly. "He is too boring in his own right. Dutiful, yes. Filial, of course. A hard worker. No doubt capable of good things. But no spark of glory. Not a warrior. Not a poet. A conscientious official, a right-hand man, not an emperor."

I look down at the cold snow between us. "My son is very young," I say.

"The Emperor took the throne at eight years old," says Qi. "Your son is already twelve years old with a young enough father to go before him and pave his way."

I raise my eyes to her face. "I do not want this future," I tell her.

"You do not wish to be a consort to an Emperor? A mother to an Emperor? You do not wish to be the Empress Dowager, the greatest woman at court, one day?"

I shake my head.

"Then you're a fool," she says.

"I saw Yong poisoned," I tell her. "By his own brother. For the chance to take the throne. I do not want a life of ritual and grandeur. I want to live here, in the Garden and be happy with my son by my side, a princeling and nothing more."

"Too late for that," she says.

We stand in silence for a long time before I speak again. "I never wished you ill," I say to her. "You or your son."

"Too late for that," she repeats and steps backwards into the doorway, a eunuch appearing by her side to close the door in my face.

I turn and look at Yan.

"She'll still be consort to an emperor," says Yan, without much pity.

"That's not what she wanted," I say.

Yan shrugs.

"Is this what I will have to live with?" I ask her. "Hatred and fear? All the other women looking at me with loathing, hoping that Hongli will die so that a child of theirs can supersede him? The constant fear that Yong will be poisoned again?"

Yan sees my eyes fill up and steps forwards, slipping her small hard hand into mine, the way she used to when we were barely more than children. "One day at a time," she says. "Do not think of everything all at once."

Our hands still clasped, we trudge back through the snow together. I keep my eyes on the ground, for the path is slippery.

"The Jesuit is here," says Yan.

I look up quickly. Giuseppe is standing in his usual space, as the dusk grows around us. I hesitate, then let go of Yan's hand and walk over to him, her presence a safeguard.

"I saw the Prince leaving," he says. "Is it true?"

I nod. The wind is stronger now. I shiver and pull my too-thin wrap about me.

"Take mine," says Giuseppe.

I step backwards.

He holds his heavy outer coat out at arm's length. I take it, careful not to touch him, and drape it around me. The warmth is immediate. Without thinking I nuzzle into the heavily furred collar and at once the scent of him overwhelms me. With a jerk I let the coat fall to the ground and run back towards my palace. Behind me I hear Yan panting to keep up with me. I look back. Beyond her stands Giuseppe, the dark furs of his coat still lying in the white snow at his feet, mingled with the silken folds of my wrap.

I wait till Yan has crossed the threshold before pushing the door shut so hard it shakes in its frame. Two eunuchs and a maid come running to see what the matter is.

I turn to look at Yan. Her eyes are serious.

"You should have told me," she says.

Invitation to Reclusion

LAURA FOUND ME WITH AN old sketchbook in my hands, one finger tracing the lines of the greyhound I once drew for the Kangxi Emperor.

"He was a kindly man," I said. "Gruff. An old warrior, not a polished courtier. He loved a good feast, the hunting grounds, his ladies, all the pleasures of this world."

"Yong may be different," she said. "In all the years we have been here the Pope has never relented regarding the ancestral worship."

I nodded, still tracing the lines with my fingertip. Prince Yong was a man of duty, a hard worker, a man committed to equality and erasing corruption. I was not sure how much artistic pleasures would soften him towards Christianity now that he was about to be crowned Emperor, although I knew there was a part of him that responded to the beauty of nature.

"He may be more stern," she said. "Less lenient towards the Order."

I looked up at her.

"Time to choose, Giuseppe," she said. "Your vows or home."

I looked back down. "That is not the choice."

"There is no other choice," she said gently and for a moment her small hand covered mine, her touch at once comforting and a burden to me.

"I cannot leave you here alone," I said.

"I have already chosen my path," she said. "My vows are made. As should yours be after fifteen years here."

I looked up at her. "To whom did you make your vows?"

She looked away for a moment, her eyes on the half-finished Madonna and Child altarpiece, Guo's face now surmounted by a golden halo. "The Brotherhood, of course," she said very quietly. "Who else?"

I found myself walking the streets each night after my work was done. Beijing was familiar to me by now, its endless busyness always a strange contrast to the tranquillity of the Yuan Ming Yuan. Street vendors called out their wares as palanquins hurried past, their fortunate occupants hidden from view, while their bearers sweated, cursing at anything in their way. When I had first come here there were so many sights that were new to me that I would sometimes stop in the middle of a street and find a little place where I might crouch down and sketch something: a face, the blurred outline of motion, an attempt to capture the lives swirling around me. But I had whole sheaves of such sketches now and my surroundings were familiar to me. So I did not pause, only walked and walked until I was tired enough to sleep without thinking.

Perhaps Yong would have been content to leave matters as they were, the Brothers permitted to serve at court but not preach their gospel further abroad. But as the Kangxi Emperor lay dying a final rivalry broke out among the imperial sons. Even though Yong had clearly been indicated as the heir, an imperial cousin, Sunu, tried instead to have the eighth prince Yunsi crowned.

"This can only mean trouble for us," Father Friedel warned the Brothers when we were gathered together. "Sunu and his family are converts to our religion. It may go hard with us if Yong sees Christianity as the source of such disloyalty."

We awaited news and sure enough the Sunu family were exiled for their disloyalty to Yong. When members of the family were found to be preaching the Gospel in their place of exile Yong acted promptly. An edict was issued placing all members of the Order under house arrest. Our work for the Imperial Family was to cease at once. We were obliged to stay within the precinct of St Joseph's. My first thought was of Niuhuru, of being unable to see her. I found myself pacing in the tiny garden, thinking only of that other Garden, which Niuhuru would shortly leave as she entered the Forbidden City as a concubine to the new Emperor. Father Friedel counselled us all to have patience and to offer up our prayers, but the turn of events led to turmoil within the Order. There was nervous whispering everywhere, even during mass and the spacious refectory felt claustrophobic now that we knew there were few other places we could go except back to our own small and plainly furbished cells to sleep or pray. One of the astronomers who had served the Jesuits for some years now chose to return home rather than take his vows and be obliged to stay in a country he increasingly considered dangerous. Meanwhile the copper-engraver Brother Matteo Ripa had determined to leave also, although in his case he intended to take with him four young Chinese Christians, converts he was proud of. Removing them from the country would require some careful subterfuge in the current climate. Ripa had in mind to return to Naples where he would train the young men as priests and then send them back to China as missionaries.

Father Friedel, convinced of the necessity of patience and the belief that we might yet soften Yong's attitude through excellence of service, determined that the time was right to send Brother Arailza home.

"He has never really enjoyed his work here," he told me. "And has never yet won imperial preference. In all honesty, Giuseppe, Arailza's skill as a painter is not as great as yours and I believe that you have had some signs of imperial favour shown to you, which may yet stand us in good stead. You intend to stay, I hope?"

I watched the preparations for departure and saw the travellers' excitement grow, wondered what it would be like to travel to the South and back to Macau, to see a ship rocking on the waves and know that, God willing, I would see my home city and family again in a year's time. Even Brother Arailza seemed to brighten at the thought of returning home, even though my preferment over him must have hurt his professional pride. For some days I thought of my journey here and even found old sketches I had done on board the ship: the sailors at work, Laura half-dozing on deck, the far-off shore. And yet I knew that each step of the journey would take me further away from Niuhuru. If I stayed here there was some chance that Yong would eventually relent, that I would see her again.

"I cannot leave without bidding farewell to… to those I have known and cared for here," I said to Laura.

"And if we are never released from house arrest?" she asked softly.

"At least I will not be far away," I said, although my heart was heavy at the idea of spending the rest of my life within these narrow precincts.

It was Laura who took it upon herself to read me the two letters I received from my brother telling me of the death of my parents. They had been sent almost a year apart but had somehow arrived together and when I opened the first I found myself unable to read it. Laura's voice trembled when she read each one and I submitted to her embraces, her looks of concern, her reminders that I must care for myself. She did not allow me to forget to eat or drink in my sorrow. I nodded and thanked her and assured her that I was well enough. Strangely I did not think so much of the moment of our parting, instead small memories of my childhood would come to me at odd moments while I was working. The size of my father's hand wrapped around my own and his rough brown beard, which I would pull when sat upon his knee. My mother's scoldings, usually followed by some small sweetmeat, her tugging at my clothes to try and make me more presentable when visiting elderly relatives. Even while momentous events occur all around us, our lives are made up of such small details. When Matteo and his converts as well as Brother Arailza and the astronomer left us I bid them all farewell and put away my sketches of the sea.

That night I left my scholar's black clothing in my little room and instead donned the brighter robes of a well-to-do Manchu man, a man free of the burdens and expectations of the Brotherhood. I slipped out of the gates unseen, flouting the rules of our house arrest.

The streets of Beijing flickered with lanterns and the little fires of stallholders. I walked among the busy crowds and passed over a few coins for bread and meat, for a long stick of candied crab-apples, tart and sweet all at once. I walked first one way and then another, not aiming for any destination.

"A man should have company, so late at night."

I looked down at the hand on my arm and the set smile of the girl to whom it belonged. She watched me hesitate and her fixed smile grew a little broader.

"Come," she said and I followed.

Perhaps I thought that if I only saw her in the dim light of a lantern, her long black hair might convince me that I held Niuhuru in my arms and that I would be sated of this impossible desire. Perhaps I knew already that I would never leave this place and that therefore I must take the vows I had avoided for so long. Perhaps I thought I should be reminded of what I was giving up.

It no longer matters which of those is true. I returned to my room and when I awoke the next morning I wore my scholar's black and told the Brothers that I would take my vows whenever they so wished.

I knelt and heard my voice speak the words of the vows and yet they did not seem to come from my mouth.

Almighty and eternal God, I understand how unworthy I am in your divine sight. Yet I am strengthened by your infinite compassion and mercy, and I am moved by the desire to serve you.

I had knelt like this only a few days before, my forehead touching the ground as I heard Prince Yong proclaimed the Yongzheng Emperor, his former name now taboo even to those who had known him well. Now I knelt to repeat the words I had so long evaded, with Laura's serious eyes on me.

I vow to your divine majesty, before the most holy Virgin Mary and the entire court of heaven, perpetual chastity, poverty, and obedience in the Society of Jesus.

As I raised my eyes I saw the painting I myself had undertaken on the chapel wall, saw Niuhuru's hand. I thought of her standing on the bamboo path the first time I saw her, felt the weight of her body in my arms as she fell from her horse at the hunt, recalled the touch of her lips on mine under the willow tree. Last of all I thought of her standing with the other concubines by Yongzheng's golden throne as I raised my eyes from the ground and saw my foolish dreams turn to dirt.

I promise that I will enter the same Society to spend my life in it forever.

As the robes of imperial yellow were placed about Yongzheng's body, so the high vermillion walls of the Forbidden City claimed Niuhuru and immured her within its endless corridors.

I understand all these things according to the Constitutions of the Society of Jesus.

I did not need to hear the murmurings of the congregation behind me as the words came to an end, barely even saw their lips moving with good wishes or the beaming face of Father Friedel as I left the church.

Therefore, by your boundless goodness and mercy and through the blood of Jesus Christ, I humbly ask that you judge this total commitment of myself acceptable; and as you have freely given me the desire to make this offering, so also may you give me the abundant grace to fulfil it.

With the edict of house arrest still upon us I could only work on the chapel. I created the illusion of a cupola on the flat ceiling as Brother Moggi had asked, completed the pillars with the semblance of a marbled finish, then continued the work on the walls. One panel contained a *trompe l'oeil* showing a doorway leading to a room filled with beautiful objects, from scrolls and fine books to a cabinet of curios and a vase filled with peacock feathers on which a ray of sunshine shone. Brother Moggi invited a local scholar, Yao Yuanzhi, to view it. The scholar reached out a hand, as though he might enter the room portrayed, then started back when he perceived that there was no doorway, only a wall, cold to the touch.

"It is like a fairytale," he exclaimed, much to Moggi's amusement and delight. I smiled at his pleasure, although I could not help feeling my spirit sink at the idea of henceforth painting only to amuse locals with pretty illusions or for the contemplation of the Brothers, my days spent more and more in prayer to be released from this prison-like existence.

"I have brought you a little gift," added Yuanzhi. He held out a little polished stone, a reddish colour with many stripes to it. "I gather you have a collection," he added approvingly. Collecting such stones to appreciate their natural beauty was a pastime amongst the literati here, I knew.

"Thank you," I said. "You are too kind." In truth, what he had taken for a scholarly pastime was only a further sign of my struggles here. My collection of little pebbles did not come from across the empire and beyond, rather each was a reminder of the Garden. It had become a habit with me to collect a little stone from there each time I saw Niuhuru, a concrete reminder of an illusory desire.

Among the silken-soft petals in the Garden of my memories there is one flower made of cold stone, a flower taken from the wall panels of St Joseph's. Where the other flowers are warmed by the sun, even now beneath my hand I feel as I did then the unforgiving chill of marble petals.

May God have mercy on my wretched soul.

The Endless Palace

PEERING OUT OF THE SWAYING palanquin I am reminded that most of Beijing appears grey from a distance, for the roof tiles give the mostly single-storey buildings a uniform appearance. But our destination shines at the centre of this grey city, its red walls and swooping golden tiles reminding all who see them that this is the residence of the Son of Heaven, the Forbidden City, which houses thousands of eunuchs and thousands more maids and other servants, hundreds of craftsmen and courtiers, hundreds of women and yet only one man. When night-time comes a call goes out across the palaces, a warning that all those who do not reside here must leave at once. At night only two men are allowed to be here: the on-duty court physician and the Emperor. Any other man found here at night will be executed.

The blood-red outer walls tower so high above us that I cannot see their tops without being blinded by the sun. Dazzled, I lower my gaze. The great red and gold gates swing open and our many palanquins and cartloads of goods pass through. We travel through endless vast courtyards until we reach the Inner Court, our new home. The palanquins separate, clatter away down one tiny pathway or another, delivering each of us to our new palaces. Here we ladies will be separated by hard stone and high red walls, not water and pebbled lakeside paths.

The sounds of imperial life are sharpened here, each footstep, voice and movement accentuated by the hardness of the materials around us. The golden roof tiles stamped with roaring dragons, the marble-carved clouds entwined about pillars, doors opening onto doors onto doors. The endless, endless hard cobbles where once there was soft grass beneath my feet. High walls are everywhere. When I touch them my fingertips come away stained red from the powdery pigment used to paint them.

"Your garden, my lady," announces the eunuch who first shows me my new home.

I look about me in silence. A courtyard. A solitary sombre pine. Pots of flowers, falsely bright against the hard stone. Dark pitted rocks, twisted as though by some giant malevolent hand.

"All the way from the south of the empire," the eunuch assures me, awaiting my praise, my pleasure.

I turn back into my rooms of my palace. No expense has been spared, every comfort has been arranged for me. I wonder briefly which still-living concubine of the Kangxi Emperor once called this palace home before being swiftly relegated to some distant part of the Forbidden City as his last breath left her unwanted and invisible for the rest of her life.

What freedom I had is gone. If I stand, squatting servants rise from their corners, ready for my command. If I sit, they crouch back down, waiting to be summoned.

Lady Nara, since she was already Yong's Primary Consort, is now made Empress Xiaojingxian. My own name and rank is changed to Consort Xi, a new name for each woman, our previous identities left behind as we take up our new positions. Lady Qi is also made a Consort. I wonder how often she counts the steps between Consort and Empress, how she intends to become a Noble Consort and then an Imperial Noble Consort.

It takes Yongzheng a while to soften his edict regarding the house arrest of the Jesuits. Only once members of Sunu's family have been executed does he relent and allow them to serve at court again. I ask to see the coronation portrait, believing Giuseppe may be tasked with showing it to me but he is not there. I stand before the portrait of my husband, the Son of Heaven on the imperial throne, his yellow robes of state draped in silken folds about him. I reach out a hand and touch the silk canvas, knowing that Giuseppe must have touched this very point, that it was his hand that held the brush to make this stroke, and this one and this one.

"Come away," says Yan softly. I follow her back to the walls within walls within walls that now make up my home. There is nowhere else for me to go.

I stand with Kun in the courtyard of my palace and spread my hands. "Whatever you can do, Kun," I say.

He turns on himself, looking around the space. When he meets my gaze I know that my sadness and sense of loss is reflected in his eyes. We have left something beautiful behind and this place, awe-inspiring as it is, is no substitute for the tranquillity and delicacy of the Garden.

I see Kun outside every day afterwards, as he tries to bring a softer touch to the space, filling it with multiple pots of flowers, adding ornamental grasses to the base of the pine. He brings a metal sculpture of a heron and adds a wide brass basin, which he fills with water and tiny water lilies. He makes as much of a garden as is possible in this hard space.

I eat and am watched. I sleep and am watched. Where Yan would turn her eyes away discreetly when I sat to empty my bowels, here there are many more servants and they watch me closely, the better, they think, to serve me. I try to dismiss them when I wish to be alone and a few, so few, will leave my presence and the rest will simply crouch in corners, waiting for my next command, ignoring my desperate need for solitude.

When I find that solitude is impossible, I try to lighten my days with familiar faces. I invite the other concubines to sit with me. They come, but something has changed. We were friendly nobodies, once, concubines to a distant prince, kept in a soft world of flowers and water. There was no need for jealousy or suspicion. Now we are concubines to an Emperor, in a hard world of imperial glory and opportunity. Daughters who were once indulged are now dismissed as useless, for what is needed is sons, many sons. And it is my son who has been shown favour. The gossips do not even bother to lower their voices when they say that Kangxi gave the throne to Yong so that Hongli might become Emperor one day, it is considered common knowledge. Where there was once sibling rivalry between the many brothers of Yongzheng, any courtier worth the name would now swear that the name concealed within a golden box and placed behind the throne is my son's. And so the women I invite, who once treated me as a pet, perhaps even daughter-like, certainly no threat, now look at me warily. How has this woman, considerably their junior, leap-frogged them to a path destined for imperial power? The conversation is stilted and they refuse my offers to play mah-jong, even though I know they still play amongst themselves. My own son, filial and good-natured though he is, visits me, bows, brings me gifts and is gone again, a young man eager to assist his father, to explore the empire that will one day almost certainly be his.

My son reaches manhood. I am promoted again, given the title of Noble Consort. With each change of rank my robes reflect my status, each rank a brighter shade of yellow, headed inexorably for the imperial yellow that is my destiny because it is my son's. And time passes, even within these unending walls.

The Empress, Lady Nara, dies. A dutiful woman, a kindly woman.

I wear white. I set aside jewels and I join with the visits to temples to honour her name as she is interred with all due ceremony in the Western Qing Tombs.

"Are you ready?"

I look to my left, where Lady Qi stands beside me, her long hair loose, her face set in a mask. "For what?"

"To be made Empress, of course."

I don't answer.

"Who else should he choose?" asks Qi. "You are already a Noble Consort. You are the mother of his favoured son."

I swallow at the bitterness in her voice. This is what I dreaded, what I wished to avoid. Women who have become awkward around me or worse, those who now actively hate me for straying into their path to greatness. "I have no wish to be Empress," I say.

"You will forgive me if I do not believe you," she says. "You say one thing but events prove you wrong, again and again."

I am summoned by Yongzheng and kneel before him.

"You are to be made Empress," he tells me. "I will have it announced." He waits for my smile, for my kowtow. Perhaps he hopes for some closeness to emerge between us again, as it once did so long ago in a different place to this.

I stay kneeling but I do not kowtow. I do not smile. "I do not wish to be made Empress," I tell him.

His smile fades. "Why not?"

I shake my head. "I do not wish for such an exalted position," I tell him. "I beg you to choose someone else. You could choose Lady Qi," I add, thinking that the honour might appease her.

Yongzheng frowns. "Nonsense," he says. "Why would I choose her?"

I don't reply. Does he know nothing of Lady Qi's desire for power? I can see that he is displeased with my stubborn silence.

"Very well," he says at last. "You will not be made Empress."

I feel my shoulders sag with relief and hurry to perform a kowtow. "Thank you," I murmur.

But he has not finished with me. "You will, however, be known as my Primary Consort," he rules. "You will oversee the conduct of the other ladies of my court and you will carry out such duties as must be undertaken in the temples and during festivities."

I sit back on my heels, aghast, as he stands and leaves the room. He has made me Empress in all but name. When the announcement is made I see Qi's eyes slide towards me. I know without her saying so that she thinks me a liar, a backstabbing liar who claims not to wish for power and yet inexorably rises towards the ultimate position of power.

Embarrassed at my superior role over women older than myself, instead I try to befriend the new concubines, who are now in my care. Fresh-faced, glowing at being chosen to wed a still-young emperor, I find quickly enough that they regard me with fear mixed with resentment. Having passed my thirtieth year, I am already old to girls more than ten years my junior. They fear me because I am highly ranked but they also dislike me for having already produced a son who is all but certain to reach both the throne and the imperial yellow which everyone here craves for themselves or their offspring. Where is the room for them, where is the space that they must claim if they wish to reach higher levels of glory? They are angry, too, that there is no way to become Empress because I have refused the position and so, without even taking the role, have blocked the path to it for those younger and

187

more beautiful, more fertile, more ambitious, than I. They squirm in resentful silence in my presence and I do not know what to say to break the invisible barriers between us. Instead I let them go and do not invite them again, no doubt to their relief as much as mine.

I sit alone, watched in silence, until I begin to think I will go mad.

I take my place on a carved throne and watch as hundreds of girls kneel before me in a courtyard much like the one I knelt in many years ago. This time I am the one to choose, for it is time my son was married. He has been named Prince Bao of the First Rank. I tremble at the thought of choosing these girls' destinies but my face must stay still and calm, my choices must be firm.

I glance down at the paperwork containing their names while the Chief Eunuch, vastly more experienced in this task than I, whispers delicately in my ear.

"Lady Fuca. An excellent family. Well bred. Gracious in her manner, no sign of arrogance, a dutiful demeanour to her superiors and elders. Well versed in etiquette. Filial. An appropriate choice for the Prince's Primary Consort."

I look the girl over. I am choosing a future Empress, a woman who must carry a heavy weight and carry it without seeming burdened. Who will feel destiny creeping closer every day and who cannot hope to escape it. I am choosing my son's future happiness. I swallow and incline my head a fraction.

The Chief Eunuch's loud voice echoes around the courtyard. "Lady Fuca! Chosen as Prince Bao's Primary Consort!"

The girl sinks to her knees and performs a formal kowtow to me and when she rises I see her face is a little flushed, but she seems content. This is a girl whose family fully expected such an honour, who have moulded her for this life. I whisper a prayer that she may be happy, that I have chosen well, as she is led away to her new home within these walls.

Other girls are chosen. Few stand out for me. Lady Gao. Lady Zhemin, a relative of Lady Fuca. Lady Su, a girl from a lesser background like my own, looks startled to be chosen. A frightened slip of a girl I hesitate from choosing, but when her name is called out, Lady Wan's face lights up in a radiant smile and I can only surmise that she has romantic notions of marrying a prince. I hope she will not be disappointed.

I pause. My son is young. He has many years ahead of him to add to his ladies. There is no need to choose any more. I shake my head slightly but the Chief Eunuch bites his lip, considering.

"Perhaps one more?" he murmurs discreetly. "For an auspicious number?"

I sigh. The eunuchs are obsessed with everything being auspicious. Numbers, animals, flowers, days… the list is endless. I nod wearily and look about the courtyard. The girls stand motionless in their expectant ranks. One girl catches my eye. She is beautiful, as they all are of course but right now, among a sea of anxious faces, hers stands out. She has a dreamy expression, her eyes are lit up with some interior happiness. I think yes, here is a girl who can find the good in life and who may be content in this strange place. I indicate her with a golden nail and the Chief Eunuch nods, agreeable. She is a Manchu and from a good family.

"Lady Ula Nara! Chosen as Secondary Consort for the Prince!"

The girl's face drains white and her eyes meet mine in shock. Any happiness she had a moment ago is entirely gone. She drops to her knees but does not complete the elegant kowtow to me, her future mother-in-law, that she should. Instead she crawls forward a little and addresses me directly, breaching all protocol. Her voice shakes so badly I can barely make out what she is saying.

"I do not wish to marry the Prince, my Lady. I beg you to let me return to my – to my family."

There are gasps among the girls. Heads turn.

I feel my stomach turn over. I have never heard of such a reaction to being chosen. I don't know what to do. I glance for help towards the Chief Eunuch, who is both appalled and furious.

"How dare you question the Emperor's Primary Consort?" he screams at her, his face red. "How dare you refuse the honour that has been bestowed upon you? You have been chosen and you will take your place among the Prince's ladies!"

He makes a tiny gesture to me and I rise, causing all the girls to drop to their knees. I begin to leave the courtyard but cannot help looking over my shoulder to where the girl Ula Nara kneels on all fours on the cold cobbles, her head down and her body shaking with sobs. The other girls stare in helpless fascination.

"Ignore her, my lady," advises the Chief Eunuch. "Some of the girls behave very oddly when they are chosen. It is only nerves."

"But what if she was promised elsewhere?" I ask, the thought only now coming to me. The moment when she paused before saying she wanted to return to 'my family', as though she meant to say a name?

He is remorseless. "What marriage could possibly be as advantageous to her as one to your son, the Prince?" he asks.

If she was in love with someone, I think, but do not say it. *If there was someone whose name she barely dared whisper, whose scent overwhelmed her, whose touch she longed for.* But I know better than anyone that such a thought is irrelevant here, where a connection to the Imperial Family is all anyone could ever wish for.

I am called to Yongzheng from time to time but whatever connection we once had has long gone. He has become 'the Emperor,' his brow ever more furrowed with his workload and his concerns. He wishes the empire to be well-run and all he can talk about is how it might be managed better, how corruption must be driven out and more stringent laws and taxes passed to ensure good governance. I admire him for his dedication but I do not understand all of what he talks about, nor do I find intimacy in it. So I lie quietly in his arms and when I am dismissed I call for Yan and she administers the Cold Flower, so that I will not be taken with child. I cannot find it in myself to desire another baby, to bring a warm, living being into this chilled world.

I embolden myself and tell Yan that I wish to see Giuseppe. Here in the Inner Court of the Forbidden City, I know full well I may never see him again if he is not summoned to my presence. We do not have the freedom to find one another by accident among the streams and flowers of the Yuan Ming Yuan.

"Are you sure?" she asks me.

"Yes," I say, although my voice shakes a little.

When he arrives I am seated on a throne in my receiving hall, a formality that I thought would give me courage but instead makes me feel awkward, as I look down on him. He gives a small nod when he sees me, as though he can see the choice I have made and understands it, or at least I hope he does. His bow is deep and graceful, as formal as my choice of seating. I hear my voice crack as I begin speaking.

"You are well?"

"I am well, your ladyship," he says.

I struggle to think what I can say to him. Nothing I want to say to him is possible. "I saw the coronation portrait, it is very fine."

He gives a faint smile. "I seem to have refined my technique so that it has become acceptable rather than inauspicious."

I nod. The silence stretches out between us.

"You have seen the other portraits commissioned by His Majesty?" he asks at last.

"No," I say. "What portraits?"

"I call them *masquerades*," says Giuseppe, smiling a little more. "It is a word from my country meaning masks. The Emperor dresses as one thing or another and is painted."

"Dressed as what?" I ask.

"A travelling monk. A hermit. A poet or musician. Such things."

I frown, unable to imagine Yongzheng dressing up as any of these things. "Why?"

He thinks for a moment. "Perhaps he feels burdened by his role," he says. "For an emperor so dedicated to his empire, some respite must be necessary."

I think of the endless papers in Yongzheng's study and the endless notations in the vermillion script used only by Emperors on them, of his tired face. I nod. "He should not work so hard," I say. "He should enjoy some time without work, but he hardly ever does."

"Perhaps he has the portraits to make him think of other things he might be doing, other lives he might have led?"

I consider other lives I might have led. Of a life in which I would be free to take Giuseppe's hand and walk away from all of this. What other lives does my husband dream of? A life where he, the Son of Heaven, owns nothing? A life where he can retreat to gentle pastimes of music and poetry, rather than the endless unfolding papers of state? I shake my head a little to bring me back to the here and now. "And you are well? Your own life is happy?"

He does not answer me at once. His eyes do not meet mine and at last he says, with great gentleness, his eyes steady on the floor between us, "I try to be well. I took my vows when the Emperor was crowned."

"Vows?" I ask, although I know already from his tone that this is not something I should pursue.

"The vows required by the Brotherhood, the Jesuits," he says. "Poverty, obedience and chastity."

I knew before he said the word what it would be, the tiny pause before he spoke that final word told me. What else might a priest vow? "You took your vows when the Emperor was crowned?" I repeat.

"When you left the Garden," he says and his eyes meet mine.

I am summoned to one of the great receiving halls in the Outer Court. My palanquin bobs and sways while I consider for what reason I may be called upon. I am not aware that I have left undone any of my duties. I expect to see my husband but I am mistaken.

"A concubine has been found guilty of taking a lover," the Chief Eunuch tells me.

I can't help it, I feel a chill in my stomach and have to fight not to clear my throat before I speak. "A concubine?"

"One of the old ones," he says dismissively. "A minor concubine to the previous Emperor. She was selected from the Daughters' Draft the year before he died."

I think of a girl, somewhere between thirteen and sixteen years of age, chosen as a bride for an old man. She might have been selected as his companion once or twice or possibly not at all before he died and when his last breath left him she would have been hustled away into some dreary back palace, away from us new ladies, we who had the good fortune to be chosen for a living, breathing, emperor. One of us lives now in what used to be her palace and her days are so empty as to be desolate. She may live another fifty, sixty years or more and never be touched, never be loved, never have any hope at all of advancement, whether through children or through her own charms.

"With whom was she having an affair?" I ask. There are no men allowed within the Forbidden City overnight and who would she come into contact with anyway, in the Inner Court? The maker of perfumes, the robe makers, the shoemakers? Most of these within the Forbidden City are eunuchs, skilled in such tasks. The monks of the many temples? Surely not.

"A eunuch," says the Chief Eunuch, his face appalled at this breach. While he himself does in fact have a wife, the only reason for the eunuchs' very existence is to keep well away from the Emperor's women.

I think of Yan and Kun, of a love that made an impossible leap and found itself somehow safe, wrapped in a warm embrace, blessed by some unseen deity who took pity on the fate of mere mortals and their suffering here on earth. I picture for a brief moment this unknown girl and her loyal servant, clinging to one another in their need for love and I feel my heart grow heavy.

"It is a matter for the Emperor," I say, knowing this to be untrue. If it were, I would not have been summoned.

The Chief Eunuch shakes his head. "The eunuch was under my jurisdiction and he has already been beheaded at my command. The girl comes under your jurisdiction. Her fate is in your hands."

"The Emperor to whom she was married is dead," I say.

"She was unfaithful to his memory," he says.

I am silent. This is not an argument I can ever win. There are too many dynasties and centuries of such rules for me to overthrow them in one conversation with a eunuch.

From the folds of his robe appears a white silk scarf. "You may give her this," he says.

I do not touch the silk. I am aware of what he is implying. I try to imagine how I can stand, face to face with this girl, younger than myself, and suggest to her that she should take her own life for having been unfaithful to the memory of an old man she probably saw a handful of times in her short life here before he died. I can feel my eyes welling up with tears.

The Chief Eunuch has spent his life in service to this court. He has risen to this position of power because he knows what to do at every moment, on every occasion. He is not unprepared for my weakness. "Does your ladyship wish for me to take the matter into my own hands?" he asks.

I hold out my hand and he gives me the silk. It is so soft, so light that I wonder if it is capable of the task for which it has been made. "Which palace?" I ask and he steps outside the receiving hall, to speak with my bearers and direct them.

My own palace is sumptuous, of course. I am all but Empress. The courtyard palace where we stop, somewhere on the furthest boundaries of the Inner Court, is a sad affair by comparison. The bright paints adorning the walkways are faded and cracked, peeling here and there to show the weathered wood underneath, grey with years of neglect. A few half-hearted flowers struggle to grow in the shaded light but most are fading as autumn creeps closer. The walkway which winds its way around the entirety of the courtyard has loose boards.

I dismount from my palanquin and stand by it, uncertain. I am very conscious of the white silk of the scarf I carry, its soft folds now crumpled from being gripped in my damp palm.

"An Empress? Here?"

I turn quickly. On the opposite side of the courtyard a woman has appeared on the walkway. She is wearing a robe that might once have been grand but is now faded, like her surroundings. "I am here – " I begin.

"For the bad one?"

"For the Lady – "

"I know who you are here for." She spits. "The young one. The fool who got caught."

"Where is she?"

Slowly, the woman makes her way round the walkway until she is near to me. Up close, she is quite old. She must be one of the Kangxi Emperor's first brides, her face covered in fine wrinkles, her eyes hooded by drooping skin. Her voice grates, cracks. "What are you going to do with her?"

I try to regain some authority. "That is not your concern," I say. "Where is the girl?"

She grins at me, showing a missing tooth, the others yellowed with age. "Where is the silk scarf?"

I hold it closer to my body but she catches the small movement and suddenly her face is serious. "It's true, then?" she asks and her voice quavers. "She must die?"

"Where is the girl?" I ask more loudly.

"She is not so much to blame, you know," says the woman. "She was so young when they chose her. Perhaps they thought a young one would warm an old man's bones, but he barely saw her before he died and then she was all alone."

I look about me to see if I can find someone else to speak with. I do not want to hear what I already know, about the unfairness of what I am doing, about the rules which govern all of us and which some simple girl has fallen foul of. I want this to be over.

"We are all alone," adds the woman, her voice an unending sing-song, reminding me uneasily of childhood stories about witches and their curses. "Alone and forgotten here."

"You are cared for as honoured ladies of His Majesty's late father," I say.

"We are forgotten," she says. "As you well know. None of us leaves this place. Our walls were once the walls of the Forbidden City, with his death they have shrunk down to the walls of this courtyard."

"I need to see the girl," I say.

The woman raises her chin. I turn to see a girl standing on the walkway where the woman first stood.

"Come here," I say too loudly.

The girl makes her way towards me, avoiding the loose boards with an unthinking familiarity that saddens me. She edges past the older woman with a bowed head, coming to stand in front of me, looking down at me from her place on the walkway. She is quite short and her frame is delicate. Her face is very pale, as though she has not seen sunlight for many months, even though summer is now coming to a close.

"Ladyship."

"I need to speak with you alone," I say.

Her small hand extends, indicating a dark doorway into the palace. I step up onto the creaking walkway and enter, hearing her move behind me as she follows. I do not turn to see if the old woman has followed us. Instead I stand still and gesture that she should come round to face me, which she does, standing before me in the poor light, her eyes fixed on my face.

"You should know that your conduct leaves me no option," I say. "Do you have something to say?" I expect a denial or begging for my mercy but instead the girl continues to stare at me in silence. "You don't deny your misdoing?" I want her to deny everything, to suddenly prove, somehow, at this late moment, that she was innocent, that there has been some mistake.

"I loved him," she says. "And he loved me. No-one had ever loved either of us."

I want to speak but I cannot. I want to say something – perhaps to threaten her to beg for mercy although I know that no mercy will be shown – perhaps to beg her to lie. But my throat is closed. What she has spoken is probably nothing but the truth: that since either of them had come to the Forbidden City neither had been shown kindness, nor tenderness, nor love. That somehow they found such things in one another.

"You know he is dead?" I ask. I curse myself for the hard tone that struggles out of my cramped throat. I want my question to frighten her into lying to save her life but she only keeps her eyes fixed on me.

"Yes," she says simply. And then, "May I join him?"

And it is I, all-but-Empress, who am silenced by this nobody-concubine's grace and power. I hold out my hand and she draws from my sweating grip the silent white silk, turns and walks away into the dark recesses of the other rooms of this forgotten and damned palace.

I dream of the Yuan Ming Yuan. I walk through the bamboo-lined path where I first met Giuseppe and the bamboos turn from their delicate green to a dark red as I brush past them. I pause by the lake where Hongli used to play and the water turns muddy at my approach. I follow a tiny path and it leads me on and on, twisting and winding to nowhere. I try to change direction and the path is always the same. I wake sweating and have to sit on the side of my bed, my bare feet cold on the floor so that I can believe that it was only a dream. When morning comes I send a messenger to Yongzheng and ask for permission to go to the Yuan Ming Yuan. I have not seen it for so long that I am beginning to forget it and I want to be there and reassure myself that the bamboo leaves are still green, that the water is clear and the tiny path will take me back to my old home, the wisteria-covered palace.

But the messenger returns with my husband's refusal. He says that it is autumn, too cold to spend time in the imperial summer garden. He looks forward to a summer visit there with me, next year. I think of the snowball fights Yan and I had there when it was my home year-round and want to disobey him, but I know that protocol does not allow for me to leave the Forbidden City without his permission. I am stuck here, with my dreams and the consequences of my actions.

I ask to see Giuseppe again, send word that I wish to see whatever his latest work in progress is. When he arrives it is with two eunuch apprentices, who carry with them a huge hand scroll. Such a scroll would usually be viewed little by little, but I ask to see the entirety of it. It takes them a long time to unroll the whole length of and when they do it stretches the length of my receiving hall. It shows a landscape and trees on a plain filled with horses, with mountains rising behind it.

"*One Hundred Horses*," says Giuseppe. "A commission from His Majesty."

The horses are beautiful and of many varied colours. Some play together, others eat grass, some even race one another. In the distance are two men on horseback, perhaps hunting or rounding up the herd. I admire the painting for some time.

"This horse seems different from the rest," I say at last. In the centre of the scroll, although set a little way back, under the shadow of a tree, stands a brown horse. Unlike the well-fed and healthy horses depicted with their companions elsewhere on the scroll, this one stands alone, its gaunt sides plainly showing its ribs, its head hanging dejectedly.

Giuseppe looks at the scroll for a moment in silence. "He is," he says.

"He seems unhappy," I say. "Lonely."

Giuseppe's eyes leave the scroll and come to settle on mine. "He is," he agrees.

I drop my gaze. "You may leave us," I say and he bows and leaves the room before his apprentices have even finished rolling up the scroll, scurrying after him even whilst trying to bow to me.

"There is no need for you to see the girl," rules the Chief Eunuch. "It is done and she will be disposed of. You have done your part, my lady." He is pleased with me perhaps, glad that I am revealed as a woman who will act as is right and proper, who will carry out even the harder parts of her position and do it without mewling to him that it is too much.

I shake my head. "I gave her the silk. I need to see her," I say and once again my palanquin makes its way towards the forgotten palaces.

I follow the Chief Eunuch's splendid robes into darkness and more darkness and then my eyes see what there is to see. Two little feet dangle helplessly from the ceiling, one faded blue silk cloud-climbing shoe still attached, the other fallen to the ground. And higher still there is something too horrible to be looked upon, perhaps I catch a quick glimpse of a mottled face or perhaps it is only my shamed imagination and I stumble into the dingy light of the courtyard and vomit spatters down onto my own silken shoes and I retch and retch until there is nothing left in me and retch again and all the while my falling tears mix with the stinking mess at my feet.

The Maze of Yellow Flowers

THE NORTH-EAST SECTION OF THE Garden became unrecognisable. Where once it had been a peaceful place of tiny paths set alongside lakes and wandering streams, with miniature hills and tall trees, now the ground was torn up for as far as the eye could see. Hongli had received permission from his father to do with the Garden as he wished.

"It will be the greatest garden the world has ever seen, Giuseppe," he told me. "It will be like a fairytale. My father has already ordered the famous Southern Gardens to be replicated here. And you, Giuseppe, you must create for me a Western Garden."

"A Western Garden?" I repeated, uncertain of his meaning.

"Yes!" he said, eyes bright with enthusiasm for his new plan. "You must build me mansions, a maze, spouting fountains. Like the ones you used to show me when I was a boy."

I thought back to the books I had shown him when he was a child, curious about my homeland: the copperplate engravings of grand palaces around Europe, of spraying waterworks. I shook my head a little. "They would look odd here, your highness. Out of place."

"You said that in the West they are building Chinese gardens."

"Yes."

"You said they had become fashionable and that all the great lords had one."

I sighed a little. He remembered everything I had ever mentioned, even in passing, it seemed. "Yes, Highness."

He laughed. "Then a Western Garden shall be fashionable here!"

"I am not an architect, Highness. I could have Brother Moggi assigned to the task?"

"No," he said decisively. "I want you, Shining. Besides, you will have the Lei family to help you," he added. "They have been architects to the imperial family for generations. They will take care of any details with which you need help."

"Should they not be in charge, then?" I asked him.

He shook his head, stubborn. "I have chosen you," he said and smiled his broad smile, the one I remembered from his childhood.

I thought of the little houses I had once built for him by the lakeside, made of scraps of wood, tiny pebbles and reeds, how as a child he had found them entrancing. Perhaps his excessive trust in my abilities as an architect sprang from that childish admiration in my ability.

I tried to warn him. "It will take years, Highness," I told him. "Possibly many years. And there will be much disruption to the rest of the Garden. It will take many, many taels of silver as well as an army of workers."

But he was a young man with a young man's enthusiasm, and furthermore, a young man who knew that he was destined for greatness, that although the current work had required his father's blessing, one day it would require only his own orders for his desires to be made reality. "Ask for what you need, and it is yours," he told me and was gone.

He was not to be dissuaded. I let a little time go by in case he should change his mind, but again and again he would return to the topic until at last, sensing my reluctance to begin, he ordered me to bring him books on Western architecture. These I begged from Brother Moggi and from them Hongli chose a selection of buildings that seemed to please him.

"This one, I think Giuseppe, and this also. But perhaps with a wall more like this one and a roof more like that. And the fountains could be like a clock, like a sundial – a water dial!"

I wondered at the strange collection of buildings he was creating in his mind. Certainly they would look like nothing recognisable from my own city. Their component parts did not fit together into a whole, they were like buildings drawn by a child, who adds any element they see fit, regardless of its intended purpose. I comforted myself with the thought that, at any rate, the so-called Chinese buildings in the gardens of the nobility of Europe were probably equally incorrect in their dimensions, their details, and their proximity to one another.

"So you will begin at once, Giuseppe," he told me with an air of finality that I did not dare to disobey.

"Your father?"

"He is busy with reforming the administration of the empire," said Hongli. "You will see little of him, Giuseppe, he works so hard. But he has given me his blessing to turn the Yuan Ming Yuan into something truly magnificent. He says it will be a place for him to rest, when he has the time."

I thought of Yongzheng when he was only a prince, how his taste had been for the simple in nature; the delicate blossoms of early spring, the bold colours of summer, the gentle decline of autumn in all its fading colours, the soft snows of winter. Buildings had certainly sprung up under his instructions, but for the most part they were built for practical purposes. A full complement of administrative offices and receiving halls had been built at one of the entrances to the Yuan Ming Yuan, so that he might work there uninterrupted and to enable greater efficiency when receiving and sending dispatches to and from the Forbidden City. Otherwise his preference was for smaller buildings, perhaps a little pavilion perched by the side of a lake, a dock at which to moor a rowing boat. Even the temples he had ordered built had been small by imperial standards, gently set into their surroundings so that it seemed at times that they might have grown there like the plants which were allowed to creep up around them. What Hongli had in mind was building on an entirely different scale. I looked at the selection of images that he had chosen and tried to imagine them within the setting of the Yuan Ming Yuan. They seemed odd, like something imagined rather than real and I wondered whether my own eye had changed in the years I had served here, whether I had forgotten these buildings of my youth, which after all had once been as familiar to me as the sweeping golden rooftops of the Forbidden City were to Hongli himself.

When I did see Yongzheng it was fleetingly. He visited us only once or twice during many months of work and I was struck by his pallor, the dark marks under his eyes.

"There is little time for rest," he acknowledged when I remarked on his appearance. "I try to make do with two *shi*, if I can."

"Four hours is a very little amount of sleep, your majesty," I said.

"There is much to do," he said wearily. "The administration of the empire has been neglected. There is much corruption that must be weeded out. My father was a great man but he was not much interested in such things. But it is the small things that make a difference, that will give us important powers for the future. We need more arable land to feed our growing population. There are too many children without families and they must be provided for. I have ordered that there must be more orphanages built. They will be paid for from the pockets of wealthy officials. It is their duty to model how people should behave, to show charity. The imperial examinations have only been available to certain families, but they must be made available to all." He sighed. "And our borders are always under threat. They cost millions of taels of silver just to maintain."

I nodded. "But your father lived a long life, Majesty. I am sure you will have much time in which to complete all of these works. Perhaps you can proceed at a slower pace and have time to enjoy yourself as well, perhaps spending more time here in the Garden – or at any rate," I added with a smile, "the quieter parts of it."

He looked about him at the chaos of Hongli's plans being put into action and gave a small smile. "The Garden is in good hands, Giuseppe," he said. "And for myself, I will hope to equal my father's long reign. My physicians give me daily doses of an elixir of immortality. I am sure it will fortify me for the task ahead. And now I must go, there is still much that I must accomplish today."

I bid him farewell but something of his weariness stayed with me and I thought of him often after that, though I saw him infrequently. I was of the opinion that he drove himself too hard, but he had always been a dutiful man even when he was only a young prince and could have pleased only himself. I knew from court gossip that he rarely spent time with either his children or indeed his ladies, although I could not bring myself not to feel a silent gladness that Niuhuru saw little of him.

I told Brother Moggi of Hongli's plans and enlisted his assistance. He agreed readily enough but flung up his hands in despair when I showed him the odd mixture of styles and buildings Hongli had chosen.

"Madonna mia, none of it fits together!"

I sighed. "I know," I told him, "but it is what he wants. We have no choice in the matter. Can it be done, or not?"

"It can be done, but it is an absurdity," he said, his usual cheerful demeanour affronted by this approach to architectural planning.

"I do what I am told," I replied. "That, at least, I have learnt in my time here."

"There is a new Brother who has arrived recently," said Moggi, looking over the drawings. "A Brother Michel Benoist, French. He is a hydraulic engineer. You will need him for the fountains, I will send him to the site."

Brother Benoist was a serious young man, still overwhelmed with his new surroundings. He nodded at my description of the fountain I wished him to design, which would spout water at each of the twelve hours of the day, but he looked taken aback, as had Moggi, at the rest of the designs.

"Think of it as an Emperor's whimsy," I said. "You need only make it work."

I saw him from time to time for many days afterwards, sat out of the way amongst the chaos of the building works, his shoulders hunched while he attempted to sketch the interior workings such a fountain would need, his brow growing ever more furrowed.

The Lei family had served as architects to emperors for generations. They, at least, were neither surprised nor discomforted by imperial decrees, however unusual. My first meeting was with Jinyu, who had taken over from his father as the chief imperial architect. He carried with him sheaves of paper and a worried frown.

"Thank you for your help," I said. "I am not an architect myself, I am a painter. But Prince Bao has been kind enough to entrust the making of a Western Garden to me and I will need all the help I can get."

He nodded and gestured to an assistant, who sprang forwards with a large box, which he opened to reveal a beautiful little model of one of the lakeside pavilions, made in Yongzheng's time as prince. "This is how we work," he informed me. "First the sketches, then we create the models, made to scale so that the Son of Heaven or the Prince may see how the buildings will appear when completed and request any changes before work begins."

I nodded. "They are wonderful," I said. "How do you make them?"

Jinyu's worried frown smoothed a little. Perhaps he had been afraid that I would insist on strange foreign ways of working. "We use clay, wood and paper," he said and reached out to the small model. Gently, he lifted away the roof, to show beneath the walls and interior rooms that made up the building inside. "Everything can be altered according to his majesty's command," he said.

I smiled, thinking that the generations of service the Lei family had offered to more than one dynasty had taught them well. They knew that an emperor's command could easily be rescinded on a whim and were ready to respond. "I like your models," I said. "These are the first drawings of what the Prince has requested. His father has given him authority over this project."

Jinyu studied my drawings for many days, along with the original copperplate engravings that had inspired Hongli, trying to become accustomed to the very different style of architecture he and his family would be required to deliver. We walked across the landscape discussing materials, while various assistant scribes took down his muttered notes on costs, timings and the labour required. His knowledge relieved me, for even though the structures were foreign to him, he quickly understood what would be required. We even visited St Joseph's together, so that he could see a Western-style building. He drew many sketches and asked even more questions, not all of which I could answer, although I did my best and also read to him from such books on architecture as we had available to us, fumblingly translating technical words.

"I did not think to learn much in the way of architectural terms when I learnt your language," I confessed to him. "I am afraid I am a poor interpreter."

He managed a small smile. "Rather a poor interpreter than none at all," he said and issued every greater streams of notes to his hardworking scribes, noting especially the heights of the buildings and the great weights of the materials we would expect to use, for stone usually made up only a small part of his usual range of construction supplies. I grew to like and trust Jinyu over time, for all his serious demeanour, for he was a hard worker and a superb craftsman and did not resent Hongli's having chosen me as the originator of his Western Garden. We built a friendship of sorts, immersed as we were in the same project, with no way of escaping the imperial demands made of us until it was complete.

Brother Benoist stood by my side in a state of disbelief. "How many labourers are there?"

I stood amidst swirling clouds of dust and looked about me. There were so many workmen I could not even count them all, I would have had to refer to the long lists of men, animals, silver, tools and more that we had been granted for the works to commence. Surveyors hurried to measure the land and mark it out. Tiny models of the Prince's future pleasure ground had been created by the Lei family for us to consider. Many of the workmen's heads were all but invisible to me, hidden as they were in the trenches they had dug for the foundations of the palaces I was creating.

I shrugged. "As many as are needed," I told him. "Whatever is needed, we have been granted."

He shook his head. "This is madness," he said.

"Have you found a way for the Fountain to spout water to mark the hours of the day?" I asked him, returning to the task in hand.

He nodded. "That is not the difficult part, the difficult part lies in building a reservoir which will feed it with water," he told me. "An ugly reservoir is unlikely to please the Prince. He will want everything to be pleasing on the eye, he has no idea of the practicalities involved."

I considered for a moment. "We can still create an attractive building around the reservoir," I told him. "Something like this, perhaps." I took out one of my books, showing engravings of Western palaces, those that had taken Hongli's eye.

Brother Benoist shook his head. "This is how we are choosing the buildings to be created?" he asked, disbelieving. "Choosing them from a book rather than designing something appropriate to their function?"

"They have no function," I reminded him. "Their function is to please the Prince's eye. No one will live here. No one will use the rooms within them. Perhaps they will wander through the maze. Perhaps they will admire the Clock Fountain. But these are not real buildings."

"They are illusions," he said, his practical engineering approach offended by the commission. "Fairytales. Absurd."

"They are his childhood dreams," I told him, my tone defensive.

"Father Friedel says the prince behaves as though he were your son," he said, a little curious.

"He is all the son I will ever have," I told him and had to turn away as my voice cracked.

Hongli made frequent visits to our works. He was active in his admiration, leaping into foundation trenches, the better to see the work up close. On one occasion he attempted to dig a trench himself, his silk robes growing muddied while his attendants looked on in horror. He wanted to know every detail, listening to complex explanations of how each building would be erected, how the waterworks would be arranged and the exact carvings to be made on the stone walls of the maze.

"And will people really get lost in it?" he asked me, laughing.

"For a little while," I told him.

"Make it harder!" he said, his eyes bright with mischief, looking back at Lady Fuca, his Primary Consort, who had accompanied him, along with his other ladies. They stood well back from the mess of our works, a huddled group of fluttering silks and bejewelled hair, but when Hongli waved them forwards they tiptoed towards us, their high shoes unsuited to the building works around us.

"Giuseppe is building a maze in which you will get utterly lost," he said to Lady Fuca. "I will have to come and rescue you. You will be wandering there until it is dark!"

"I know you would rescue me before dark fell," she said placing one delicate hand on his arm and smiling up at him. "You would not leave me to wander alone and afraid."

He covered her hand with his broader one and gave her a tender smile. "I would run to your side at once," he assured her and for a moment the two of them gazed at one another, oblivious to those around them. Behind them I saw the other ladies giggle together, although one looked away from their show of the affection. I wondered whether Hongli was aware that his obvious love for Lady Fuca caused jealousy amongst the other young women who had perhaps hoped for a Prince's favour when they had married him.

"We will return soon," Hongli promised me. He broke off a yellow flower from a straggling bush that had survived the works so far and tucked it into Lady Fuca's already-laden hair. "The maze should have imperial yellow flowers planted all about it."

I bowed as they left and made a note to myself about the flowers, one of many hundreds on a never-ending list of tasks still to accomplish. Hongli had also asked for an illusion on a scale I had never yet created. Vast awnings on cloth, to be mounted on frames near one of the buildings, then painted to resemble, far off, a little village. I had suggested building a small village but Hongli still remembered a *trompe l'oeil* painting I had done for him as a child and insisted that one should be incorporated into the Western Garden. The outlines must be put in place to ensure the correct perspective required for the illusion to work and even then it would still require most of the imperial studios' many artists to complete the work in good time. And the entirety would have to somehow be sheltered from the elements. It made me sigh just thinking about the work and planning required.

I took to arriving onsite each day before dawn, in the hopes of a few moments' peace before the men arrived. In the early days I would catch a glimpse of the deer grazing by the lakeside or see the night creatures returning to their homes. Hedgehogs and badgers snuffled through the half-built foundations and over piles of earth while bats swooped past my ears, returning to their daylight perches. But as time wore on these animals made themselves scarce, moving their burrows to other parts of the Garden, away from our noise and destruction. From where we worked, I could see only mud or dust, as the rain decided, piles of materials and felled trees, deep holes appeared everywhere while the air was filled with shouts and the curses of hardworking labourers. The plants and even trees were trampled on, felled, ripped out or moved elsewhere until our location was nothing so much as a barren wasteland. I thought longingly of the soft blossom and waving willows, calm lakeshores and shy wildlife only a few minutes' walk away but never found the time to leave the works and find some peace. Besides, I found out soon enough that the peace that I longed for was hardly to be had within the Garden at all. The Western Garden was the most ambitious of Hongli's projects, but other works were taking place across the length and breadth of the Yuan Ming Yuan. Larger palaces, a Southern Garden replicating those in the South of the empire complete with huge dark twisted rocks. More administrative offices, grander temples. A vast field of pots filled with lotus plants and tended to daily by the gardeners, the better to create a glorious view of flowers come the summer. The Garden I had first encountered when I arrived here was changing, slowly but surely, into something else entirely. I missed the delicacy I recalled from twenty years ago. I remembered how I had first seen it, the sensation that I was the first to discover each little pathway, charmed by its air of secrecy, as though it were a garden forgotten by the world outside.

I returned to St Joseph's from time to time and for once found pleasure in the silence of the lengthy prayers.

"The exterior design is all yours," Brother Benoist told me as he delivered me the drawings indicating the interior workings of the fountains. "I am tired of it already. It has given me too many sleepless nights."

"I had in mind something classical," I told him. "Perhaps twelve women, each pouring water?"

But when the time came for me to create the design I found that each woman became Niuhuru. Again and again I cast my mind back to the Grecian and Roman ideals of womanhood and dutifully outlined their form and yet each had something of her. Their hair fell straight rather than in artful curls, their eyes took on her almond-shaped delineations until my sketches were blurred with lines drawn again and again, while little clumps of soiled bread gathered beneath my table, smudged with the charcoal they had erased.

My suffering was ended by Xiyao. He stood behind me to view my progress and visibly recoiled when I showed him my designs.

"Naked women are an unsuitable subject matter for an imperial building," he told me.

"They are not naked," I pointed out. "There will be drapes of fabric carved into the stone, to cover their modesty."

Xiyao was adamant. "It will not be approved."

"The Prince wants a Western Garden," I told him. "This is a very classical design for a fountain. I have seen scores of them in my home city and further afield, with far less clothing."

"Not in China," he told me firmly and I gave in, in part out of relief at no longer struggling with thoughts of Niuhuru.

Instead I thought back to the illustrations I had seen of the Gardens of Versailles, with their creatures from Aesop's Fables, each spouting water at a given time. I drew a design incorporating twelve seated figures, made up of enrobed human bodies with animal heads, each one a creature from the Chinese Zodiac. Brother Moggi raised his eyebrows when he saw them.

"Are you sure the Brothers will approve such a heathen theme?" he asked, his voice echoing slightly in the quiet of the chapel of St Joseph's where I had chosen to sit in a pew and contemplate the final design.

"I no longer care," I told him. "I am tired of the noise and dust and confusion of the works. They are never-ending. The Garden used to be a peaceful place."

I woke half-blinded by a bobbing lantern held too close to my face while one of the brothers shook my shoulders.

"Brother Castiglione! Wake up!"

I shielded my eyes from the lantern. "What is it?"

"You are summoned by the Emperor!"

"At night?" I knew full well that the Forbidden City was locked up at dusk, that no-one entered or left.

"The guard said it was urgent."

I stumbled into my clothes and followed the lantern outside, trying to judge the time. I had already completed the prayers of Matins before returning to my rest, marking the deepest point of night, or so it seemed to me. Yet there was no sign of dawn. Outside a palanquin stood ready, surrounded by guards and two lantern bearers. Their faces were pale in the darkness and I looked behind me to see if others of my brethren were to join me but it seemed I was summoned alone. I took my place inside the palanquin and it was lifted at once, its bearers breaking into a full run so that I clutched at the sides to steady myself. I had never been carried at such a pace before and I found myself afraid. Was I, a man, really to enter the Forbidden City at night? For what purpose? Had I in some way offended Yongzheng? I thought with a sudden shudder of the portrait I had painted years ago of Niuhuru, standing startled outside her home, her eyes fixed on me. Had it been found somewhere and hinted at something more than had ever taken place between us? And even as my mind protested, so something small and cold inside me thought of our lips together and acknowledged that I had certainly offended against the emperor and now I was about to be punished for it. Was this how executions were arranged? Was this how my life would end, summoned in the darkness to meet my maker in silence and secrecy? My knuckles grew tighter on the sides of the palanquin as I was carried closer to my destination. I heard the challenge by the guards on the gate and the muttered response from my escort, then the heavy sound of the gate to the Forbidden City opening.

The bearers ran on. I could not stop myself from looking out. I had never seen the Forbidden City at night and it was an eerie place, seeming larger even than it was by day now that it was empty of its usual bustle. Here and there lanterns burned and by their light I glimpsed silent guards standing immobile on their watch as my palanquin raced past them. We passed each of the great halls as we headed towards the Inner Court and suddenly we were out of the wide-open spaces and into the never-ending pathways between the palaces of the imperial family. I felt the cold settle into my stomach as I recognised Niuhuru's palace and believed my fears to be made real. I took a couple of slow steps from the palanquin, almost braced for a guard's heavy hand on my shoulder but the guards and bearers stood still, their faces devoid of expression. The small figure of Yan appeared in the doorway, urgently beckoning me in.

Inside the sudden brightness of many lanterns burning dazzled my eyes and for a moment I thought that time had somehow reversed, for Yan and Niuhuru stood before me, their faces white with fear and behind them in the alcove of the bed, panting for breath, lay a young prince. For a moment I believed I was seeing Prince Yong as he had been when his brother had sought to poison him to eliminate him from the rivalry for their father's throne but then I heard Yongzheng's voice behind me and fell to my knees. When I looked up the Emperor's face was pale and I could see the fear of the women reflected in his eyes.

"Shining. I am grateful to you for joining us."

I rose. "Majesty. I am at your service. What has happened?"

His voice shook before he mastered it. "My son is ill. His mother believes him poisoned and she begged me to summon you. She says you were of great use to her when I myself was poisoned."

I turned back to the bed, now seeing Hongli's face where I had mistakenly seen Yongzheng's. In a few strides I reached him, knelt by his side and saw to my horror that within his mouth his tongue was black. I looked up over my shoulder to the three faces hovering over me. "Lady Qi commanded the services of a physician when you were ill, Majesty, perhaps we can summon him now?"

The Emperor's face darkened. "I believe Lady Qi's son Hongshi to be behind this," he told me and even in my horror I noted that Yongzheng was already disowning his own offspring.

I glanced at Niuhuru and saw tears falling down her face. "Send for the imperial physician," I said, speaking as though I was confident in my orders. "There must be something that can be done."

"He is on his way," said Yan.

The physician's face drained of colour when he realised that he was tasked with saving the known heir from poisoning. But he set to, his eunuch assistants working smoothly at his side, brewing foul-smelling liquids and grinding strange concoctions.

"You will report to me on his progress," said Yongzheng to me. "I must speak with Hongshi."

I bowed as he left us and then turned, helpless, to Niuhuru. "I do not know what to do," I confessed to her.

"I am so afraid," she whispered. "If he dies…"

I held my hand up to stop her. "He will not die. Do not speak it."

"But…"

"Do not speak it!" I said and the physician turned to glance at me, a foreigner raising his voice to the Primary Consort of the Emperor. I ignored him. "Yong… the Emperor survived," I said, conscious of the taboo of having spoken his old name. "He was strong and Hongli is younger and certainly no less strong. He will fight this."

I did not know a night could be so long. The brightness of the lanterns inside the room stung my eyes and more than once I looked out into the darkness of the courtyard and hoped that I would see the dawn, something to give me hope and yet the darkness all around us seemed endless, our false light a mockery of Hongli's blackened tongue and closed eyes. I wished all of us could sleep, that we could escape this night and still it wore on.

When the dawn finally came I told Yan to open up the doors and windows.

"It will be cold," she objected.

"I cannot breathe," I told her. She flung open the doors and windows and the chilly autumn air rushed over us as Hongli let out a moan that had us all running to his side.

"He is awake," cried Niuhuru and it was true, his eyes flickered open and he blinked at us before closing them again. To my relief I saw his tongue seemed a more natural colour and he seemed to breathe more easily.

"Is he over the worst?" I asked the physician.

"I believe so," he replied. "The dose must have been small or he must have eaten less of the dish than his poisoner would have wanted."

I thought of the food tasters, the tiny strips of silver that were always included in every plate of food for the imperial household, how the eunuchs swore that poison would turn them black at once and reveal hidden dangers. "How could he have been poisoned?"

Niuhuru's voice was harder than I had ever heard it, her face hidden from me, buried in the silk coverlets covering her son. "He was practicing archery with Hongshi, who offered him water from his own water bag just before Hongli came in to eat. Perhaps he thought we would think it was the food at the meal and not the water that harmed him, but Hongli already felt sick before he began to eat."

I thought back to the elegant young man who had presented himself so correctly to his grandfather the Kangxi Emperor, hoping for favour, who had instead been passed over for his younger half-brother Hongli, the child prodigy who had broken all protocol to sit on his grandfather's lap and chatter to him of his passions. I remembered Lady Qi's desire to be Empress Dowager one day and thought that her son would surely have been raised with ambition burning in his heart.

"What will happen now?" I asked.

The physician began to list the curative and strengthening substances and treatments that Hongli must endure, how rest was imperative, how certain energy lines must be stimulated to return him to full health. But Niuhuru was not listening. She stood up and when she turned to face me I saw both terror and rage in her face.

"She tried to kill my son," she said. "She has gone too far."

Niuhuru rarely wore full court robes but in the great receiving hall of the Outer Court she took her place beside Yongzheng and I saw the might of an empire about to come crashing down on any individual foolish enough to believe they might shake its foundations. Lady Qi, her face white and her hands shaking, was made to stand before them. Her son was nowhere to be seen.

"The son of this miserable woman has been banished from the Forbidden City," began Yongzheng. For a usually quiet-voiced man, the echoes of his pronouncement filled the huge space without difficulty. Lady Qi fell to her knees, as though about to beg for mercy but the Emperor continued speaking as though he had not seen her.

"This unworthy son's name has been stricken from the *yudie*."

Lady Qi let out a wail of horror.

I turned my head to a courtier I knew and spoke under my breath. "*Yudie*? 'Jade plate'?" I had not come across the term before.

"The imperial genealogical record," he whispered back. "He is removed from the record of the Emperor's offspring."

"We can only hope," continued Yongzheng, "that this dishonour will lead him to take the only possible action expected of a man."

Lady Qi screamed.

I looked to the courtier, uncomprehending while around us the court stood in silent acceptance.

"He will be expected to take his own life," murmured the courtier.

I looked at Niuhuru's face, set in a mask. When she spoke her voice was controlled. "Lady Qi will be removed from her palace and will join previous ladies of the court in the back palaces."

Lady Qi crawled towards the throne, her voice a sobbing pant. "I ask for mercy. For my undeserving son and for myself, his unworthy mother."

"No mercy will be granted," said Yongzheng. He rose to his feet as Lady Qi was grabbed by guards and dragged from the room, her screams echoing around us. The room quickly emptied and I made my way towards Niuhuru. I did not speak, only looked at her.

"She found my lack of ambition suspicious," said Niuhuru and up close I saw that her voice had not trembled only because her jaw was clenched too tightly. "She thought I must be ambitious in secret, to have risen so far. But why would any woman wish to risk the life of her son by rising above others who crave power? To achieve what?"

I shook my head. "We cannot know what fate has in store for us."

Niuhuru let her hand touch my sleeve for a brief moment and I saw that she was shaking. "I cannot live like this," she said. "I cannot, Giuseppe."

"Come back to the Yuan Ming Yuan," I said in a low voice, knowing the offer was meaningless. "I am making a Western Garden for Hongli. He will get better and he will be happy again."

She tried to smile but her lips did not move as they should and her eyes filled with tears. "I was so afraid," she whispered. "I thought…"

"He will be well," I assured her and I allowed myself to lay my hand over hers for the briefest of moments before she nodded and hurried away, leaving me standing in the great hall. I tried to quieten my emotions, breathed deeply.

"You must be a great comfort to Lady Niuhuru," said a quiet voice.

I turned, startled, for I had thought the throne room had emptied entirely. Just behind me stood one of Hongli's consorts.

"Lady Ula Nara," I said, bowing. "You must be relieved that the Prince is making a recovery."

I thought she might smile, or nod in agreement but she met my gaze without expression. "Lady Fuca is by his side," she said.

"Of course," I agreed. "Although I am sure he would find the care of any of his ladies a comfort at this time."

She blinked slowly, as though my remark was foolish. "His Highness only has eyes for Lady Fuca," she said.

I smiled as kindly as I could, noting that there must be some rivalry between the young consorts. "Considering what has just happened, it is best to put aside rivalries if possible," I suggested. "We must take love where we find it and be content with what we find."

She looked down at my sleeve, where a few moments ago Niuhuru's hand had lain and my own hand had covered hers. "Take love where we find it," she repeated, her voice distant, her eyes glazed as though seeing something far away.

I felt a little shiver of fear. What inferences might an unhappy young girl make of what she saw between Niuhuru and I, what use of such glimpses might she make? "I will leave you now, your ladyship," I said and bowed. I walked away, fighting the desire to turn my head to see if she was still watching me, certain her eyes followed me as I left her.

Hongli was recovering, I heard, so that my heart lightened each day that I received the court reports on his health, although I was certain I would not see him for a while, as the imperial household closed ranks around their future emperor and the household physician would barely let him out of his sight for fear of a relapse of some kind. I sent him a little painting of an auspicious sleepy hedgehog in the Yuan Ming Yuan, the sort of thing he used to want me to paint as a child and in return was sent a message urging me on with the works in his new Garden. His father the Emperor could not come himself, I was told, for he was once again plunged into the endless paperwork and reform of the empire in which he had buried himself. I thought of how pale, and how much older he had seemed, despite having reigned only a short period so far. It seemed to me that his Elixir of Immortality was misnamed, if it could not even keep him in good health now, in the prime of life.

I had begged Kun's services as chief gardener for the Western Garden and Niuhuru had granted his release from her services. He frowned at the drawings I showed him.

"I know, it is not the kind of garden you are used to," I said. "But I want you to manage the garden elements around the buildings, Kun. I trust you."

He smiled. "I will do my best."

"I know you will. It must look odd to you," I added. "But the gardens of the West are very formal. They are mostly developed around circles and lines and the designs are to be followed to the letter."

"Where are they supposed to be viewed from?" he asked.

I nodded. I had expected this question. Kun was used to designing tiny scenes within the imperial gardens, each one to be viewed from a particular place, sometimes a section was to be framed with a moongate, a circular opening in a wall which forced the eye to see the garden as it had been created, a rock placed just so near a tree, a path winding out of sight, leading the gaze. The Yuan Ming Yuan was full of small artificial hills which restricted what could be seen, alongside tiny walkways which tempted the visitor to follow them to yet another elaborately created visual masterpiece disguised as only the work of nature when in fact it had taken much labour and sometimes whole seasons to achieve the desired effect.

"They are to be viewed from above," I told him. "That is the best effect of their shapes, their designs. And the viewer should be able to see for long distances, not one small scene but many, one after another, to show the grandeur of the Western Garden in its completeness. To impress them with the greatness of the Son of Heaven and all his dominion."

"It seems plain," said Kun. "Most of the plants are without flowers. Just bushes, cut into shapes?"

I thought of the great water dragon Kun had fashioned for Hongli when he was a child, the tiny painted gingko leaves made to look like fluttering butterflies. Cutting green bushes into balls and cubes was hardly making the best use of his talents. "He does want yellow flowers all around the maze," I said. "You will have to content yourself with those, Kun."

He nodded and collected up the drawings I had made. "I will need many men," he warned me.

I spread my hands. "The Prince will give you whatever you need, you know that," I told him. "Ask and it is yours."

I watched him walk away, a quiet figure amidst the chaos of the site and not for the first time I envied him. Kun always brought with him a sense of calm, of contentment, of joy in the small things. And somehow fate had smiled on him in bringing him Yan and making their love into something possible, no matter how unlikely it had seemed at first. Their daughter Chu was grown to a woman now, known by all of the ladies of the court for her exquisite embroidery, her nimble fingers recreating in silk the flowers her father coaxed from the earth. I wondered how one impossible love had been made possible while another was forever out of reach.

The men were almost finished for the day. I walked to the lake's edge to wash my face before returning to the site. I nodded to Jinyu, who was engaged in rolling up the scrolls depicting the buildings we were engaged in creating. Already the water reservoir was in place, now about to be hidden behind a cascade of stone carvings and flourishes to conceal its true function of providing the water for Brother Benoist's clockwork fountain. The stone statues waited, their bronze heads cast with mouths agape but as yet empty. Facing the fountain was an elaborate viewing platform, where the Emperor might sit in comfort to observe its workings. The workmen were packing up their tools for the night, for dusk was creeping in.

"You are not done, Shining?" asked Jinyu, seeing me pull a large ball of string out of my pocket.

I shook my head. "I am trying out a new layout for the maze," I told him, fixing one end of the string to a little wooden stake and pushing it into the earth.

He looked at the wide area of flattened earth surrounding the already-built central point of the maze, a small stone pavilion. "Do not get lost!" he chuckled and told his men and the workers to leave the site.

I smiled and waved him goodnight, then took up a little bundle of the wooden stakes. The design was already drawn up, but often, I had found, designs changed when they took up their place in their appointed locations, as though the place itself had plans of its own and the results were often better. I had already had lanterns placed around the pavilion so that I might work on it in the half-darkness. Hongli had said that he wanted to walk the maze by night, with flickering lanterns making the paths of the maze still less certain than in daylight. I thought that perhaps if the maze were to be used by night I would benefit from seeing how it might look at night. In truth I also knew that I wanted time alone, that the long noisy busy days tired me and that the Brothers' not unreasonable expectations that I should devote more of my time to prayers and theological conversation wearied me even more. With the workmen gone the Garden was at least quiet again even if my immediate surroundings were hardly in keeping with the rest of the Yuan Ming Yuan: here were no streams or lakes, no little pathways and delicate flowers. But as the men's voices faded into the distance I could at least begin to hear the croaking frogs from the nearest lake and the last songbirds' twitters before they regained their night's nesting spots.

For a while I walked steadily, my little bundle of stakes slowly diminishing while my string wound this way and that, creating imaginary pathways that only I could see in the dim light of the lanterns. At last I stood within the pavilion and looking down saw a woman's form standing outside the area I had marked out.

"May I walk with you?"

Her voice shocked me, it had been so long since I had heard it here. "Where is your palanquin?" I asked. We were some distance apart but the silence around us meant we could hear each other clearly.

"I told the men to leave me at the temple to pray. I said I would return to them when I was done and then I walked here."

"In the dark?"

She laughed a little. "I have walked the Yuan Ming Yuan enough times to walk it with my eyes closed."

"There might have been a new stream or lake dug since you were last here."

"Then I would have drowned."

"A risk."

"A risk worth taking."

"For what?"

She was silent.

I gestured in the dim light that I would join her. "May I guide you through the maze?"

She shook her head. "I thought those who walked in it were supposed to get lost. You should stay there and I will try to reach you."

I smiled. "You may try to walk it alone, if you wish."

"Where do I start?"

I gestured. "There will be a main entrance there. Then you enter and all of the pathways are designed to confuse you, to have you wander lost."

"And if I succeed?"

"Then you should reach the pavilion at the centre," I said. "Your son wishes to hold celebrations at night here. He thinks all his ladies should run along the paths holding little lanterns while he waits in the pavilion to reward the winner."

"Reward her how?" she asked and I heard her smile.

I did not answer. I did not trust my own voice.

"My son is a romantic," she said, walking forward to the starting point I had indicated to her. "Will he give Lady Fuca a guide to the maze, do you think? So that she may reach him first? He is besotted with her. I am happy for them both."

"Not all his ladies are so happy," I said.

She paused where she had reached what would one day be the gate to the maze. Her voice was sad. "I chose that girl," she said.

"Ula Nara?"

"Yes."

"I am sure it is seen as an honour for the girls to be chosen," I said.

"She begged me on her knees not to choose her," said Niuhuru. "I let the eunuch persuade me it was only nerves. But I knew it was more than that. I walked away from her while she knelt on the ground sobbing."

"I don't know her background," I said.

"She was promised to someone else," said Niuhuru. "She was in love with a young man and I chose her to marry Hongli."

I thought of Ula Nara's glazed expression, as though she was forever looking at something I could not see, how she had spotted something between Niuhuru and me that we had believed was hidden. "I am sorry for her," I said.

"I thought she would forget him," said Niuhuru. "But she has not."

We stood in silence for a moment and then Niuhuru began to

walk through the strings I had laid out. I watched as she paused before choosing each new path to take, as she realised mistakes she had made and heard her chuckle softly to herself. I leaned my hands on the pavilion's carved ledge and knew that when she reached me I would be unable to resist taking her in my arms. I felt myself gripped with a strange sensation of mingled fear and desire.

She took her time. Once or twice I saw her hesitate before a path that would have led her to me and then turn away, as though she, too, was half-afraid of what would happen when she succeeded. At last, coming close, I saw her hesitate before she lifted up her face to look at me. I stood in the pavilion and looked down on her. It had grown fully dark and I was grateful for the many lanterns I had ordered lit, not because they had guided my work nor her steps but because now we could clearly see one another's faces. I am not sure how long we stood like that, each of us searching the other's face before she stepped forward, standing at the base of the pavilion, her pathway to me clear. I moved from my spot to the top of the stairs and held out my hand to her.

"Niuhuru," I said and heard her low answer, "Giuseppe," before a shout came from the darkness beyond the maze, a man's voice, desperate.

"Ladyship! Ladyship!"

I took her hand then, but not in the way I had intended, the two of us trampling over the string pathways to reach the voice and when I saw the guard I knew something terrible had happened.

"Hongli?" gasped Niuhuru.

The guard shook his head. He was a big man but he looked afraid and he had broken out in a sweat. "The Emperor is ill."

My mind was befuddled as though I had been drinking. "Ill?"

"On his deathbed," panted the man and then all three of us were running in the darkness.

My horse kept pace with her palanquin without difficulty, even though the bearers ran as though their lives depended on it. In the darkness all I could hear was their panting breath and the hooves of my mount. I wished that she could ride with me or I with her, anything so that I could be close to her and speak with her, to know what was going on in her mind. The distance to the Forbidden City had never seemed so great.

Yan was waiting, hovering anxiously on the walkway of Niuhuru's palace while behind her Hongli paced up and down. Kun, better at managing his emotions, squatted in the courtyard, rising to his feet as we entered. Too late I thought that we should not have arrived like this, side by side, in the pale dawn when I should have been in St Joseph's and Niuhuru should be within her own palace, since the gates of the Forbidden City had barely opened. But Hongli did not comment on this. Instead he knelt before Niuhuru and asked for her blessing. White-faced she gave it and at once Hongli was guiding her back to her palanquin while he took to his, calling to me over his shoulder.

"Wait here, Shining. I will have news sent to you at once. You must manage my mother's household until my return."

I nodded but he was already gone and I entered her rooms, uncertain of what to do. Certainly there was no need for me to manage anything, for Kun and Yan were in charge here and so I allowed Kun to hustle the servants away to their tasks while Yan motioned to me to sit, for I was pacing in front of the window. She stayed with me, fetching me a cup of hot tea before quietly retreating to her embroidery in a corner of the room. She faced away from me, towards a window, and did not speak to me, for which I was grateful, for I could not have formed words. My mind was only a jumbled mass of half-done thoughts. What did I hope for? That somehow things might change? The only change to come was one I could foretell well enough.

Time slipped by. I watched the sun slowly move across the sky until the growing darkness outside warned that I would soon have to leave the Forbidden City. I felt a great weariness come over me. At last the words that had been swirling inside of me all of the previous night in the Garden took shape. I spoke out loud, addressing myself to the soft glow surrounding Yan's work, a little lantern lighting only her hands. I thought that I must say the words within me, that if I did not speak them now, to someone, to anyone, that something in me would die.

"I dream of her," I said, and saw Yan's back stiffen at this sudden moment of truth. "I don't mean that I fantasise about a life together," I added. "I do not sit like some lovelorn boy and imagine that one day I will take her hand and walk away with her, that we will leave the Forbidden City with her son's blessing and that I will take her home with me, back to Milan, where my mother will embrace her as a daughter-in-law. I am not a fool."

Yan turned as I spoke and now her eyes were fixed on me. She had always been small, as though a little stunted in growth, but her eyes were very dark and there was a sharpness to them, as though she saw through the lies fools might try to tell her, as though she saw into what you said and understood something beyond mere words.

"I dream of her," I repeated. "I sleep and she is there. I can spend my day working and I would swear to you that she has not crossed my mind, that my thoughts were empty of her. And yet as my eyes close, so she is there. I do not summon her, I try not to be so weak. But she is there, Yan, she walks in my world. If I have painted the hunt, I see her through falling leaves in the forest. If I have painted some noble courtier's dog, she caresses its fur. If I walk by day in the Yuan Ming Yuan, where she no longer is, that night I will walk there again and she will be by my side. I dream of her, Yan."

In a quiet corner of my memory palace, there sits a stunted little figure, who sews and sews and whose dark eyes see all truths. I visit her often, kneel by her side to hear her speak, to remember again the fierce joy I felt on hearing her reply.

"If she has not visited the Emperor's bed willingly these many years it is for fear that he will hear her speak your name in the darkness. When she dreams of you."

I opened my mouth to ask her more, to beg her to sate my desire to hear Niuhuru's feelings but behind Yan the door opened and Kun's face left me in little doubt of his news.

"The Yongzheng Emperor is dead," he said. "Hongli is named the Qianlong Emperor."

The Palace of Motherly Tranquillity

S CARLET AND YELLOW LEAVES FALL into the black and white world of our mourning. Our robes are white, our hair hangs loose, seeming blacker now that it is bereft of jewels and flowers.

Everywhere we go there is chanting and incense. Rows upon rows of monks chant for the passing of the Yongzheng Emperor and to bring in the reign of the Qianlong Emperor. At first the chants are soothing, they block out unnecessary conversations and unwanted thoughts. But soon they begin to grate on me.

"Close the windows," I tell my servants and my rooms descend into deeper gloom as they try to shut out the noise. A useless effort, anyway, for I am required, as Primary Consort to Yongzheng and as the mother of his successor, to attend more ceremonies than I knew existed. I kneel and bow, light whole fistfuls of incense. I try not to choke in the swirling clouds of perfumed smoke that surround the court as we move from one ritual to another.

I watch as the women who were once my peers lose their palaces and status to make way for a new generation of court ladies. Lady Mao, who first welcomed me to the imperial family. Ning. Zhang. Chunque. I think of them all, playing mah-jong by the lakeside in the Yuan Ming Yuan, greeting me without jealousy. Qi will already be there, locked in a world of bitter grief after Hongshi killed himself. Even the younger ladies, who joined the court after Yongzheng took the throne, are not spared. Some of them are still in their twenties. All of them are taken away to the back palaces on the very edges of the Inner Court, where no-one ever visits, to join whichever crones of the Kangxi Emperor still live. I shudder in fear at the idea that one of them will be caught in an affair and that I will have to pass sentence again. I think to remonstrate with my son, but this is how it has always been, how it always will be. Only I am allowed to stay within the central complex of palaces, by virtue of having inadvertently birthed an emperor.

The most desirable palaces in the Inner Court do not sit empty for long. The Palace of Eternal Spring is given to Lady Fuca, my son's newly-enthroned Empress. She takes up her destined post without apparent fear, perhaps made confident by my son's evident love for her. Lady Ula Nara is located nearby to her, her face frozen in silent misery since the day I took away her smile. Little Lady Wan, a delicate girl, fills her palace garden and hair with flowers, apparently happy with her lot although Qianlong seems to treat her more like a sister than a concubine. One by one the palaces are filled with young women, the consorts of our new Emperor, each one ready for a lifetime of petty rivalries and struggles for promotion through the uncertain ranks of imperial favour.

I do not cry. My eyes water from the incense and yet the tears will not come. I sit and tell myself all of Yongzheng's virtues as a man and as an emperor and still there are no tears. My eyes are red from the smoke. No doubt the courtiers will think that I cry in my rooms and my servants must think that I cry when I am in the temples. But I do not cry. I try to remember the first time I met Yong, when he was only one prince among many princes and I was just a child. I remember his frown looking over my cold naked body and his covering my shame and still, I cannot cry.

My son comes to me. He, too, has bowed and burnt incense in vast quantities.

He kneels before me and I put my hand on his head. "Are you well?" I ask.

He looks up at me and I see tears well up in his dark eyes. He is still a young man and he has a warm heart. Given his grandfather's long reign, he might have expected to keep his father for longer. For a moment he is silent. But he manages his voice so that it emerges steady when he speaks. "I am well, Mother." He rises and sits in a carved chair by my side. "I have arranged for you to move palace," he tells me suddenly, as though to change the mood.

"Move palace? To where?" For one frightening moment I think I, too, am to join the women in the forgotten palaces, to be made invisible since my husband is dead. But of course I have forgotten. I am now the Empress Dowager, the greatest woman at court. Even the Emperor must kneel to me. There is no higher position.

"I have chosen a new palace for you. It is the largest amongst the ladies' palaces. I have renamed it the 'Palace of Motherly Tranquillity'. You may have it decorated however you wish. Spare no expense."

He waits for my admiration and gratitude, but I only look at him in silence.

"You must have the best," he tells me, earnestly. "You are my mother. It is my filial duty to see that you are happy."

"I am happy enough here," I tell him.

He shakes his head. "You must have the best," he says and then he is gone again, to attend some essential ceremony before his coronation.

He is crowned. My son is now the Qianlong Emperor. His own childhood name, Hongli, becomes taboo just as Yong's did and I must bite my tongue not to call him by it when I see him.

I am visited by the Chief Eunuch. "His Majesty will wish to call upon you in a few days' time, in your new palace. He will serve you breakfast."

"Breakfast?"

The Chief Eunuch is in a hurry, he has much to do and does not wish to be explaining what seems obvious to him, after his many years of service here. "Yes. You will be seated at a table outside the Palace of Motherly Tranquillity, so that the entire court can see you and he will kneel before you to present you with dishes from the table, thus demonstrating his love and filial devotion for you, his only living parent. It is most important that the Emperor should be seen to be filial."

"I have not even moved yet," I tell him.

"Well, the palace chosen by the Emperor as your abode is in need of renovation," he admits. "But it does not really matter. You will be outside it for the ceremony and the façade is being worked on as we speak."

Yan wakes me in darkness and helps me to dress. I swallow when I see the imperial yellow robes laid out for me. I feel the cold silk slip over my skin and look down at the hue worn only by three people: my son, his newly-promoted Empress Lady Fuca and myself. The colour envied, strived for, desired by so many men and women over the years here and worn by so few. Raging dragons mark out their territory across my thighs while at my hem a stylised sea ripples. I take a deep breath and step outside my palace, where a palanquin in the imperial yellow takes me to my official residence.

Some of the paint is still wet, I can smell it. The large façade is bright with gold and red, with every manner of decoration, pristine in the watery dawn light. The courtyard in front of it is huge, it could hold a few hundred people. Inside there has not been enough time to do any work and the dusty rooms are empty and faded. I step outside, where the servants are laying out a table. Maids with covered dishes of food wait nearby, ready to step forward. Courtiers and guards fill the courtyard in rows of multicoloured silks, our mourning now halted to celebrate a new ruler. Behind the bright colours I can see a figure in sombre dress. Giuseppe, ready to make a sketch of this ceremony, capturing Qianlong's filial devotion to his mother.

There is a stir and everyone readies themselves as two yellow palanquins arrive, followed by many more in bright colours. As my son emerges there is a ripple of silk and a clatter of weaponry as everyone present falls to their knees, their faces hidden. Only I remain seated and upright.

Qianlong steps slowly and gracefully up the stairs to where I am sitting. My son has always had a sense of occasion and at this moment he is all too aware of the eyes of the whole court upon him. He makes a tiny gesture and a maid hurries to put a little bowl into his hands. Kneeling carefully before me, he lifts up the dish so that I may take food from it.

I take a small bite and smile at him but his face is very serious. He offers me dish after dish and I taste a little of each before setting it aside. At last the charade is over and he kneels to receive my blessing before he returns to his palanquin and leaves, allowing the court to follow in his wake. Only Giuseppe remains. His assistants have hurried away his work for safe storage. He hesitates, then approaches me.

"At least I know I will be well fed by my son, now that he is Emperor," I say, trying to sound light-hearted.

Giuseppe's mouth smiles but his eyes remain serious. "I am sorry for your loss," he says.

I take refuge in formality. "He was a most devoted and hardworking emperor," I say. "His reforms have left a great empire for his son to inherit."

There is no-one in the courtyard. The courtiers have all gone and only Yan stands by, waiting for me to give the signal to summon my palanquin from the other side of the palace. Giuseppe steps a little closer to me, reaches out and takes my hand. I almost draw back but allow my cold fingers to be warmed by him for a moment.

"He was a good man," says Giuseppe. "I will never forget his love for the Garden and how happy he was there." He pauses. "As were we."

And the tears that should have come before come now. I put one hand to my mouth to stifle my sobs while Giuseppe watches me. He does not try to comfort me with words, nor does he step closer, he only holds my fingertips in his warm hand and keeps his steady gaze on me as I weep and weep for a serious man who once forgot his duties and loved me.

The Studio of Exhaustion from Diligent Service

"A NEW PAINTER IS TO JOIN us," said Laura. I looked up. "New?"

"From France. But he studied in Rome, so we will be able to speak together in Italian."

"His name?"

"Jean-Denis Attiret."

"How old is he?"

"Thirty-six, I believe."

I nodded. "He will have a great deal to learn."

Laura smiled. "You will have to teach him," she said.

I sighed. "I am fifty this year," I told her. "And I begin to feel weary."

"Are you grown old all of a sudden?" she asked, laughing.

"I feel old," I said. "Especially at the thought of a young man who has much to learn and whom I must teach."

I was a little relieved when I met him, for Jean-Denis lacked neither enthusiasm nor talent. His works depicting animals were particularly fine and he was already accustomed to painting on a variety of surfaces, from silk to glass, which would stand him in good stead. He nodded seriously while I showed him examples of traditional Chinese paintings and explained how we had struggled to find new ways to modify our *chiaroscuro* techniques to create something pleasing to both our eyes and those of the Emperor and his people. I gave him various small commissions to carry out, that he might learn the style and he showed himself to be a quick and diligent pupil. I could not but wish I had had someone who could have shown me how to change my own ways when I had first come here, rather than struggling to find a path alone.

Jean-Denis was devout too, in a way that gave me pause for thought. His certainty of his purpose here as a missionary first and foremost, his undoubted skill as a painter wholly in the service of the Brotherhood, would protect him from the paths Laura and I had both found ourselves on.

"We would have found this work easier if we had had his piety, I think," I said to Laura.

"Easier?"

"We would not have looked beyond God for love," I said and we were silent then, together.

I knew that despite having taken my vows I continued to be a source of concern to Father Friedel, now an elderly man. The lavish gifts I received from Qianlong honouring my service worried the Father, for such honours made him think that I was less devoted to the Mission and more to the court and my imperial patrons. I saw his face when bolts of the finest silk were delivered to me, when food was regularly sent from the Emperor's table. Even a sculpture of Jesus on the cross caused him to frown, carved as it was in precious jade. The seemingly innocuous gift of a summer hat turned out to be regarded as an unheard-of honour and therefore even more worrying. My growing preferment at court could be counted in paintings, for where I had created only ten works for Kangxi and one hundred for Yongzheng, I had already surpassed two hundred works for Qianlong in a shorter space of time than either of his predecessors.

"Now that the new Emperor is enthroned," said Father Friedel, "I have in mind that you, Giuseppe, would approach him with a petition to undo the severity of the edicts of his father."

"We are forbidden from discussing matters of a political nature with the Emperor," I reminded him.

"He has a filial demeanour towards you," persisted Father Friedel. "It would be remiss of us not to attempt a reconciliation towards our religion through the relationship you have built up with him since he was a child."

"I will try," I said cautiously, although privately I thought Father Friedel could well be damaging my relationship with Qianlong past repair, which seemed a great risk. I was painting a portrait for Qianlong and had a sitting the next day, although I was obliged to hide the petition in my robes, for if the eunuchs admitting me had seen such a thing they would have removed it from me at once. Once in his presence, I knelt and pulled out the petition. The eunuch attendants looked on in horror.

"What is this, Shining?" asked Qianlong.

"It is a humble petition from the Order," I said. "They ask that you withdraw the condemnation of their religion."

"I do not condemn it," he said. "I simply forbid the Bannermen and their families to convert to it."

I prostrated myself, anxious that Qianlong might take offence at my request. "We mean no harm by our request, Majesty."

He nodded. "I will read your petition, Shining."

The eunuchs were not as forgiving. I was searched every morning from then on to avoid the possibility that I was carrying similar documents. Father Friedel was relieved when some small softenings of the edict were made following my meeting with Qianlong, but I refused to intercede any further.

"I am a painter first and foremost, not a missionary," I reminded him. I could see him struggling with the desire to insist, to force my vow of obedience to the Order, but in the end he let the matter go.

Despite his enthusiasm and willing effort, even Jean-Denis found his new life hard sometimes. He was reprimanded by Qianlong for not taking well to watercolours, having been at first reluctant to give up his oils. And he did not like the food, preferring, as did many of the other Brothers, more familiar tastes from home. Laura and I had long since adopted the diet of the Chinese, for the food that the Brothers preferred seemed plain to us now and besides there was always the risk of offending the Emperor if one did not eat the food at court, since dishes from his own table were seen as a sign of preferment.

It was a hot afternoon when I heard Jean-Denis throw down a brush with a vehement exclamation in his own tongue, which I took to be a string of oaths.

"Is all well?"

"I do not know how you have borne this life with such patience, Giuseppe! You must be a saint."

I shook my head. "Hardly, Jean-Denis. What troubles you?"

"To be attached to a chain from day to day, to have time to say one's prayers scarcely even on Sundays and feast days, to paint almost nothing according to one's own taste or aptitudes, to meet a thousand other difficulties. It would make me want to return home if I did not believe that my brush were useful for the good of religion, to make the Emperor more favourable to the missionaries who preach it. That is the only thing that keeps me here!"

I patted his shoulder. "All of us have such moments," I told him. "I think perhaps you have been working too hard and been cooped up too much in the Forbidden City. I will ask permission for us to visit the Yuan Ming Yuan, that you may see something different."

As I expected, Jean-Denis recovered much of his good humour when he saw the Garden.

"It is as big as Dijon!" he exclaimed, once I had shown him the extent of the grounds.

I nodded. "It is a vast place. I have been lost here many times," I confessed.

"Does the Emperor like your buildings?" he asked, when I showed him the Western Garden.

"He likes them well enough for play," I said. "But our different storeys piled one on top of the other are intolerable to the people here, they prefer buildings to be of one or at the most two levels only. They fear they will break their necks if they must ascend so high as to a fourth or fifth story!"

We spent a long time in the Garden and made many sketches. It was a peaceful day and one that brought both pleasure in the surroundings, which I had missed, as well as some sadness for days long passed and for my youth, which I saw reflected in Jean-Denis' vitality.

"I will write home describing this place," he said with enthusiasm. "No-one at home could imagine such a place, such beauty that seems as though made by nature yet is the fruit of man's artifice."

I nodded. I myself had written few letters, only the odd request for materials or books. Jean-Denis, by contrast, was an inveterate writer, always scribbling away, much like Laura with her diary. I saw her writing in it most evenings after we had finished eating, her blonde head bowed over the pages. I knew that she must have stored many volumes of her thoughts somewhere.

"You are cautious with your words, I hope," I said to her once.

"I cannot hide my thoughts from myself, Giuseppe," she said, smiling.

"No, but from the prying eyes of others," I said.

She was silent for a few moments. "If I die before you," she began.

"Unlikely," I said. "I am considerably older than you."

"You would protect my thoughts?" she said, ignoring my interjection.

"By destroying them?"

She shook her head. "Not if it can be helped."

I nodded. "I will protect them if I can," I said.

"Otherwise I may well vanish," she said, attempting a smile. "For there would be no-one left to remember me."

"I would not forget you." I said.

"And when you are gone? We have no children to speak our name after we depart this life."

"Enough of such talk," I said. "I have only just managed to make Jean-Denis smile again."

Our days settled back into a routine, now with three of us at work, our assistants and apprentices by our sides. The studio was always busy, there was always one new commission or another to add to the many already in progress: from enamels to paintings. We spoke little to one another except when a new commission was sent and then we would gather, the three of us, to consider how best to complete the work. More and more I tried to give Jean-Denis and Laura work that I might otherwise undertaken myself. I told myself that I was being a good master, that it was my duty to encourage their works and that as they were highly experienced artists in their own right, it was only proper that we should share the work more evenly. But in truth I was growing tired. I had served three emperors now, over more than two decades. And there was something missing from my life, something I had dismissed as a young man full of ambition but which I recognised now as a lack. I had taken my vows knowing what it was I was giving up, for it already had a name, but as I grew older the yearning I felt did not diminish, as I had perhaps expected, rather it grew greater and I knew of no way in which it could be assuaged.

Father Friedel had another request for me.

"A Chinese novice has baptised abandoned children," he said. "And has now been beaten and accused as a criminal. Will you intercede for him with Qianlong?"

"You know that this may damage Qianlong's preferment for me," I told him, but he was adamant.

Qianlong shook his head, as I had expected. "Do not concern yourself with such matters, Shining," he told me and I did not see him for some time afterwards, a deliberate sign of his displeasure which only added to my weariness. It seemed to me that I had spent my life here torn between two lives, whilst longing for a third.

"Master?"

I opened my eyes and looked up at the young eunuch's worried face. I, his master, was lying on the floor of my painting studio, my eyes closed until he spoke to me. Perhaps he was afraid I had died. He can barely have been twenty and I was almost fifty. I probably seemed ancient to him.

"Yes?"

"His Majesty has a commission for you."

I stifled a sigh. "I will be with His Majesty directly," I said, waving a hand to dismiss him.

He hurried from the room and I sat up, wincing at a sudden twinge in my back. The hard floor sometimes soothed such pains but returning to my feet often undid the good work of lying still. In truth, the pain was not even so bad, but there was a growing weariness to my life that drew me to the floor and sometimes made me wish never to rise from it again. Slowly I regained my feet, gathered a few materials, stepped outside the studio and nodded to the bearers waiting with a palanquin.

The familiar rhythm of the ride brought familiar thoughts. A commission from the Emperor. Once, I would have been excited by such words. The Screen of Twelve Beauties, coronation paintings for Yongzheng and then his masquerade albums, the Western Garden, the inaugural formal portraits depicting Qianlong at the start of his reign alongside his Empress and eleven concubines: all of these had been both challenges and honours such as should have pleased any court painter of ambition. But in the past few years my enthusiasm had waned. I wondered how long my life would be and whether I would serve yet another Emperor one day. It was unlikely, I supposed. Qianlong was in the prime of life with a magnificent and wealthy empire at his command. He might well expect to live as long as his grandfather. For a moment I thought, *I will die serving him,* and despite my fondness for him it seemed as though someone had pronounced a prison sentence over me. To continue to be at the whim of a monarch who might demand anything of me, who was not to be gainsaid, whilst longing for something I could never be free to choose... but we had arrived.

Qianlong, as I had expected, was exuberant. "Shining!"

"Your Majesty."

"I have a commission for you. Something special."

I bowed.

"My rooms and gardens are to be entirely refurbished. Entirely." He was already unrolling a scroll to show me details of plans. I recognised the seal of the Lei family, newly released from their work on the now completed Western Garden and its palaces.

"*Studio of Exhaustion from Diligent Service*," I read out loud.

"Yes," he said. "I have renamed it. I think it suits me, don't you?"

"Yes, Majesty," I said, smiling a little. The idea of Qianlong being exhausted from anything seemed unlikely.

"There is a private theatre within the complex," he said. "I wish you to decorate it inside. You may use whatever design you think best. I trust your judgement entirely."

I bowed. Qianlong was fond of saying such things and no doubt meant them, although he could also suddenly change his mind and insist on some entirely different motif once work had already begun. "Your Majesty is kind."

He beamed. "Tomorrow I am taking my mother to the Yuan Ming Yuan," he said. "It is a long time since she saw it and so much work has been done to beautify it. She will scarcely recognise it!"

I thought of the first time I had seen Niuhuru, how I had been lost and wandering through the Garden, with few landmarks to guide me. How since Qianlong had taken the throne one building after another had appeared – not just the Western Garden and all the palaces he had commanded me to create but across the whole of the Yuan Ming Yuan: temples, walkways, pavilions, new offices, palaces, bridges, boathouses equipped with magnificent dragon-headed boats and more. "I hope the changes will be to her liking," I said.

"She will be delighted by them," said Qianlong.

The space I was shown into was large and had fine proportions. Set against the back wall and jutting out into the room was the stage itself, a miniature pavilion on which the actors could play out their stories. The rest of the room would be set out with comfortable seating – chairs or cushions according to the Emperor's command. It was unfinished; the delicately made bamboo flooring was still being fitted while the ceiling and walls were bare of any decoration: my commission. I stood for a few moments with my hand resting on the empty wall, my eyes drawn to the plain ceiling above me. I felt devoid of inspiration. I considered various scenes, various auspicious symbols. Remembering Qianlong's delight in my works of *trompe l'oeil* I sketched a bamboo fence, inset with a circular open gate, a moon-gate as they were called, through which further buildings and gardens could be glimpsed, leading the viewer to fancy themselves in a garden looking outwards rather than inside a building. A pretty enough idea, but it did not interest me much. I spoke with my apprentices, explained once again the concepts of forced perspective, had them mark out key points on the walls so that they might begin the work under my guidance. I thought back to my first efforts at introducing perspective, how much I had struggled. Since then Xiyao had written a treatise on the subject. I had worked with him on it and now its use was more and more widely accepted.

"And the ceiling, Master?"

I looked up at the empty expanse above our heads. Perhaps a blue sky, with soft clouds? But that would not be detailed enough, not of enough interest. I closed my eyes and of course she was there, as ever, the way I had first painted her, the wisteria of her little fairy-palace falling about her.

"Wisteria," I said. "Growing across a bamboo *pergola*." Without thinking I had used my own tongue for the word. "A gazebo," I clarified. "Made of criss-crossed bamboo with the wisteria trained to grow across it. It will add to the illusion of being seated in a garden."

The apprentices nodded eagerly and continued their work. I watched their bustle, their enthusiasm for the project and felt nothing. The work was not of interest to me. I had painted such illusions too often, the magic of them had gone, for I saw only the artifice behind them. I had come here wanting to do something magnificent and nothing I had done felt important enough.

Laura listened to my complaints about the Studio and shook her head. "You had better hope Qianlong does not decide you must refurbish all the rooms in the Forbidden City," she teased. "There are supposed to be nine thousand, nine hundred and ninety-nine of them in all. You are lucky you are only refurbishing the Studio."

"Why not just have ten thousand rooms?" I asked.

"Ah, they say that Heaven has ten thousand rooms," said Laura. "And that it would be presumptuous of the Emperor to have more rooms than there are in Heaven."

I shook my head. "All I need is a quiet place," I told her. "Even the painting studio is always full of apprentices. They make my head ache with their endless questions."

"You will need to find a secret quiet place," said Laura. "There must be one amongst the nine thousand, nine hundred and ninety-nine that will suit your needs."

"Where do you go when you need silence?" I asked her.

"There is a little garden behind the church," she said and I saw a blush rising on her cheeks.

"You go there alone?" I asked her, knowing the answer already.

"I go there because it is the place where I am happiest," she said and turned away, back to her own work.

I wanted to warn her, to tell her that what there was between her and Guo was forbidden, but I could not find it in me to remind her of what she already knew. The only happiness I could achieve was in my work and it wearied me.

"Nonsense," said old man Lei, patriarch of the Lei family, when I said as much. "Your scroll depicting the hundred horses is a treasured piece in His Majesty's collection. And many other examples of your work are highly praised. And I understand that Nian Xiyao has dedicated his book, *The Science of Vision*, to you, in admiration of your ideas on perspective."

I smiled. He was a kindly man and took a more practical approach to his own work than I perhaps did. His family had served the emperors of China for generations and he knew their work would outlive us all. But when he was gone I lay on the floor of my studio again. I could not think of the theatre with excitement. It bored me and my own boredom saddened me. I thought of Niuhuru, even now being taken to the Yuan Ming Yuan by her son and wondered if she, too, would feel that the place she had once known had somehow disappeared beneath too many layers of beauty, like a known acquaintance transformed into something otherworldly for a part in the opera, making one squint to recognise them under the costume and extraordinary makeup and somehow unable to see them at all.

"The illusion is wonderful," said Jean-Denis when he viewed the work in progress in Qianlong's theatre. "Will you instruct me further in its execution? I know the essentials, of course, but you are a master at it."

I nodded without replying. Jean-Denis' enthusiasm should have been pleasing to me, but it only added to my weariness, reminding me of myself at a younger age. I oversaw the work on the theatre each day and as each day waned I returned to my studio and lay alone on the floor, gazing at the colourful ceiling tiles, my mind so unwilling to think that I did nothing but count them, over and over until they seemed to swim before my eyes. Thirty of them, all the work of a craftsman who had cared about each and every one, or perhaps had not. Perhaps he had outlined every shape while his eyes saw something else, a life he had never been able to achieve.

"Qianlong has issued a death sentence on five Dominican missionaries," said Father Friedel, his wrinkled face pale. "We must stand by our

Brothers in Christ. Will you intercede with His Majesty on their behalf?"

I shook my head. "He will refuse," I said simply. "You must know him better than this by now. My preferment as a painter, even his kindnesses in my regard, do not mean that he will listen to anything from me concerning the Order."

As I had expected, when I steeled myself to beg for mercy, Qianlong only shook his head. "You do not understand our customs, Shining," he said without rancour. "Continue your work. We will not speak of this again."

The missionaries were executed and I saw Father Friedel's disappointment, but I was used to the Order's disappointment in me as a missionary by now, it meant little enough.

"Shining!"

Fortunately when Qianlong came on an unexpected visit the studio I was not, in fact, lying on the floor. "Your Majesty. I am honoured."

Behind him were a group of his ladies, all looking about them with curiosity. I called for refreshments and had some of my apprentices unroll scrolls of works in progress. I watched them as they peered at the scrolls and pointed, commented on a painting showing the hunting season and smiled as they identified known faces.

"I believe you are enchanted by my ladies," said Qianlong, teasing. "Perhaps one of them has caught your eye?"

The women giggled.

I smiled. "They are all charming, Your Majesty, but I am quite sure they only have eyes for you. I am an old man and they are far too beautiful for me."

Qianlong was laughing. "But you must choose one!" he cried. "You, who have a painter's eye, must say who is the most perfect!"

I thought of Qianlong's own mother, her face now a little worn from when I had first seen her, strands of grey in her hair and yet to me more beautiful than any of the ladies present, exquisite as each one was. "I have not looked at them so closely, Majesty," I said. "I have been counting the tiles on the ceiling."

"Have you now? And how many are there?"

"Thirty, Majesty," I said.

Qianlong made a fuss about counting each and every one and laughed heartily when I was proven correct. "You are too good, Shining," he told me, clapping me on the back. "Surely even a priest may *look* at a woman?"

I smiled but did not answer and Qianlong grew serious again. "I am writing a new edict," he said. "You are to be made a Mandarin."

I shook my head. "That is too great an honour, Majesty," I said, thinking of the Brothers and their horror at the very idea of my being made a senior official. Such a change in my status at court would only remind them once again that I was not as dedicated to their missionary efforts as they would wish, that I was being rewarded as the painter I was, rather than the priest they still hoped I might be.

Qianlong shook his head at me. "You see, Shining," he said. "You are too good. Too modest. I will not force you to accept it now. But one day you must, you know. It is the post of Mandarin or marriage to a beautiful lady, you will have to choose!"

I endured more of his teasing for a while, but when he had gone I dismissed all of the apprentices. I thought of how relieved the Brothers would be that I had turned down such an honour. They would praise me for my devoutness, for my obedience to the Order.

"He treats you with great respect," said Jean-Denis, perhaps a little over-awed.

I nodded. "I have known him since he was a baby," I said. "They place great importance on respect for their elders here, even when they outrank them. He was taught to bow to his tutors as a boy, even though they all knew he would be Emperor one day."

"Do you think," began Jean-Denis but I waved him away.

"I am very tired," I said. "Perhaps we should finish for the day."

He nodded and cleared away his tools, then stood waiting.

"I will join you soon," I said. "Hurry or you will miss prayers."

He hesitated for a moment, before scurrying away. His devotion to Our Lord was true and honest and I knew that he found peace in prayer.

When he was gone I lowered myself to the floor, counted the tiles above me, and wept.

On a low stone wall of the Garden of Perfect Brightness where all my memories now reside there sit discarded, side by side, a crucifix and the bright red hat of a Mandarin. Either might have been my motive for decades of service in a land far away from my birth, yet neither are what held me here so long.

Vast Empty Clear Mirror

"YOU WILL BE ENCHANTED," PROMISES my son, riding alongside me. He has insisted that we should ride on horseback together to the Yuan Ming Yuan. I am nervous about seeing the Garden again. I wish I were his Empress, quiet and untroubled in a palanquin a little way behind us: she does not remember the Yuan Ming Yuan of the past, my son will not eagerly watch her face to see her every reaction to the changes he has wrought.

Yongzheng spent a little time there during his brief reign but rarely brought any of his ladies back there once we had arrived in the Forbidden City. Qianlong has deliberately kept me away, intent on completing the Western Garden and its palaces before I am to see them. He knows nothing of the evening I spent there with Giuseppe and anyway I saw little of the works: towering creations of carved stone in the half-light alongside still-open trenches, bundles of plants waiting to be planted. My eyes were fixed on Giuseppe and on the strings that might take me to him. I know that Qianlong has not just had works completed in that small area, either. He has incessantly told me of new buildings and bridges, of improvements to waterways and the enhancing of views: manmade hills focusing the eye on what should be seen rather than the eye being free to see what it wants. But my son is brimming with pride and I determine to like what he has done. It is still the same place, after all: there will be waterways and flowers, little paths and birdsong and I will go back to my own little palace to see the flowering wisteria. So I smile at him and nod my head as we ride away from the Forbidden City and towards the Garden, a vast procession of guards and courtiers and officials, Qianlong's own ladies, eunuchs and maids. We are to stay in the Yuan Ming Yuan for a few days, the better to enjoy all its new delights.

"There is even a surprise for you," says Qianlong, his eyes gleaming.

The roads have been improved, the earth pounded down and made hard, with straighter ways and well-managed planting to either side. The carts at the back of our procession will do well here. The Grand Palace Gate and its surroundings, have been enlarged and refurbished, the red doors freshly painted, studded with brass that gleams from polishing. As the doors swing open I see late blossoms, delicately planted terraces of flowers, a pathway turning to the left and one up ahead and my heart lifts a little. Yes, it is more managed and a little grander but it is much as I remember it. All will be well.

Qianlong calls for silence, he halts our procession and calls just a few of us forwards: myself, the Empress, his other ladies, a few courtiers of high standing. We are perhaps thirty people.

"The rest of you will enter by the Western Gate," he decrees. "I wish our party to enjoy a surprise I have arranged."

The vast procession moves away from the gate, trundling onwards to the where my old home lies. It takes a little while for the sound of them to die away. I hear birdsong and cannot help but smile. My son beams back at me.

"Now we must approach quietly," he says. "Come!"

I think that perhaps he has brought some animals here who are shy: swans and their cygnets, deer and their fawns. We walk quietly along the little path that turns to the left. There is a courtyard of low-built buildings which did not used to be here and although they are elegant enough I believe they are probably storage rooms for gardening implements and other such necessary but unbeautiful objects. On the other side of them will be one of the larger lakes, with a tiny winding path that one can follow throughout the Garden, a walk I often used to take Qianlong on as a child. He would play on the edge of the water, a stick in one hand, poking at the tadpoles and reeds while the gentle sunlight shone down on us and I looked this way and that for a glimpse of Giuseppe's robes. We step out of the courtyard and I turn right, onto the winding path.

Ahead, a cacophony of noise suddenly erupts. More than one of the ladies shrieks. I stand still, blinking.

The entirety of the road before us is lined with red stalls, each manned by a eunuch dressed as though he were a market trader. Up and down the road pace their customers: courtiers in their finest clothes, laughing amongst themselves at the role they are playing, mock-bargaining with the eunuchs, who offer their wares: grilled meats and bowls of hot noodles, caramelised fruits on long wooden skewers, pretty fans and table-games with intricately carved pieces, hairpins, cooling juices and warming teas. In a long winding row by the lakeside, blocking the view of the water, stand singers and musicians, performing a popular song. From the trees hang caged birds, perhaps to provide birdsong, although their inhabitants only flutter from one part of their cages to another, ruffled by the noise from below.

Qianlong is laughing. "You are surprised! I knew you would be. I know my ladies cannot enjoy the market streets of Beijing and so – I have created them here for your pleasure!"

Lady Fuca clings to his arm and smiles up at him. "It is astonishing! May I bargain with the stallholders?"

"Bargain all you wish," says Qianlong, waving her towards the endless red stalls, bright with streaming pennants. "But you know that all they have is yours to command."

The other ladies and the courtiers come forwards, exclaiming at the stalls, the music, the gaiety. They immerse themselves in my son's play-world as though they were children, sipping drinks and pretending to haggle over the non-existent prices of a fan or a silken scarf.

I try to look through the wall of musicians and glimpse a new raised wooden walkway that juts out onto the lake, culminating in a pavilion. I think to move towards it, to reach a quieter area but Qianlong is already at my side.

"Noodles?" he asks and I have to follow him, to express pretend outrage at the price the eunuch says the noodles cost and applaud Qianlong when he beats him down to a something more acceptable. I have to eat the hot noodles and drink the broth, I have to exclaim when a eunuch acts the part of a pickpocket and robs the Emperor himself and is taken away by eunuchs dressed as guards, I have to smile so that my son will be happy with his surprise.

At last I take his arm. "Your Western Garden!" I say, with great brightness. "I have not yet seen it! Take me there." I hope for a long quiet walk around the Sea of Blessings, to leave behind the noise and the madness, but Qianlong waves the courtiers and ladies along with us, nodding to the musicians to accompany us, so that I cannot escape at all.

The palaces of the Western Garden tower above us, immoveable and strange to me in their squat stone heaviness, incongruously topped with blue or green glazed roof tiles in our own style. The fountains spout gurgling water for us, the maze has the ladies giggling as they fail to reach Qianlong, laughing at them from his pavilion. I rest my hand on a small carved flower of the maze's walls and watch them.

Beyond the main palaces I see a tiny village, far off, the houses more modest in their appearance but still in keeping with the Western architecture I have seen so far.

"There is even a village?" I ask Qianlong.

He is delighted with my question. "Walk closer to it," he urges me.

I do so, only to suddenly realise that the village is an illusion, a painting on such a vast scale and using a trickery of sight such that it appears real and yet is only an image. "Did Shining do this?" I ask.

Qianlong is all smiles. "He did," he says. "I commanded it and he had more than a hundred painters brought here from the imperial studios to complete the work. He says it uses *forced perspective*," he adds, proud at knowing the technical terms Giuseppe uses. "It makes an illusion, to trick the eye and see what is not really there."

I nod. I wonder whether these buildings make Giuseppe homesick, whether these are the sights of his childhood. Has building them exhausted his last remaining memories of his homeland? Perhaps he considers the whole thing a playground for the child he once knew, a fairytale made real in stone but still an illusion.

I try to find some peace in the Garden but it is almost impossible. When I suggest boating a gigantic boat is summoned, lavishly painted and surmounted with a dragon's head, nothing like the little rowing boats we once paddled here and there. Naturally it is not made for just a few people, so a crowd climbs aboard. The musicians follow us in smaller but no less lavish boats, so that the singing goes on endlessly, adding to the chatter of the courtiers. At last I clasp Qianlong's arm and ask him if I may visit my old palace.

"Of course!" he agrees.

At once our party changes direction and we make our way back across the Garden, heading South-East. Tiny wooden bridges that I recalled walking over have been replaced with sturdy new covered bridges complete with marble steps grand enough for our entourage to sweep over. Buildings are everywhere, rising from little meadows, woodlands and even the middle of lakes. The emptiness and wildness of my memories is now gone, the little streams and secret hollows that

Yan and I once explored are opened up, over-planted and no longer tucked away but boldly on show for all to see. I stay silent while the ladies and courtiers heap praise on everything that has been done here.

At last we reach the Nine Continents Calm and Clear, my old home. The palaces around the little lake have been refurbished, I am told, and there has been a lot of new planting but in comparison to other areas I am relieved to see that it is still recognisable: the islets still circling the lake, bridges linking each, the great willow trees.

"You will stay in the largest palace, of course," says my son. I look across the lake at the palace that used to be Lady Nara's, Yongzheng's Primary Consort when he was only a prince. I remember Yan dressing me to meet her, my anxiousness that she might be angry at my arrival and jealous and instead meeting a kindly, sad woman in mourning for the loss of her child.

"I would rather stay in my old palace," I say.

"Nonsense," says Qianlong. "It is tiny! It is hardly fitting for you now that you are the Empress Dowager. But we can go and look at it, if you would like to."

I nod.

Slowly we walk along the lakeside until we stand before it.

"The wisteria is charming," says my son. "We had to cut it back of course, it was threatening to envelop the whole palace! But I have given orders for it to be re-trained more delicately. As you can see."

I stand a little ahead of the crowd, so that no-one can see my face. I think of the little fairy-palace I was brought to when I was only a child and glad of a fairytale to soothe my fears. Then, the wisteria covered every part of the building, the hanging flowers a purple mist of loveliness. Now the vine has been cut back so that the palace can be clearly seen, the wisteria reduced to a thin snaking shape along the front, nothing more. My eyes fill with tears and I have to stand looking at the palace longer than is necessary to clear them and be ready to face my son.

"I have increased the number of gardeners three-fold," he tells me as I turn to him. "The Garden must be perfect in every way."

I nod.

"What do you think?" he asks.

"You have done so much," I say. "I do not know what to say."

He smiles broadly. "There is so much still to be done," he says.

Lady Nara's old palace is large and every comfort has been arranged for me. I am treated with too much care, as though I am an elderly lady. I have not yet reached my forty-fifth year, but tonight I feel old. I sip hot tea and allow myself to be wrapped in overly-thick furs against the possible chill of a warm spring night. At last I dismiss most of the servants so that I can hear the silence I have been denied all day. Yan kneels before me to remove my too-high shoes and when she catches my eye she makes a little face that shows what she thinks of the day we have passed.

"Do you remember when we first saw how big the Garden was?" I ask and she nods, silent. I go to sleep early and sleep badly, my mind a jumble of little red stalls and endless songs.

It is still half-dark when I leave my bed, leaving the unwanted furs behind. In bare feet I walk along the lakeside, feeling pebbles and grass, a sensation denied me for many years now. At last I find the shelter of a willow tree that will shield me from view. The ground is hard and cold but it feels familiar. I look out across the lake and see a duck escorting her ducklings between the reeds, hear her quack anxiously when one seems briefly lost. Above me in the tree I hear a crow caw and its mate answer. As the sun rises more birds sing and I close my eyes, the better to hear their sounds and the lap of the lake's water on the shore. Slow tears roll down from my closed eyelids as a great grief wells up in me and cannot be contained. I know, now, what the rest of my life will be like. It will be music everywhere and the illusion of simplicity while living a life absurd in its luxury. It will be always accompanied apart from perhaps a few brief moments, growing ever rarer, when I can slip away like this. I will have to accept lavishly unwelcome surprises from my well-meaning, generous-hearted son, for he will not listen to my desires, certain that he is right. The Garden will grow both ever grander and less precious to me. Those tiny moments in my life when Giuseppe has held my fingertips or stood close to me will grow fewer and fewer until I barely see him from one year to another. I will forget what it is to thrill to another's touch.

I am not permitted to indulge in either fading memories or growing fears. I see eunuchs and maids in the distance, hurrying on errands. The Garden is waking and I must return to my rooms, where Qianlong joins me for breakfast.

"There is so much we can do!" he tells me. "We must go on a Southern Tour, to view the empire. You must come with us to Chengde in the autumn, I know my father did not greatly care for the hunt but the fresh air will be good for your longevity and I will ensure the journey does not greatly tax you."

"You may travel without me if you wish," I tell him. "I do not wish to be a burden to you."

He kneels before me. "You are my mother," he reminds me reproachfully. "It is my filial duty to make you happy. You need only ask and it will be done."

I look down on his bright eyes and place my hand on his head in blessing.

What else can I do?

The Garden of Perfect Brightness

"WILL YOU ENJOY THE HUNT?" asked Laura, watching the servants packing up my painting implements.

I nodded. I had accompanied the hunt many times during Kangxi's reign, since he was a keen hunter. It was a refreshing novelty to leave behind the formality of the Forbidden City and make our way into the woods of Chengde for the autumn hunting season. Yongzheng had shown little interest in its pleasures; he was not a man for outdoor pursuits despite his love for nature and perhaps he found it hard to forget the fear he must have felt in watching his son nearly die there. In any case it was some years since the court had departed in such pomp for the hunt. Qianlong, a keen hunter, was all-afire with anticipation.

"We may even kill a tiger," he said and I had to laugh at the same words coming from his older mouth, for they brought back an image of his child self, hopping from one leg to the other in excitement. "You will paint the hunt," he instructed me.

I bowed. "With pleasure." Certainly there was much scope for painting during the hunt, with animals as well as people set in a more untamed scene than could be found either within the walls of the Forbidden City or the ever-more-managed perfection of the Garden.

"My mother will accompany us," said Qianlong. "Indeed it is primarily for her benefit that we are going to Chengde. The fresh air and nature all around her will be most beneficial to her health."

I nodded, although everyone who knew Qianlong knew he loved to hunt and that his mother's health was nothing but an excuse to resurrect the old rhythm of attending the hunting grounds every year, as his grandfather used to do. But privately I thought that perhaps Niuhuru would enjoy the visit to Chengde, that being close to her childhood home and seeing familiar landscapes might bring her pleasure and that the natural world around her might offer a sense of the freedom that her ever more exalted positions had slowly eroded.

Jean-Denis looked me over. "Very grand," he said, smiling in genuine admiration tinged, perhaps, with a little jealousy.

I looked down at the brightly coloured, lavishly decorated blue silk robe I wore, marking me out as Mandarin of the Third Rank. "I could not refuse it again," I said. "The Emperor insisted." I did not say that this time the edict had come from Niuhuru, that for reasons of her own she had added her voice to Qianlong's to insist that I accept the honour. Qianlong I could refuse, claiming that my vows forbade ostentation or the seeking of worldly praise, but Niuhuru's distant command I found harder to ignore. Perhaps a part of me hoped that being granted such an honour, being known as a favourite of the Empress Dowager, would allow me more opportunities to see her, however briefly. I knew that this honour was a worry to the Brothers, that they saw in it confirmation of their fears that I was not truly one of them, that I was somehow apart, unmotivated by the religion they hoped to disseminate and therefore harder to control.

"And the hat," said Jean-Denis, eagerly. Perhaps in my new attire he saw the heights to which a man might aspire, if his work pleased the Emperor.

I turned the hat in my hands, its black upturned brim surmounted with a jewelled button and threads of red silk. Cautiously I placed it on my head. I had grown used to my severe black robes, their plainness.

"You are one of them now," laughed Jean-Denis. "You are become a Chinese after all your time here."

I nodded slowly, my own face serious. "I think I have been one of them for longer than I knew," I say.

Before we left I went to find Laura. She had always been annoyed at being left behind during the hunting seasons and had pored over my images from the hunts with a wistful expression.

"I am too much in the city," she told me. "I get tired of the noise of it, the busyness. I long for the clean air, the natural surroundings of the countryside. The silence."

"As do we all," I said, thinking of the Yuan Ming Yuan.

She was not to be found in any of the main church buildings and I had almost given up on finding her when I was reminded of the garden she had mentioned and went in search of it. It was situated to the rear of the building, a tiny plot of herbs with some of the vast southern rocks so much admired in the capital. I could not see Laura and was about to turn away when I saw two shadows on the ground ahead of me, the figures casting them hidden by the rocks. I opened my mouth to speak but then closed it as the two shadows touched, then became one embrace. I heard a low murmur and Laura's voice responding, too soft to hear what she said. Quietly I left the garden, thinking of the one moment when my own lips had touched Niuhuru's. I wondered if I would ever again have that experience, if my whole life would be marked by that one moment and the impossibility of it ever being repeated.

In Qianlong's theatre the works were progressing well. Above my head the wisteria now bloomed, twining delicately along bamboo supports, offering a glimpse of pale blue sky beyond. To my right, the wall was beginning to disappear into a formal moon gate shaped with curved bamboo and beyond it a garden scene was emerging, complete with buildings beyond and a pair of magpies who perched on its fence in the foreground. I nodded to my apprentices who, encouraged, continued their delicate outlines and preparations for flowering peonies and a crane caught tending to its plumage. I stood, considering the overall effect, when I became aware of Kun standing by my side.

"Is the Empress Dowager well?" I asked him. Any unexpected glimpse of Kun or Yan always made my heart beat a little faster in fear that Niuhuru might be unwell or in any danger, since they stayed so close to her side.

Kun nodded. "Her Majesty wishes you to know that she will be at the hunt," he said.

I smiled. "As will I, Kun. You can tell Her Majesty that I hope I will have the pleasure of seeing her there."

He nodded. His eyes travelled around the room, taking in the wisteria ceiling and the garden-illusion growing ever more real as its colours and shapes took shape. "It is like her old palace in the Garden," he said at last, raising his eyes to the ceiling.

I nodded. "Did Her Majesty enjoy her recent journey there?" I asked.

"She cried," he said bluntly. "She crept away at dawn to try and see it as it once was but there is little of it left as she recalls it. As we recall it," he added, looking directly at me and bowing before he took his leave.

The procession gathered in one of the vast outer courtyards of the Forbidden City. Palanquins, horses, guards, huge carts filled with tents, weaponry for the hunt, clothing, food and more, while endless courtiers joined the area with their own possessions. The Chief Eunuch looked exhausted and was no doubt quietly cursing Qianlong's enthusiasm for the hunt, thinking of his father Yongzheng who had been content to remain at home and not move thousands of people and everything needed to care for them to a place several days' distance from the usual facilities required to maintain a court in good order.

I waited patiently, sat astride my own horse, with two apprentices behind me in a covered cart, which held my painting materials. Jean-Denis, also on horseback, looked excited.

"I had not thought so many would be travelling."

I nodded. "It is something of an undertaking to move the court."

"There will be no-one left here!"

I smiled at his lack of knowledge. "These are just the favoured ones and everything needed to keep them happy. There will be many hundreds left here in the City."

"Make way for the Empress Dowager!"

An open yellow palanquin bobbed towards us and our cart was forced to one side. I looked towards it and saw Niuhuru. Her face was pale and she looked tired. I waited for her to see me but she was not looking about her, her eyes were fixed ahead.

"Make way for the Emperor!" came the call and Qianlong's own palanquin came bobbing along, empty, for he was on horseback, riding just before it, his smile open and happy. There was a jolting and jostling as everyone prepared to leave, for while all of us had been ready to depart since before the dawn, the Emperor himself could not be expected to wait for even a moment. Slowly the procession began to creep forward, the vast outer gates of the Forbidden City swung open and our journey had begun.

"It will be a great opportunity," said Jean-Denis, his face still beaming. "I will attempt to capture the motion of the horses, as you have shown me." He was always keen to be praised for his work, to carry out commissions that might earn imperial approval. I saw in him my own ambition from many years ago and wondered if he sometimes resented my own status above him, the fact that all the best opportunities were given to me before any other artist. The horses, in particular, were a favourite subject for Qianlong and he had praised my work in depicting them at full gallop, for lending the sense of movement which no doubt recalled for him the thrill of the hunt.

"Forward!" came the call from up ahead of us.

I watched Qianlong's palanquin follow him out of the main gate, saw the twin palanquins of Niuhuru and Lady Fuca bobbing behind it. I thought of Kun, describing Niuhuru's visit to the Garden. *She cried. She crept away at dawn to try and see it as it once was but there is little of it left as she recalls it. As we recall it.*

"I find I am unwell," I said suddenly. "I will leave you to paint the hunt on this occasion, Jean-Denis. Should the Emperor or anyone else ask for me, you can tell them that I am growing older and the cold air of the mountains would not do good things for my cough."

Jean-Denis looked bemused. "Your cough?"

I coughed loudly. "My cough. I would not wish to be unable to serve the Emperor through worsening it."

"But the cart, the apprentices…"

"I leave them all in your capable hands, Jean-Denis," I said. "You will do well, I am sure of it." We had barely made our way through the crimson gates but I turned my horse's head left and made my way along the wall of the Forbidden City, gaining entrance through the Eastern Gate.

I had perhaps thought Jean-Denis foolish for believing that all the inhabitants of the Forbidden City would be gone, but certainly the place was suddenly grown quiet, with only a few bored looking guards here and there, no doubt sulking at missing the adventure of the hunt. The odd official tasked with some boring errand scurried past. Inside, I knew from past experience, those residences now left empty would be cleaned or even refurbished in the absence of their owners. There was no let-up in work allowed for those maids and eunuchs who were left behind. And some palaces still held their unwanted occupants: older concubines from Yongzheng or even Kangxi's reign, all too aware of today's departure and their exclusion from it, their palaces full of silent resentment.

The Palace of Motherly Tranquillity was not silent. Its exterior had been painted and gilded to mark Niuhuru's official arrival, but I knew that the interior was still being refurbished and no doubt now, with its mistress away, the works could be done with greater speed and less discomfort to her, ready for her return. I noted two members of the Lei family engaged in consideration of changes to be made and painters mixing pigments while maids brought out all manner of furnishings to be cleaned and freshened.

"Shining? I thought you were at the hunt?" Kun had arrived with his own apprentices, now busily uprooting withering summer flowers, which would be replaced with the autumnal colours of chrysanthemums, grown in a nursery elsewhere and now about to take pride of place as they burst into bloom.

"I thought of what you said about the Empress Dowager's visit to the Garden and found I could not leave," I said. "I need your help, Kun."

The refurbishment of her rooms took less time than I expected, leaving Kun and I perhaps ten days before the return of the court. Still, time was short and I was glad that I had been able to prepare in my deserted studio. When the works were done I dismissed her household servants, telling the Chief Eunuch's deputy to use them elsewhere while final touches to decorative panels were made. He did not ask questions.

In the cold dawn light Kun swung open the carved and painted doors to Niuhuru's palace. We were confronted with her receiving hall, an over-large room with a raised platform at one end. A screen stood behind it, painted with imperial dragons while auspicious objects surrounded the carved throne where she was supposed to sit. It was a rigidly formal space.

"She hates it," said Kun.

I nodded. It was everything Niuhuru had never wanted.

"What is it you would have me do?" asked Kun.

"I need you to make me a half room," I told him. "A hidden room." I had learnt from the Lei family and I showed him a tiny model I had created.

He looked at it in silence and then lifted his eyes to mine.

Kun was a fast worker. It took him only a day, with my help as his inept assistant, to create the wooden framed-walls of a room that sat behind the empty space of the receiving room's throne. The room was not large, it allowed a person to walk perhaps six or seven paces before they had to turn again in either direction, but cunningly its back wall stopped only a hand's breadth from a window of the palace, while its two side-walls enclosed the space entirely. In front of the window Kun and I pasted strips of white silk onto a light bamboo framework which created a new wall, its shimmering height reaching to the full extent of the high ceiling and meeting the floor below it. Light poured through the silk, creating a giant blank canvas of a wall.

"Now my work begins," I told Kun. "Your only remaining task is to disguise the outer walls so that no-one will know this room is here." I mixed simple paints and showed him how to use them to cover the walls and door of the hidden room, then despatched him to source hangings and scrolls to be used as decoration, masking the space we had created entirely. When he had done, I thanked him and told him that now I would work alone. His only task was to warn me of the court's progress, should they for some reason return early.

I had seven days.

The white silk glowed with the hidden light of the window behind it. Alone in the little room, I cast my mind back to the first time I had seen the Garden. How the first vistas of flowers and carved bridges had given way to ever more beautiful sights as it revealed itself, the shimmering waters and delicate buildings hidden here and there, the quick fleeting life it harboured as all around me dragonflies glittered and frogs flashed their bright skins leaping to shelter as I passed. How, breathless and overawed, lost and dazed, I had come across an avenue of bamboo and within it caught my first glimpse of a face that had become, for me, something greater than I could put a name to.

I lifted up my hand. The brush touched the silk, giving it colour, taking from it light.

To paint with love is different, I found. In my lifetime I had painted to please a master, to prove myself, to complete a commission. To find a way to bridge two worlds, to please three emperors, whether young or old. I had painted, rarely, for my own pleasure, although usually when doing so I was trying to gain a new skill or solve a problem of perspective, colour or light. To paint without commission, without fear of a critical eye, to paint freely as you wish to paint and to do it as a gift of love… it is different. I painted what there had been between us over many years and what could not be said. I painted my memories and watched as the grey dawn light bloomed to sunrise through the silk, casting a golden light on a landscape now lost. As the day grew brighter the colours grew so vivid they seemed to ripple as the heat does in summer and when sunset came its pink-flushed hues touched the silk with a greater art than I would ever possess. In these moments the scene I was painting seemed to come alive and I would step back and cease my work, for it seemed to be creating itself without my intervention.

When it was done I stood alone and looked at the work in silence. A spring day blew wispy clouds across a deep blue sky and a light breeze rippled the surface of the lakeside, only a few steps away. Across the lake could be seen a small building, perhaps a little temple, a simple affair half-hidden by crooked pines. A haphazard path might lead there, although its outline was unpaved and faint among the rising willow trees and delicate pink blossoms that lined the water's edge, the grass a pale haze in the golden sunshine. In the closest shallows rushes came up between grey boulders and here, with his back to us, a little boy crouched, one hand gripping the boulder so that he might stretch out further with his other hand to touch the glistening green of a wary frog's back. By his feet was a tiny model of a fisherman's hut, something made with scraps of wood bound with rushes.

I thought of Niuhuru and how she would stand here, also alone, seeing her past come back to life before her eyes and knowing that I had offered her all that I could ever give: my art and my memories, bound up in love for her.

Exiting the room, I closed its small door behind me and ran my hand over it. Outside I found Kun, planting gnarled bulbs in the garden, ready for spring.

"Yan may need to change the servants," I told him. "Some of them will question where the space behind the receiving hall has gone. There may be gossip, whispers."

He nodded. "The household is in Yan's command," he said. "I will tell her as soon as they return." He stood, letting out a little groan as his back straightened. "I have a gift for you," he said, walking away from me. I followed.

We came to a little tucked-away building at the back of the palace and Kun gestured.

I stood in silence trying to take in what he had done. A small but complete weeping willow tree stood before me. Its sturdy trunk was artfully woven from new-cut willow branches, while as it rose to a height almost twice that of a man delicate branches fell downward as though trying to touch invisible water. But this was no bare winter tree. All along each branch trembled delicate willow leaves. Frowning, I approached the tree, squatted down and took one leaf between my fingers. It was a tiny scrap of green silk, cut to the shape of a willow leaf and embroidered with its delicate veins, its stem bound to the branch with a thread of green silk. I thought of Yan and Chu, their embroidery silks around them, delicate fingers adding the final touches to the work of Kun's calloused hands.

"It is for the room," said Kun. "As though it grew by the lakeside."

I looked up at him. "It is beautiful. A work of art, Kun."

His lined and sun-burnt face creased into a gentle smile.

"How did you know, though?" I asked, standing up. "What was in the room?"

His smile deepened as he hoisted the tree across his shoulders to bring it back to the palace. "What else would you paint for her?" he asked.

There is a tree in my palace of memories, a softly weeping willow set by the edge of the lake. Its rough trunk was woven by a man with a good heart, each tiny silk leaf embroidered with a silent kindness. A love that seems impossible can be made possible by such things.

Two Songbirds in a Cage

THE SERVANTS HAVE ALL BEEN changed, at Yan's strange command. I do not care, I am too weary to mind the new faces. I had barely had time to get accustomed to all the extra servants given to me when I moved into this palace. I cannot imagine what they find to do all day, but the Emperor's Mother must of course have more servants than anyone could know what to do with. I lie on my bed and try to rest, glad to be rid of the endless unsteady rocking of my palanquin on our journey here although Yan continues to bustle in and out, carrying cushions and silken coverlets.

"What are you *doing*?" I finally snap.

Yan only smiles. "Preparing a room."

"For what? Can't one of the maids do it? Come and sit by me Yan, fan me a little. It's stifling in here after the mountain air."

She shakes her head, stubborn as she has always been, determined on her chosen course. I sigh and rise, open a window hoping for some sense of the outdoors but there is only my walled courtyard garden, a few pots of flowers scattered about, which only serve as a reminder of how little nature is allowed here.

Yan is standing behind me when I turn back. "What?"

"Come with me," she says.

"Where?"

"The receiving hall."

I make a face. She knows what I think of sitting high on a carved throne in my own home. But she has already gone and I follow her, whining like a child. "Can't I just rest, Yan? What do you need me for? Arrange whatever it is however you want it."

The receiving hall is quiet, there seems to be no-one about. The walls appear to have been altered, enclosing the space behind the throne but then half the palace has been moved around and turned inside out in my absence so I do not even comment on it until Yan touches the wall with her fingertips as though she somehow expects it to move.

"What are you doing?"

But the wall does move, it opens up into a door that was not there a moment ago and Yan disappears into it. I step after her and gasp.

Beneath a weeping willow tree are piled silken cushions and beyond the cushions… I stand and stare while behind me I am faintly aware of Yan closing the hidden door, leaving me alone.

Slowly I sink down onto the cushions, taking my place where Giuseppe wanted me to sit and view his masterpiece. For it is his work, I know it at once. A dragonfly skims past my little son's crouched back. Further into the centre of the lake's rippling surface, beyond his reach or interest, a lotus flower opens up its heart to the sun.

I sit in the room all day and when sunset comes I call Yan and dispatch her to find Giuseppe before the Forbidden City is closed for the night.

"You wish him to come now?" she asks. Dusk is falling and no man must be found within the Forbidden City after darkness, on pain of death.

I meet her gaze. I have no secrets from Yan. "Tell him to come to the Garden," I say. "Tell him I will be waiting."

I know that if the door opens it will be Giuseppe himself who stands there and that he will be here because we have both made the same choice. I stand by the panel and rest my hand on it, waiting to feel his presence on the other side.

"Shining."

I rose up and followed Yan without challenging the summons, knowing who had sent her. We slipped into the Forbidden City's Inner Court just before darkness fell. As I entered Niuhuru's palace I heard the cry go out across the City to lock up for the night, the warning to any outsider, to any man, to leave this place or lose his life if he is found. In all my years serving here, I had obeyed that warning without question.

The throne was empty. I had not expected otherwise. I knew that I had not been sent for to receive her praise and bow, to murmur a courtier's thanks. The palace was quiet and Yan slipped silently away, leaving me alone in the red-gold light of new-lit lanterns.

I stood by the wall, adorned with a painting of two songbirds in a cage, their feathers almost touching. I allowed my palm to rest gently for a moment against the panel. I tried to quiet my breathing, to think upon the step I was about to take and yet all I could hear was my own heart's beat, or perhaps that of another.

They say that the Forbidden City has nine thousand, nine hundred and ninety-nine rooms, one room less than the Halls of Heaven.

But here within the walls of my memory palace, there is another, hidden, room, one half-step closer to Heaven.

I hope you have enjoyed *The Garden of Perfect Brightness*, which forms part of a series set in China's Forbidden City. Each book can be read alone but many characters recur throughout the series. The chronological order is:

The Garden of Perfect Brightness

The Consorts (a free novella which you can download from Amazon)

The Fragrant Concubine

The Cold Palace

Author's Note on History

THE YUAN MING YUAN (GARDEN of Perfect Brightness) was a
pleasure garden over 800 acres in size (300 hectares). Originally
a hunting ground for the Kangxi Emperor, he gave it to his son, Prince
Yong, who began to develop it as a country estate and who lived there
with his consorts and children until he was made Emperor.

When Prince Yong became the Yongzheng Emperor he used
the Yuan Ming Yuan as his summer palace and as a retreat from the
Forbidden City and his heavy workload as emperor. He took his duties
very seriously and died quite young after a short reign, possibly from
overwork (he slept only four hours a day) and possibly as a result of
poisoning from taking an Elixir of Immortality.

The Qianlong Emperor, who had grown up in the Yuan Ming
Yuan while his father was still a prince, went on to develop the Yuan
Ming Yuan into an extraordinary pleasure garden. Full of exquisite
buildings, miniaturised landscapes, scenes from fairytales, a 'shopping
street', as well as a Western Garden which included a maze, various
palaces and a fountain for which he commissioned Giuseppe
Castiglione as architect, the Yuan Ming Yuan was written about by
the Jesuits and other foreign visitors to China as being one of the most
beautiful and extraordinary landscapes ever seen. The grounds were
almost half water-based, including large and small lakes and streams,
all connected together.

The Yuan Ming Yuan was burnt to the ground in 1860 during
the Opium Wars. Today there are none of the original buildings left,
only the stone ruins of the Western palaces (which were made of stone

unlike the wooden Chinese buildings) remain within the grounds of the park, situated in the suburbs of north-west Beijing. It is still an exquisite place to visit and you can find a link to photos of my research trip there: just visit the book's page on my website.

Giuseppe Castiglione was born in Milan and trained as a painter from boyhood until nineteen, showing great talent. He was recruited by the Jesuit order, who insisted that he should take Jesuit vows and commit to living permanently in China, after various previous painters had returned home, annoying the Kangxi Emperor. He arrived aged 28, eventually took his vows very late (just after Yongzheng took the throne) and did indeed spend his whole life in China, serving three consecutive emperors. He died after fifty-one years in China and his tombstone bears an inscription extolling his virtues ordered by the Qianlong Emperor. The Kangxi Emperor named him Lang Shining, as his name was difficult for Chinese people to pronounce. He was an expert at *trompe l'oeil*, which the Chinese found an extraordinary effect. Through working with his own styles and Chinese approaches and using a combination of Western and Eastern materials, he managed to create a Western-Chinese form of painting that is now highly thought of artistically. *The Shining Inheritance*, by Dr Marco Musillo, covers his life and work as well as his artistic legacy.

It took several years between being recruited and Castiglione reaching China, due to some initial training with the Jesuits, followed by a prolonged stay in Portugal (to paint the Portuguese royal family) and then the long voyage to China, which I have mostly omitted so as to concentrate on his time in China.

The Emperor's mother's real name was recently found to be Zhen Huan, but Niuhuru was her clan name and I have used it here because

I have used clan names for all the concubines in my stories, since many of their personal names are lost. She was the daughter of a fourth-ranked military official. Sources from the time remarked that she was very tall and the only surviving portrait of her as an older woman shows her with grey eyes. She was made concubine during the Imperial Daughters' Draft to Prince Yong, who at the time was a well-regarded son of the Kangxi Emperor but not the Crown Prince. The existing Crown Prince was eventually demoted by his father for dubious sexual practices and a lack of seriousness. With over thirty sons, there was a period of considerable rivalry, before Prince Yong was eventually made heir, in large part because the Kangxi Emperor had taken a liking to Yong's son, Hongli (later known as Prince Bao and then as the Qianlong Emperor). Niuhuru therefore went in her lifetime from being the minor concubine of a prince to being the mother of the Emperor, which made her the most important woman at court and the only person to whom even the Emperor had to bow. Niuhuru lived until she was eighty-four and her son Qianlong treated her with huge respect and care. She was known to chastise him for the overly-lavish celebrations he put on for her birthdays.

There is no mention of a romance between Niuhuru and Castiglione, although her son was described as 'filial' towards Castiglione (a serious obligation in China) and late in life she insisted Castiglione accept the honour of being made a Mandarin. They would have known each other for many years as both of them spent a great deal of their lives in the Yuan Ming Yuan. I wanted a personal reason for Castiglione being the first painter to really try to find a way of creating a bridge between Western and Chinese styles of painting.

The Qianlong Emperor went on to have the longest reign in the Qing dynasty and his era was probably the height of the dynasty, the last in China's imperial history.

Laura Biondecci was a real woman, the only woman we are currently aware of who joined the Jesuits to serve in China as a painter. Castiglione acted as her mentor and some of her works may have been attributed to him, including the painting of Guo Feiyan mentioned in the text. She kept a diary in Italian all her life, which was only found in the 1980s in the archives of the Southern Church in Beijing. She met Guo Feiyan in Beijing and it seems the two had a reciprocal romantic relationship. She painted Guo as a Madonna for an altarpiece in the Southern Church, possibly the first Chinese Madonna ever painted, although the image was destroyed in a fire.

Jean-Denis Attiret's frustrated outburst is taken directly from one of the many letters he wrote home (quoted in The Four Horsemen Ride Again: Portraits of China by J.F. Kearney). His description of the Yuan Ming Yuan, an extract of which is included at the start of this book, contributed to a craze for Chinese-style gardens in Europe.

The Kangxi Emperor's response to the Papal Bull is quoted verbatim from Dun Jen Li (1969), *China in Transition*, 1517-1911. Van Nostrand Reinhold.

Lady Fuca died quite young and Qianlong was devastated at her loss: this is covered in *The Consorts,* a prequel novella.

Ula Nara eventually went mad and was banished from court. She died within a year. More of her story is told in *The Fragrant Concubine* and *The Cold Palace* in my Chinese series.

There were actually more than one Jesuit Missions set up in Beijing and more than one church, but I wanted to focus on Giuseppe's experience and therefore I have only described St Joseph's Church (Dong Tang), which still exists in Beijing, as does Castiglione's gravestone in the Zhalan Cemetery, carved with an inscription written by Qianlong himself. The Qianlong Emperor gave the most money ever donated by an emperor for a European funeral for Castiglione's burial and had him posthumously raised to the rank of Vice Minister.

Maids and eunuchs sometimes married and adopted children.

The majority of the artwork referred to exists (with the exception of Castiglione's fresco of the Garden of Eden in chapter one, his first painting of Niuhuru and the final painting of the Yuan Ming Yuan for Niuhuru's 'hidden' room) and most of the chapter titles are taken from works of art, both Castiglione's and by other artists. I have altered the timing of when he completed some of the works to suit my own needs. The Studio of Exhaustion from Diligent Service was actually Qianlong's retirement complex within the Forbidden City but a lot of the decorative work in his theatre was in Castiglione's style, especially the *trompe l'oeil* work and the wisteria-covered ceiling.

There is a legend that Heaven has 10,000 rooms and that the Forbidden City has 9,999 *and a half* rooms. The half room intrigued me right from the start of planning this novel and so I gave Giuseppe the opportunity to create it for Niuhuru.

The text of Giuseppe's vows is taken from the www.JesuitVocations.org website.

I have occasionally adjusted the timings of real events to suit my fiction, for example Hongli's birth occurring after Giuseppe's arrival rather than before.

Biography

I MAINLY WRITE HISTORICAL FICTION, AND am currently writing two series set in very different eras: China in the 1700s and Morocco/Spain in the 1000s. My first novel, *The Fragrant Concubine*, was picked for Editor's Choice by the Historical Novel Society and longlisted for the Mslexia Novel Competition.

In 2016 I was made the Leverhulme Trust Writer in Residence at the British Library, which included writing two books, *Merchandise for Authors* and *The Storytelling Entrepreneur*. You can read more about my non-fiction books on my website.

I am currently studying for a PhD in Creative Writing at the University of Surrey.

I love using my writing to interact with people and run regular workshops at the British Library as well as coaching other writers on a one-to-one basis.

I live in London with my husband and two children.

For more information, visit my website www.melissaaddey.com

Current and forthcoming books include:

Historical Fiction
China
The Consorts
The Fragrant Concubine
The Garden of Perfect Brightness
The Cold Palace

Morocco
The Cup
A String of Silver Beads
None Such as She
Do Not Awaken Love

Picture Books for Children
Kameko and the Monkey-King

Non-Fiction
The Storytelling Entrepreneur
Merchandise for Authors
The Happy Commuter
100 Things to Do while Breastfeeding

Thanks

MY GRATEFUL THANKS GO TO Dr Marco Musillo, an expert on Giuseppe Castiglione's life, author of *The Shining Inheritance*. His clearly-demonstrated point that Castiglione was a professional painter recruited by the Jesuits, rather than a Jesuit who could paint, showed me a very different person to the one I originally imagined. To Professor James Millward for his expertise on the Qing era and encouragement and to Elizabeth Scheuerman of Rochester University, NY for her wonderful article on Laura Biondecci, giving me insight into a fascinating woman and a whole new character, who no doubt deserves her own book. Professor Mark Elliott's book *Son of Heaven, Man of the World* on the Qianlong Emperor has continued to stand me in good stead. Their collective scholarship gave my imagination a wonderful basis to work from, although of course both errors and deliberate fictional choices are mine alone.

I am immensely grateful to the University of Surrey for funding my PhD: it has been a very precious gift of three years of creative freedom to explore not only this story and my craft, but many other creative outlets as well. This book is dedicated to my two supervisors, Paul and Rachel, with huge thanks for all their encouragement and interesting questions, their insights and knowledge generously shared for three years. It's been such a lot of fun: I would start the whole thing again tomorrow.

My beta readers, as ever: Camilla, Elisa, Etain, Helen: it's always fascinating to see a book through new eyes. Thank you to artist Kate

Newington, my beta painter, who practiced painting on rice paper so I could see what it was like as a canvas.

Thank you to my family who accompanied me to Beijing and shared in my research there: especially Seth for demonstrating exactly what a little boy playing in the Yuan Ming Yuan would be like! My gratitude to Ryan for holding the fort in China on numerous occasions so that I could step back into the past unimpeded.

Printed in Great Britain
by Amazon